AWARDS AND PRAISE FOR

HOPE FARM

Winner, 2016 Barbara Jefferis Award
Shortlisted, 2016 Stella Prize
Shortlisted, 2016 Miles Franklin Literary Award
Longlisted, 2017 International Dublin Literary Award
Longlisted, 2016 Indie Book Awards
Longlisted, 2016 Australian Book Industry Awards—
Fiction Book of the Year

'Peggy Frew is an amazing writer and *Hope Farm* is a great novel that captures the pleasures and difficulties of being both a parent and of being a child. The complex story of Silver and Ishtar and their fraught relationship is beautifully written, acutely observed and, best of all, completely absorbing. I could almost feel the crisp Gippsland mornings, hear the birds warbling and smell the stale dope smoke. *Hope Farm* is elegant, tender and very wise.' **Chris Womersley, award-winning author of** *Bereft*

'Elegiac, storied . . . aligns itself with other novels in which children—out of rashness, anger or even ignorance—act out to terrible consequences. As with Briony in Ian McEwan's *Atonement* or Leo in L.P. Hartley's *The Go-Between*, these decisions are usually compounded by circumstance . . . Frew does not want to pass judgement though. She understands that the sadness of childhood is to grow up in circumstances over which you have little or no control.' **Jessica Au,** *Sydney Morning Herald*

'Reading [*Hope Farm*] made me feel as though I'd lived it. So darn clever.' **Clare Bowditch**

'Frew's deceptively slow-burn tale of a teenage girl—adrift, bewildered, seeking solidity—moves inexorably to its climax, laying bare a certain darkness at the heart of the alternative lifestyle. But it's the tale of a survivor, too.' **Luke Davies, award-winning author of** *Candy*

'At this point it could be too early to call it, but I'm thinking this could end up on my top 10 books of the year list . . . Beautifully written, difficult to put down, hard not to feel the ache.' *Geelong Advertiser*

'In its exploration of maternal, sexual, unrequited and platonic relationships, *Hope Farm* is a finely calibrated study of love, loss and belonging.' **Thuy On,** *Sunday Age*

'[An] assured exploration of that awkward moment between childhood and the teenage years [as well as a] devastating critique of the treatment of unwed mothers in the '70s.' **Margot Lloyd,** *Adelaide Advertiser*

'Frew is a gifted writer, evidenced here by finely balanced observations and atmospheric description . . . Silver is poised at the beginning of adult understanding and Frew handles the challenge with deftness. Silver's insight and compassion are juxtaposed with naivety and the idealistic force of her first crushes.' **Ed Wright,** *Weekend Australian*

'Absorbing . . . A beautifully told story of courage and survival, *Hope Farm* is about growing up, belonging, and long-kept secrets.' **Carys Bray, author of** *A Song for Issy Bradley*

'[*House of Sticks* is] the kind of tune that hovers in the air well after the last note has sounded.' **Sunday Age**

'An accomplished and compassionate portrait of contemporary family life in all its delights and drudgery.' **Sunday Tasmanian**

'Her [Frew's] prose is deceptively powerful . . . *House of Sticks* is vivid and contemporary on the page.' **Weekend Australian**

'Peggy Frew's crystalline eye observes the shoreline of domestic life . . . Helen Garner meets Henry James in this suburban gothic, where innocence can turn to menace in a moment, love to resentment, and trust to prickling suspicion.' **Kate Veitch**

Peggy Frew's work has appeared in *New Australian Stories 2*, *Kill Your Darlings*, *Meanjin* and *The Big Issue*. She has published two other novels, *House of Sticks* and *Hope Farm*, and is also a member of the critically acclaimed, award-winning Melbourne band Art of Fighting.

PEGGY FREW

ISLANDS

ALLEN&UNWIN
SYDNEY·MELBOURNE·AUCKLAND·LONDON

First published in 2019

  This project has been assisted by the Australian
Government through the Australia Council,
its arts funding and advisory board.

Allen & Unwin
83 Alexander Street
Crows Nest NSW 2065
Australia
Phone: (61 2) 8425 0100
Email: info@allenandunwin.com
Web: www.allenandunwin.com

 A catalogue record for this
book is available from the
National Library of Australia

ISBN 978 1 76052 874 4

Internal design by Sandy Cull
Set in 12.2/17 pt Adobe Garamond Pro by Bookhouse, Sydney
Printed and bound in Australia by Griffin Press

10 9 8 7 6 5 4 3 2 1

 The paper in this book is FSC® certified.
FSC® promotes environmentally responsible,
socially beneficial and economically viable
management of the world's forests.

FOR MICK,
FOR CLAUDIA,
AND FOR ROWAN

You were a girl, thin and young, with veins that showed blue through your pale, pale skin, and your hair was reddish-gold and really you were still a kid when we saw you last.

You were a girl and you were only fifteen, and you looked younger. Long legs, grey eyes.

You were a girl, a sister and a daughter, and we knew you. At least, we thought we did.

There was a house. In the city—town, we called it, but it was a city and still is, the city of Melbourne. There was a house with two storeys and a tall shaggy tree in front and wisteria looping behind. A house on a hill.

There was a house on a hill in the city and it was full, of us. We were a family. A mother, a father, two daughters.

There was a house on a hill in the city and it was full of us, our family, but then it began to empty. We fell out. We made a mess.

We draped ourselves in blame and disappointment and lurched around, bumping into each other. Some of us wailed and shouted; some of us barely made a sound. None of us was listening, or paying attention. And in the middle of it all you, very quietly, were gone.

And there was an island. Not too far from the city and the house on the hill—about two hours in the car. Since before you were a baby we went there for our holidays, and one of us goes there still.

Ah, the island of your childhood. The beach is small, even at low tide. The rock pools are small and round and shallow. The dunes are mostly low, but they rise as they approach the point and the formations of red rock—soft, waxy-feeling, carved in places with laborious initials, love hearts, swearwords—that the beach is named for.

In the high dunes there are silvery runner grasses, semi-buried, their sandy roots hidden, sturdy and enduring. There are squat mounds of a kind of succulent, its stems stubby and juicy, its pink summer flowers threadbare and brave.

Between the beach and the houses, in the wide band of ti-tree, shadowy and dense and tunnelled through with soft paths, there are beige and grey branch-ceilinged rooms filled with dapples and bark and scatters of very small, dry, minty leaves. There are fat tongues of interwoven creepers, and papery thickets that smell of ants. There are tiny glades—carpets of unblemished sand, a log seat, magic circle of sky, squeaky-stemmed shoots, bright green, bearing tiny blue flowers, a sudden, miniature, mossy hill. Islands within the island, whole and private worlds.

Here on the beach is where you were brought as a baby, were held and kissed and set down, the bodies of the adults like rocks at the corners of your eyes, their voices thinning away, the waves and the air and the sand all shimmying their infinite particles and you breathing, reaching.

Here, up at the house, in the garden, is where you stood, a naked toddler in a tin tub, water escaping your fists, rolling silver down your pearly skin, your grandmother kneeling by you in the smell of lemons and earth.

Here on the concrete porch in the white sun is where you lay, nine, ten, eleven years old, and read books and ate stone fruit, the juice dripping into the cracks.

Here, back down and through the gate and over the fire track, are the morning glory vines, their spreading leaves a rich and European green, their violet blooms ready to darken and wilt almost as soon as they are picked. Here is where you crouched with a drooping flower behind your ear and watched through twisted grey branches your mother walk away along the beach.

Here—on the beach, in the dunes, in the scrub, in the garden, in a dry, hot, inland paddock that you galloped across on a pony with a helmet fallen over your eyes—here is your island. Nobody else can know it.

But there wasn't only you.

—Here on the beach on a grey day is where I walked heavily in dirt-coloured sand, by clouded unlovely waves, a thirty-six-year-old woman in the last year of my marriage.

—Here is where I, the good son, the good husband, mowed the lawns and pruned the roses and got sweaty and sunburned and hot with fury because nobody ever noticed my efforts, my steadiness, my loyalty.

—Here is where I crossed the lawn in my old bare brown feet, my secateurs held loosely at my thigh, the skin of my arms wrinkled and slack. Here by the gate is where I breathed the cottony sweetness of the blossoms on my lemon tree. And here on the path is where I cried, alone.

—Here in the dim scrub is where I hid beside you with my own morning glory flower, and watched our mother, and awakened to something I did not want. And here is where I stood without you in the soupy water of a dam, my feet slimy and my chest full of sadness. Here is where, older now—an adult, a young woman—I walked one cold May afternoon, miserable and drunk, and started a conversation with a stranger. And here is where, even older, with children of my own, I stood in a windy night on the back porch of a house on the other side—the ocean side— of the island, and thought of you.

Here, on the beach, in the dunes, in the scrub, in the garden, on wet black Settlement Road at first light, under rows of cypresses, and in spider webs and in waves and in the flights of birds, and in the silent inching open of the moon behind clouds and through clouds and alongside stars and in nights more blue than black, and in the sometimes low moon round and yellow over the innermost paddocks and the dams and chicory kilns and quietly grazing sheep and cows, and in waddling echidnas and shy nibbling wallabies—here is the island, over and over again.

Here is your island, and here are ours—your mother's and your father's and your grandmother's and your sister's.

Islands, towns, beaches, houses. Bedrooms, kitchens, parks at night. Mothers, fathers, mirrors, dinners. Christmases, bodies, paintings, horses.

The world swarms, and this is just our world, the world of our family, the world of our own making. It exists in us, and in the places where we reach across to each other. The world swarms in every direction. The world swarms, and somewhere you are in it.

PART ONE

ISLAND STORIES

SURF BEACH

They arrive late. Straight away the kids run out the back, even though it's cold. June and Paul carry in the bags, the boxes of food, the esky.

Paul sweeps back the curtains and opens the windows and clean, damp air courses through the rooms.

When their first child was a baby that slept all night and most of the day as well—the magic baby, they called her; they tiptoed, unbelieving, waiting for the spell to break—they rediscovered each other's bodies in this house. It was summer and they drank beer on the front porch, wet-haired, the heat of the beach still in their skin. They made lazy meals: salads and cold meat, omelettes. They touched like they had only just met. Everything tasted fresh—nip of beer, cucumber, cheese, the briny flavour of the sea on their kissing mouths.

A new life. Their life together. As if such a thing had never been done before. But what June feels now isn't derision, or wistfulness, or the fond humility of an older woman looking back—because she's not wiser; if anything, she feels less knowing, less sure of herself—what she feels now is wonder. At her own certainty, her boldness. She is staggered by it.

In and out of the shrubbery the children pelt. The evening is wild, the sky loaded. June bends to the esky, reaches to the fridge. There is the smell of the vegetable crisper, earthy and stale.

She thinks of the house that had been her grandmother's, on the far side of the island, the bay side—the pantry with its scuffed and dented storage tins, its dustings of spilled flour, its ancient cans of beetroot slices and asparagus spears. The permanence of those things. Even after Nan died they stayed, untouched, while different people used the house, bringing their own food. June's father, her uncle, aunt, cousins. Small or large groups—a cousin and her lover lying sticky-thighed in Nan's bed; a family with small children whose footfalls drummed the worn carpets like echoes.

She thinks of the week she spent there alone, in her twenties, during the exhausting and seemingly endless process of uncoupling from her first boyfriend. The black nights, the drinking. The phone calls.

She thinks of Anna. Always Anna.

Paul cooks pasta, and the children eat and fall into bed only halfway changed into pyjamas.

June washes the dishes, her own face there in the window every time she looks up. The night swirls. She takes a coat and goes onto the back porch.

From over the dunes comes the thump of waves. The beach of her childhood dazzles in her mind, sheltered in the bay, with its tumbles of red rocks that left a coating of colour on hands and feet and the seats of bathers. Afternoons that lay flat and baking. The half-light of the ti-tree tunnel that led back up to Nan's, its silty path always cool.

The fears that belonged there lay partway submerged, like the cold dark dirt that was under the sand of the path, if you dug down. They came out at night, with the raking of the leaves of the lemon-scented gum on the roof, the patter of seedpods, the voices of adults from the other room. They were soft-edged, tapering, and they shrank in the daytime almost to nothing.

But this, now, is the coastline of her adult life. She is on the other side, booming and rough. Night and day this side whips with its raw wind, it hectors and shouts; it does not rest, nor let her rest.

OPENINGS

Midday, January 1988. The bay side of the island. Helen is walking along Red Rocks Beach. A dull day, dull colours, a close, grey sky. And windy—wind raking up the waves, sweeping sand against her legs in stinging rushes.

From the scrub, in the murky light, grit under their fingernails, blue morning glory flowers wilting behind their ears, Helen's two daughters watch their mother.

Anna, who is nine, plunges her hands into the cool sand. She darts a finger into a nostril, then sucks it.

Junie, who is eleven, knows what her sister wants. Junie knows that Anna wants to be close, to smell their mother's hair, to sit in her lap. She knows that to Anna the loveliest thing in the world is the place at the side of their mother's neck, a secret place you have to push back her hair to find. She knows that Anna doesn't want Helen to walk away.

Junie sees the thrust of Helen's calf muscles, the *flub* of her buttocks, the embarrassment that is her old, faded hat. There is the voice of the girls' father, overheard the night before, small with hurt: *Jeez, Hel, you're acting like you hate me.* There is tenderness like the raw gap from a fallen-out tooth, there is sadness that feels ancient, there is helplessness and revulsion and desperate want, all at once, and when out of the corner of her eye Junie notices Anna's nose-picking the slap she gives her sister surprises them both.

Helen trudges on, around the point, past the red rocks and into the curve of the next little bay. She passes the place where a particular kind of seaweed collects in knee-high mounds, loose flat pieces like oversized tea-leaves, mottled brown and white. There is a woman, a local, who gathers this weed, who can sometimes be seen bending to scoop armloads of it into a garbage bag, releasing humid gusts of salty air and explosions of miniscule, colourless, itching mites.

Helen reaches Saltwater Creek, a brackish lick, driveway-width and only inches deep where it emerges from the dune grass and meets the sea. She splats through and keeps on. She will walk for a long time; she will be gone for hours. She didn't tell anyone she was going.

In less than a year Helen will leave her husband, John, but she doesn't know this yet. She will leave him for another man, but the other man has not yet appeared, the idea of him has not entered her mind and stuck there like a burr. What has happened—what is happening—is a restlessness, an irritability with John and their daughters that, no matter how much she tries to resist it, prickles and bloats until she can't stand it, has to get away, be by herself.

She doesn't try to understand this, to think where the feeling might be coming from. She tries to ignore it. It lessens when she has time alone, and when she moves, when she walks or swims.

It's not entirely true to say that the idea of another man has not yet come into Helen's mind. She is in her mid-thirties. When she got married at twenty-two she had already slept with seven or eight men, although she never told John this. Some of these men were very complimentary. It was mostly her hair and her legs that they liked. *Nice hair. Nice legs.* One of them said that she looked a bit like Natalie Wood. These things said by these men—or boys, some of them were, and she a girl—made her feel good. As good as the actual sex, sometimes better. Lately, along with the restless feeling, she finds herself revisited by the voices of these men and boys. From folds of memory they rise, clean and sharp and completely, miraculously, intact.

They were snapshots, those compliments, light bouncing off the surface of her. They were not real. Helen looks down at her ankles, her feet entering the sand, breaking its crust with each step. They did not *know* her, the men who spoke those words.

But to *not* be known—to be met for that first time, at her surface, her skin. Just as that skin was being entered, anything—anyone—could be inside.

The voices visit her and something flutters open and all the Helens she might have been merge and swell and lift her up. The wind forces tears from her eyes, she licks her salty lips, her fingers hook the air; blindly she grins at the beach, the mud-coloured waves, the ti-tree crouched, hump-backed, on the dunes.

THE FIRE TRACK

Junie and Anna used to fight about who sat in the front seat, but now they didn't because neither of them wanted to sit there, next to John, in case he cried. He often cried in the car, and it was hard to know what might set him off. The tears seeped out without noise, and he would fumble for his hanky and blow his nose. Then he might say something, in a strangled-sounding voice. *You kids know that none of this is your fault.* Or, *You're such great kids. Such good girls.*

They were always statements, never requiring an answer, and they always made Junie feel like something was closing in, and she needed to get away.

This time Anna jumped in the back like a flash of lightning and so Junie was the one stuck next to him for the whole two hours. She rested her head on her arm, turned to the window, pretended to sleep.

Before the bridge there was a long descent. The road came out from between hills and rounded a bend and there was the water, and Anna craned between the seats and yelled, 'I can see the sea!' and Junie looked away on purpose. Everything childish, everything that belonged to the past, gave her a shrinking feeling. It was like the feeling of homesickness, right in her gut, and it was always followed by a blast of anger, which blew it away mostly, although there would be shreds left.

'I can see the bridge!' yelled Anna.

'*Shut up.*'

Nan's house had never felt small before but it did now, its walls too flimsy, someone always walking in on you. The air was full of things that people weren't talking about.

John worked in the garden, digging, pruning, sweating. Cricket scores clattered from his transistor radio. Nan picked vegetables and took them into the kitchen, her bone-handled knife taking off the ends of beans, *flick-flick, flick-flick*. Anna lay on the porch in her bathers and read *Choose Your Own Adventure* books. She ate nectarines and the juice dripped dark on the concrete. Junie could hear her slurping from the bedroom.

Between the scrubby foreshore and the back fences of the houses ran a brown dirt track. It led to a kind of dam, and it was for the fire truck, so it could fill up with water when it needed to, although Junie had never seen it do so, nor ever seen any vehicle drive along the track. Most of the houses had gates at the bottoms of their gardens, so people could go across and down to the beach, following the faint paths that ran through the ti-tree. Sometimes she did see people crossing, carrying towels and beach chairs, wearing hats—but rarely, and nobody ever seemed to walk along the track. Why would you, when there was the beach just there, and the sea, open and shining and alive with salty breezes?

Junie walked on the track. In the patchy shade, the dried mud hard under her bare feet. In hot afternoons thick with cicada drones she walked alone towards a shimmering cloud that hovered, never getting closer.

One time she opened a gate and went through it. She crept between two bushes and looked out at somebody's green lawn and white house, blazing under the sun. When she closed her eyes the shape of the house hung in orange dimness, a bright rectangle above a less-bright apron of lawn. She could smell herself, the sweat at the backs of her knees, the briny closeness of her underpants.

There was a disturbance in the space that was the lawn, and she opened her eyes again. It was a dog, a German shepherd. It came towards her with its tongue out, walking with a kind of fluid conviction. She recoiled, branches sticking into her back. Then she changed her mind and made to crawl out, to run for the gate, but the dog was already there, blocking her way. It stood over her, its hot breath soft on her face. It didn't touch her, or bark, but it didn't move away either. It was huge.

She stayed frozen in a crouch, her hands and feet in the dirt, leaves tickling the back of her neck. Once she tried to inch forward, but it moved its head, drawing in its tongue and closing its mouth. When she went back to her original position the dog let its tongue out again and resumed its steady panting.

It held her there for what seemed a very long time. Her legs ached. Ants crisscrossed her skin. Then, for no apparent reason, the dog swung its great head and moved off, sniffing away along the fence line, and she crawled stiffly out and ran.

On the fire track the afternoon was unchanged, throbbing brightly. She thought she could hear John calling but she didn't go back—she went in the other direction, towards the dam.

The water was ringed with rushes, like in a picture from a book. Dragonflies made stagey passes over it. There was a space in the reeds and she entered, her feet sinking into ooze that was warm on top but cold below. Something that might have been alive scraped against one of her toes and she lurched on, wading deeper, flapping her hands. The water slopped at her shorts.

In Melbourne, at Avoca Street, the wisteria would have let the last of its flowers down along the back fence, but nobody was there to see, to stand in its purple shade. Inside would be the Christmas tree, still wearing its skirt of torn wrapping paper. John had forgotten to put out the compost bucket and they would return to a stink and a cloud of tiny flies that pattered at their faces and went up their noses.

The ti-tree sighed. The dragonflies skimmed with indifference. She was twelve years old and nobody knew where she was, nobody in the whole world.

In Melbourne there was a house and it wasn't the same, and never would be, because Junie and Anna's mum was different, had turned into a different person. And there was a man that they would have to meet, when the holidays were over and the first year of their new lives began, flat and unforgiving.

When someone came along the track she thought it was the dog. A shape flickered between the branches and her heart clenched and she saw herself trapped in the water, the dog standing guard, panting evenly, sealing the space in the rushes with its body.

Then she thought of Greg, whom she'd never seen, but who camped in the foreshore and left dead fires and empty beer cans, and who Nan said was once a normal boy, more or less, until he went a bit funny in the head. Greg wouldn't walk on the track, she knew, but for a moment she imagined him, dirty and thin, slinking along.

It was a man, shirtless, a towel around his waist. His belly and the upper reaches of his boobs of fat were pink with sunburn. He stopped.

'You right?' he said.

Junie nodded.

The man shrugged, and walked on.

Not long after that John and Anna came.

'Jesus,' said John, 'here you are. Didn't you hear me calling you?'

When Junie didn't answer his voice got angrier.

'What are you doing? I was worried about you. Don't go off like that without telling anyone.'

There was a feeling at the back of her throat that was like sadness, but it felt good.

'Come on,' said John, but she didn't move.

'Come on,' he said, 'it's getting late. Nan'll be waiting with dinner.'

She stared down at the water. Her feet were numb.

There was shouting. There were threats. There was Anna whining, 'I'm hungry,' in the background.

The feeling in Junie's throat was changing, losing its sweetness. She tried to think of things to bring it back—singing hymns at school chapel service; burying Sam, her guinea pig, after he died—but they didn't work.

At last John waded in and lifted her up. She felt how strong he was, and where her face was pressed against his shirt she could smell his sweat. She made herself as heavy as she could. He lugged her to the track and dumped her down.

'Phew,' he said. Then he laughed. 'You duffer.' He tried to ruffle her hair but she ducked and started walking back to the house.

*

Later, in bed, Anna whispered, 'Why did you do that? At the dam?'

Junie didn't answer.

'Were you scared?'

Outside, things moved in Nan's garden. At every level—down on the ground, up in the branches of the trees, higher, in the black sky—things twitched and scuttled and flapped.

'Junie?' Anna wasn't whispering any more. Her voice quavered. 'Junie? Why wouldn't you come out of the dam?'

Something thudded on the roof. Something slithered.

Anna was crying. She called out, and the door opened with a slicing, yellow light. John's big shadow came in, and her dark little shape sprang up easily into his arms.

BOYS HOME ROAD

John wishes he'd packed that morning, left straight from work. It's harder to face at this end of the day, the dark house, the overgrown lawn, the junk mail blown into the bushes along the drive. Inside, the closed-up smell, the silence. The poor kids— and here he goes again, bloody sooking, standing in the laundry with the keys still in his hand.

He pulls himself together, enters the kitchen, puts on the light. No need to clear out the fridge; the milk will last till Monday and there's nothing else to take. He washes his breakfast dishes and wipes the bench, although it's clean already. He's been avoiding the bedroom but he will need clothes. Come on. In he goes.

Like a wind-up toy losing momentum he gathers undies, socks, t-shirts. Slower now, a pair of shorts. Sliding the drawer closed and there it is, he's run out of steam, he's oozing across the room like a glacier and opening the wardrobe and the smell of her comes at him from the empty shelves, slinks out like a poisonous gas, and his hands have gone limp, his legs have disconnected from his brain, he's lost his body completely, he's an engineless stub leaking tears.

*

University, 1968, he'd gone with her up to her room. They were meant to be seeing a film but she wasn't ready yet; she needed to find something—a jacket, a hat, he can't remember what exactly. What he does remember is the mess. Clothes on the bed, clothes on the chair, clothes on the floor. Papers, books, cups with dregs in them. She searched the place like a kid tossing armfuls of autumn leaves. *Nope, nope, nope.* Then she started pulling clothes out of the shelves, letting them fall at her feet. Eventually she found whatever it was and put it on, flashed him a smile—*Ready!*—and off she went out the door, leaving him to sit a moment longer on the very corner of the bed, the only clear bit, thinking, *Who is this girl?*

And the evening they'd met in the city. Another film? They were always seeing films; films must've been cheap—cheaper than going to restaurants, anyway. They met on the corner of Collins and Swanston, and she was wearing odd shoes. Both white, but one a sandal and the other a covered thing with tiny holes punched in the leather. *You've . . .* he said, and she looked down and didn't skip a beat, just smiled and made a flipping gesture with her hand. She kicked them both off, and before he could stop her she'd chucked them into a rubbish bin. *Those sandals pinch,* she said, *and I hate those other shoes. My mother gave them to me.* Up the steps to the cinema she floated, him following, bewildered and clumsy, and smitten.

It wasn't as though she had money for all these clothes and shoes and things she treated like shit and threw on the floor and lost and forgot. She was always broke. She'd open her purse and look in it and poke around with her fingers, because there were always a million things in there—receipts and paper-clips and broken bits of jewellery and packets of sugar from the caf, which she ate during lectures, she told him, to keep awake. She'd poke around, or just turn the thing upside down and shake it so everything fell out into her lap or onto a table or the floor, and then when there was no money she'd look up at him, surprised.

She got by though. More than that—she flew. When she walked into a lecture people turned to look; you could almost see the pages of their notes flutter as she passed. She wasn't especially pretty or anything—and weren't they all pretty, those girls, so young and lovely? Him too, with all that hair and his boy's face, and his body lean and hard—he could cry just for that, and might as well while he's at it. But Helen—what was it that made her stand out? She was tall and she stood up straight. She, for all her lack of respect for them, seemed to be good with clothes. It's always been a mystery to him—cut and fit and so on; his mother bent over a sewing pattern; *bias*, and *darts*, words like snipping scissors—but he can appreciate the finished product, when a woman puts it all together.

How many women has he admired over the years, invisibly? All those university girls in their houndstooth slacks and turtlenecks and flat shoes, trying to look like French film stars. Not an easy style to pull off, but Jesus, when one of them got it right! Breezing through the union building, her hair bouncing, her hips, her sweet round buttocks. And since: women in the street, women on the tram, women at his work—Gail, with those little boob-hugging jumpers. Mothers at the kids' school— he saw them, he appreciated them. And that's okay, it's okay to look, but jeez, Helen, you don't go and fuck someone.

He finds his hanky and blows his nose. Lets out a slow breath. The bed is tempting but he can't give in. Sitting would lead to flopping, which would lead to snuffling in the pillows for morsels of her scent, which are becoming harder to find under the accumulations of his own. Which is what? Eau de Misery. Or, no—better: Old Cuckold. Pathétique? Wait—Sad Loser, that's the one, simple yet evocative. Unwashed middle-aged man with hints of loneliness, wallowing and cheap red.

He gathers up the clothes. When he gets back on Sunday night he'll change the sheets. It's been, how long, two weeks? Three. It's getting on for late January and the kids will need to come back, to go to school again, and they—he and Helen— will need to sort something out. Some kind of arrangement. He shies away from the word, from its formality, its conviction. Can't he—can't they all—just stay a while longer in the shelter of not-quite, of haven't-decided, of not-sure?

He will have to speak to her, possibly even in person, which will mean inhaling her current perfume—New Fella, or I'm so Happy, or Eau de Lots of Sex, or whatever it is. Which will mean ripping off the pitifully thin layer of scar tissue he's managed to generate and exposing himself once more to his own helplessness, his lack of vindictiveness or outrage, his inability to, for fuck's sake, stop loving her.

Thank you, she's said, more than once, *for not being angry*. But he takes no credit. It's not an intentional gift. He keeps waiting for the anger but it's just not coming. And his bloody mother, watching. *You can't even get this right*, those cold eyes say.

Frivolous was the word his mother used, right back when he first brought Helen to meet his parents, when the Red Rocks house was still new, the rosebushes not yet planted. Helen, in an action that would become one of her trademarks, wandered off for a walk by herself and didn't come back in time for dinner. John's mum sat at the table, refusing to start without her. The lukewarm vegies, the meat in its clotting juices. His dad drifting somewhere in the background, not getting involved.

He—John—had tried to apologise, said something about Helen losing track of time, about how they ate later at college so perhaps Helen wasn't used to such an early meal, and she'd cut him off with just that one word. *Frivolous.* Rapping it out like some kind of final judgment.

At last Helen appeared, breathless, smiling, her hair wild, the hem of her skirt wet. *You should see the sunset! Gorgeous!*

His dad cutting the meat, making awkward noises in the back of his throat. His mother's murderous silence.

Helen ate three helpings and said, *Delicious!*—and to this day he couldn't be sure if she was completely unaware of, or unfazed by, or had perhaps even enjoyed his mother's silent, concertinaed rage and his and his father's squirming.

All along, she'd just breezed right past his mother, and you had to admire it, really. Those steely glares, those comments— *Girls today, any number of university certificates, but can they sew? Can they cook a dinner, or press a shirt?*—their miniscule teeth simply didn't catch on Helen, either fell short or slid off.

Once the arrangement is made parties will have to be informed. The girls. His mother. People at work. He groans at the thought of the blokes, of awkward shoulder-thumpings, averted gazes. And the women—that was worse—the gentle commiserations, the kind words, which will probably bring him undone.

He goes back to the kitchen, puts his overnight bag on the table. He opens a beer and a packet of peanuts and leans at the bench. Outside, between the shadowy mounds of garden beds—one of Helen's fads; books on the bedside table, *Landscapes for Living, Create Your Own Cottage Garden*; weekend drives to specialist nurseries—the lawn aggressively flaunts its length. He turns his back on it. The beer and salt are mineral on his lips. He feels something in his body, a dense coiling. When he was a kid he and Barry Nichols cut a golf ball open with Barry's father's hacksaw—what was that stuff that came out? Some kind of metallic tape, erupting in flat rustling ribbons, spilling unstoppably, like guts. How had it all fitted inside there in the first place?

When he goes through the back door a ripple of air brings the smell of grass, and of something that's flowering, something thick and sweet that sets his hay fever twitching. He bangs the gate and gets in the car, blows his nose, wipes his eyes.

Carlton Gardens, after one of their film nights, Helen on the dry grass, Helen's hair against her neck, the secret flesh right at the tops of her thighs, the way her hand went to his crotch, so easily, so knowingly, her body meeting his without question. *Get on board*, said her skin, her fingers, her tongue, *or get left behind*.

When he turns on to the main road and passes the void of the cemetery another memory comes. A Saturday, last winter, the girls both out—a fortuitous synchrony of birthday parties. He had done the drop-offs, good old Dad, embarrassing with his stubble, his gardening jumper, his goodbye kisses glancing off an ear, a temple; the whip of hair, the smell of shampoo and the musty innocence of the scalps of children.

Returning to the house, the feeling of calm, something fierce and orange blooming in Helen's garden, wet black branches, low, dense cloud. He could hear her in the shower. *A moment*, this was called, in the code of their marriage. To be said softly, with a smile: *Looks like we've got a moment*. His cock hardened.

Moments, scattered like jewels across the years; thinning, true, as time passed, but there still, and no less brilliant. Various bedrooms, various beds. Floors, couches—on the table here more than once, the kids asleep upstairs, Helen back on her elbows, her knees wide, her hips filling his hands. He pushed the bulge in his jeans gently against the lip of the bench. The beginning, of course, had blazed with moments, moments thick and fast, moments back to back. The beginning was like sunlight on glass—staring into it would dazzle you. He smiled. What they'd had—and what a thing, to have it still, when they got the chance, to reach back and pluck it, dripping handfuls of liquid gold.

He boiled the kettle and put coffee in the plunger, loaded the dishwasher, wiped the table and benches. He was twisting the lid back on a jar of marmalade when Helen came out in her dressing-gown, skin pink and damp, black smudges of yesterday's make-up under her eyes. He gave her The Smile, but she walked past. She stood at the window. He put the jar in the fridge and went up behind her, pressed into her, kissed her neck.

I can't, she said, but then she reached around and undid his fly, took him out and pulled up the heavy woollen gown.

She was dry and there was a soreness that brought back the feeling of boarding school, of night-time wanks, urgent, chafing, silent, the effort it took to simultaneously shut out and be wary of the shapes in other beds. He saw her hands braced on the windowsill. Her forehead bumped the glass.

Sorry, he gasped, and came.

She stayed like that, looking out, as he sagged and panted against her, and then he realised that she was crying. He put his arms around her and she turned and cried against his chest, and the more he tried to get her to say what was wrong the more she cried, until she was past talking, her face all red and swollen, her breaths jerking crazily, and he ended up leading her back to the shower and getting in with her.

They stood together under the water until she quietened. Her arms were around his waist and her ear to his breastbone, but in calming down she seemed to retreat—it was as if her thoughts were locked away, simmering, private.

He found himself mumbling like a teenager, hot with shame. *Didn't you come—was that it?*

She smiled and kissed his cheek and got out and began to dry herself. *It's fine*, she said. *It's just hormones. PMT.*

The roads are quiet—he's well behind all the other Friday evening traffic. At the island Junie and Anna will be reading in bed, in the haloes of bedside lamps, knees pointy under faded blue candlewick bedspreads. His mum will be making her way through her detective shows, or an episode of *All Creatures Great and Small*, rattling the ice in her whisky glass.

The quiet flicker of those two rooms in the darkened house, the sighing garden, the moon-pale lawn where the girls lay on rugs as fat babies, crawled and toddled and fell, bumped around on the old bike he got from a garage sale, got bitten by bull ants and ran howling, spraying tears. Where Helen came up from the beach, her damp skirt clinging to her calves, so full of life the air around her seemed to tremble.

He's fallen in behind a truck; its tail-lights sway. He rouses himself and overtakes. What did he expect, really? She breezed in, and she's breezed out again. How could he ever have thought he'd hold on to her?

The reflective posts curve off into slick darkness; scrappy trees stagger along the edge of the road; behind them lie open, sleeping paddocks. He's tired. He shouldn't have had that second beer. He turns up the radio, which is tuned to the racing station, the frenetic blare of the Friday night trots.

Something white and shining leaps into his vision, a boxy shape rearing up from the left. He brakes, swerves, recovers. It flicks past—a caravan, pulled over; a big red Land Rover squatted in front of it. He blinks and shakes his head. He must've been dozing off. Heart hammering, he puts the window down and scours himself with cool air, lifts his bum and resettles into the seat, jiggles his shoulders. Not far to go now, but he'd better watch it.

He covers the last ten or so kilometres to the bridge with the window still open, singing aloud to Van Morrison and Elvis on the golden oldies station. The bald hills crowd in and let go again, and he sails down the last stretch, the flat water below reflecting a half-moon. Past the clustered darkness of the San Remo shops and over the bridge with its tall lights, empty of their daytime perching gulls.

There's only twenty-odd minutes to go but his eyes keep blurring, his brain lapsing into blankness. Bugger it, he'll have to stop, have a quick snooze. He passes the surf shop, the bluestone house with porthole windows, takes a right at Boys Home Road.

Funny, in all his years of coming to the island he must've driven past this road a hundred times, but he's never gone down it, never seen the actual boys' home. Somewhere in his brain a few sedimentary facts and story fragments lie, all in his mother's voice. *They built it before there was a bridge; made it harder for anyone to escape. Judy Sloane's mother found one of them hiding in her garden. Couldn't've been more than eight or nine years old. Terrified, poor kid, ran a mile. All his hair'd been shaved off.*

He rolls along the gravel, past vacant lots and large industrial sheds, until he reaches it. There's no doubt about which one it is—the buildings are enormous, red brick, two spreading wings with narrow, dark windows; church-like peaked roofs, grand double doors, stained glass behind wire. What by day would show clearly as missing tiles, cracked and sagging brickwork, stains, broken glass, invasions of weeds, in the semi-dark gives only a general sense of softness. He can almost smell the crumbling mortar, powdery and sweet.

He parks the car and turns off the headlights and everything settles into flat black shapes against the sky; the grand roof-point, the low rectangular wings. Ahead, at a blockade of scraggly bush, the road makes a right turn to run alongside the water. He puts back the seat, folds his arms across his chest. He can hear the suck and glug of small bayside waves. No beach along here, only mangroves—what must those kids have thought, waking on their first mornings to look out over swampy mud and all those bare roots, like bones, like dead things?

On the edge of dozing comes a memory: driving home for the term break, second year, before Helen—before his parents moved to the island, when they were still at Churchill, in the house of his childhood. He'd gone for a counter meal with Mugger Timms and Stewie Perkins, set off late, warm and only a bit sozzled, revving the shit out of that crappy little Austin all the way through the quiet city and out onto the highway. A cold night; his legs freezing from the wind that blasted through a hole somewhere under the dashboard. Empty roads as it got later and later. Steak-and-kidney pie heavy in his gut, and the beer, but he didn't have far to go—here were the rows of cypress and the white timber fences of Salter's agistment; here was the grain silo.

He'd been thinking about home, in an idle sort of way—nothing conscious, just running images through his mind. He was doing it, as he always did, with shame, with a furtive kind of tenderness. He didn't know what was wrong with him, where it came from, this sadness, this *longing*. They were still there, his parents, in the house—they weren't even old yet, in the grand scheme of things. And he didn't want to go back in time, to be a kid again—did he? It had been such a relief to get away.

His mother in the dark kitchen with that terrible smile, her ferocious hands roaming for things to scrub and chop and stir and wipe. You never saw a woman put so much anger into chores. Turning to the window as if she couldn't stand the sight of him for one more moment.

But an earlier time, an illness, and her there in the night, a yellow lamp, her cool touch, her dry kiss on his forehead. Had he imagined that?

Thinking this way was like picking at an impossible knot.

He drifted. He thought of waking in the sleep-out, the louvred windows that on cold mornings were laced with the condensation of his breath. His mother's turnovers, the smell of cooked pastry, scalding bites, the plum jam steaming, sharp and sweet. The backyard, the woodpile, the shed, the dog run.

And then there was the moment between seeing the horse and hitting it, stomping on the brake, every muscle rigid, the steering wheel clamped in his hands—no time to turn. In the middle of the black, wet road, in the middle of the night, on the outskirts of a nothing town in the middle of nowhere, a chestnut horse appeared in his headlights, and then, *bam*, was on the bonnet of his car—skyward-raking legs, broad, upside-down belly, mane and tail and twisted neck and one huge rolling eye right in his face. Blood on the glass. Slamming forward—and if it hadn't been for the death of Barry Nichols's cousin the month before, thrown from a car on the Geelong road, he probably wouldn't have had his seatbelt on—and the terrible heaving slide of the animal, the thud of it on the road. And then stillness, a fine rain in the headlights.

It wasn't dead. When he got out and went around to look, it was lying there breathing these awful, fast breaths, and it kept lifting its head and making as if to get up. Which it couldn't, because its legs were not okay, the front ones both out at wrong angles, the back ones tucked under. *Shit, shit, shit.* Trying to calm it, reaching out a hand—*Hey, hey, it's all right*—then stepping back as it stirred afresh, and rocked and laboured, those sorry hooves dragging against the asphalt. Blood on the white blaze between its eyes. Blood on its teeth as it gasped.

Lights, and a rushing sound—a car, thank God. Braking, a door-slam, a presence beside him. No one he knew, some farmer driving home from the pub, most likely—there was the smell of booze. A glimpse of battered hands braced on blue-jeaned knees, a flannel shirt, grey hair. *Poor bugger's had it. Stay here, kid, I'll go and get help.*

The man driving off again, and something about being called *kid* ripping right into him, his legs shaking, tears running to his chin. *Don't leave me here*, he thought, and put his head down on the bonnet of the car, feeling the heat of the engine. And once his head was down he couldn't bring himself to lift it again, to face the dreadful struggle, the dreadful sounds, the blood, that red-gold coat matted and wet in the headlights.

Behind his closed eyes appeared another car—his parents' car, with his mother alone in it, in the driver's seat. He could see the back of her head, and her shoulders. She was wearing her old best coat, her trip-to-town coat, the chequered one. And he was standing alone, eleven years old, at the school gates with all his bags. The back of her head, the car, driving away, gone.

The farmer didn't return, but he must've sent the cops. Two of them, one young, one a bit older. But not much—neither of them much older than John was.

What happened mate? Just walk out in front of you, did it?

The beam of a torch swept across the road to a fence, silvery with raindrops, the wires down between two posts. *There you go. There's your answer.*

The three of them standing there, out of reach of those scrabbling hooves.

What—his voice shaking—*what do we do?*

You just hop back in your car, son. A hand on his shoulder. But there was something unconvincing in the cop's touch, his voice.

Son? I'm practically your age, he thought. And then, desperately, *Where's the farmer? Bring him back, with his old-man's hands. He'll know what do to.*

Just hop back in your car, said the cop again. *Just wait there.*

He did, and watched the two of them return to their car, the older one walking with false purpose, the younger half-running to keep up. The older one opened the door, reached in and took out a gun, a small, neat, cop's gun. The two of them walked back together, then stopped a few paces away. Their white faces through the beaded windscreen, the older one wearily pushing back his hat, rubbing a hand over his eyes, the younger one speaking, his head bent.

How unprepared they all were. Look at him, strutting his way into his twenties, kicking footies, fooling around with girls, thinking this was the world—scraping through uni, your own money, your own car. As if being an adult was about striding past and over everything.

Those cops in their uniforms, with guns. What did they know? Not much more than he did. Through the misty glass he imagined he could hear the young cop's voice, raw-edged and adolescent, full of need. *How*, he imagined him saying, *do you shoot a horse?*

RIDING

Nan took them horseriding. Which really meant that she sat in the car with the newspaper while they trundled across beige paddocks on what were not horses at all, but ponies—weary, grimy ponies with too-big saddles, and headstalls left on underneath their string-mended bridles.

It was the Easter holidays, and it was supposed to be autumn, but it felt like summer still, The Summer of The Break-up, The Summer of Helen's Boyfriend, The Summer of John's Crying.

Anna's pony was called Freckles. He—or maybe she; nobody told them which it was, and it wasn't easy to tell, Freckles being so low to the ground and heavy in the hindquarters—was like something from a museum, stuffed-looking, solid, a dusty dun with brown flecks. Freckles's head hung low and his or her ears drooped to the sides, like handlebars.

Junie's was Pancho, slightly bigger—a pinto, she knew from her *Horses of the World* book; splashes of white, tan and black. His neck was thick, his rump wide and womanish, but he had an accidental kind of beauty, his chestnut patches coppery and sleek, the chocolate lining of his ears plush, his tail proud. Junie secretly thrilled at him, wishing him hers. It didn't matter that

35

he stood like a bored soldier while she stroked his neck, that he moved his head evasively when she tried to rearrange his forelock or brush the flies from his eyes, which had blobs of black stuff at their corners. Her fingers came away from his hide covered with grey, sticky dirt; furtively she smelled them.

A woman leathered by sun and dressed in a pair of men's jeans and a flannel shirt emerged from a shed, took Nan's money, fitted the girls with helmets, and helped them onto Freckles and Pancho. The woman gave a juicy cough and spat into the dust. 'Jason'll be out in a sec,' she said.

Then Nan got back into the car and the woman re-entered the shed, and the girls waited, helplessly astride the stationary ponies.

Jason was somewhere between a teenager and a man, skinny, with a big-nosed, knobbly face, pitted with acne scars—and when he swung out of the shed, pushing back his Akubra and hitching his stone-washed jeans, Junie was overcome with a horrified, unwilling awkwardness.

'G'day, girls.' Jason grinned, hands on scrawny hips. 'Ya ready for me?'

Anna, who always worried about the wrong things and never cared about what mattered, didn't appear to be bothered by Jason's swagger, his teasing. She seemed more concerned, despite Freckles's steadfast immobility, with keeping a firm grasp on the front of the saddle. But Junie's awkwardness wouldn't go away, and was in fact worsening—she began to burn with furious embarrassment at the thought that Jason might notice, in fact probably already had, and would take her discomfort to mean that she liked him, was *attracted* to him.

'Get out of it, ya bastard,' said Jason as his horse—his was a horse, not a pony; gangly and grey, narrow across the chest—turned a skittish circle, its big pale tongue slapping at the bit.

Junie gazed off over the shimmering paddocks, willing her flushed face to cool, refusing to watch as he flamboyantly adjusted reins and stirrups.

'Rightio, girls, let's hit the road.'

There were no other customers. They were at the mercy of Jason. Off they went, him first, the pointy hipbones of his horse rising and falling. Pancho followed, and when Junie glanced over her shoulder there was Freckles, and Anna, with her clutching fingers and flapping knees, her shoulders rigid and high, her eyes full of terror and joy.

The so-called trail was a thread of dirt across the paddocks. There were no trees and the sun burned down on them. The saddles squeaked in time with the animals' steps. The heat, the light, the resigned trudging, Pancho's rubbery farts, all spoke of boredom, of reticence, of time being marked.

Junie pictured the inside of Pancho's mind as a dimly lit hollow, its walls muffling and protective, the fish-eye lens of his vision opening onto a sepia-toned view: watery swathes of grass, blank sky, the horizon unblemished but vibrating with possibilities—weather, nightfall, predators. At the centre of this cave, like the swirl at the centre of a marble, hung the image of the yellow yard, the open-mouthed shed, the drinking trough, the rope looped around the rail, the slump of a hip and the settling of one back hoof onto its toe.

She knew he was only going through the motions but she didn't care. She fixed her gaze on his ears, their curved backs, marked with fine but visible veins. She tried to let her surroundings—the paddocks, the narrow buttocks of Jason's horse, and Jason himself, fidgeting and gesticulating—slip out of focus. She tried not to hear Jason's voice. She was riding. She let her hips slide back and forth with Pancho's rhythm, rested one hand on her thigh. She saw herself: a girl on a horse, her movements leisurely and assured, her body attuned to the animal's, full of grace, and ease.

This didn't last long. Jason was not going to be deprived of his audience. His hat and his restless back, both dotted with flies, kept bobbing into view, and the waving flags of his elbows. He twisted his neck and pointed his craggy face at Junie, jabbering relentlessly.

'Racehorse, this one was. Useless. Never even ran a place. Headed for the knackers when we got 'im.' Craning past Junie: 'And you're old as the hills, aren't ya, Freckles? Always been old. Born old, and cranky.' Directing himself her way again: 'Where did youse girls say youse were from?'

We didn't. Junie stared harder at Pancho's ears. 'Melbourne,' she muttered.

'Big smoke, eh?' He had hooked one leg over the front of his horse's saddle and was nearly sitting backwards, facing her. His lips were cracked, and his tongue appeared often, wetting them. 'Big smoke.' This time the words had something extra, a lilting ridicule. 'So youse girls're on holidays, are youse?'

'Yes.' She heard herself, a city girl, uptight, restrained. She looked down at her hands, smooth, useless, the hands of a spoilt brat, a princess. *But I'm not!* She wasn't—he was making her into one, crowding her into it. She tried to get the feeling of the girl rider back, easy on her horse, or of the kid who ran through the scrub in bare feet, who swam out deep by herself, but they wouldn't come, there wasn't space.

'Youse're sisters, right?'

'Yep.'

'Thought so. Youse could be twins.' He wasn't even holding the reins any more; seated sideways, his leg still hooked, he was taking a package of cigarettes from his shirt pocket. He put one in his mouth and lit it. 'So how old are ya?'

Junie's throat tightened. She brought her shoulders forward, trying to make her t-shirt fall loosely and not show the bottle-top shapes of her nipples. 'Twelve.'

'Twelve!' He sucked on the cigarette and then let the smoke out, aiming it upwards, making a show of it. 'Twelve—and ya know what's next, don't ya?'

She gave a small, polite sound.

'Well?' He made a rolling gesture with his hand. 'Come on, what comes next, after twelve? Don't tell me ya don't know yer numbers.'

Freckles had drawn closer, his or her stubby head level with Junie's knee. Junie glanced at Anna, but she had her eyes down, her face hidden under the brim of her helmet.

Jason was not letting up. 'E-lev-en,' he said, as if talking to a moron. 'Ta-welve . . .' More hand-rolling.

'Thirteen.'

'There ya go! Thirteen. A real teenager, you'll be. And that's when ya move on, ya know?'

She didn't know. She didn't want to know. She gritted her teeth. *Shut up.*

'Oh yeah,' said Jason, something rich and gratified in his voice. 'They all do, all the girls.'

But it wasn't girls that came into Junie's mind, it was Helen, her fingers shining with chicken fat, her lips moist, smiling across the table at *him*, the boyfriend. Helen's skirt sliding up, the spill of her flesh against the chair. And the next day, when she called Junie into the bathroom to bring her a towel—*him* gone, but the feeling still there, a shrinking, a curling-in of disgust. Helen's breasts in the water, moving like they had lives of their own, the fizz of dark hair between her legs, the lips down there she didn't even try to hide.

'Yeah,' said Jason, 'they start off with horses, can't get enough of them, but then, sooner or later, they move on, you know? They move—*gah!*' He broke off, grabbing at his throat. The cigarette dropped and both his legs went up, and then he was on the ground, the grey horse dancing away with a snort.

Pancho and Freckles came to an immediate halt, as if their engines had been turned off.

Jason rolled to one side and then got up on his hands and knees, gasping and spitting. 'Jesus Christ!' He swiped at his mouth. 'Swallowed a fucken fly!'

Junie pretended not to be watching. Her mother had gone, been magicked away, and now a private seed of laughter sat right in the middle of her stomach, tender and delicious. She held her face very still, to keep it hidden.

'Jesus fucken Christ!' His hat had fallen off; his hair was dingy blond, and plastered to his scalp with sweat. He looked much younger.

'All right.' He clambered to his feet and lunged for the trailing reins of the grey horse. 'Come here, ya bastard.' But the horse, as if in on the joke that nobody—not Junie, stone-faced and immobile, or Anna, perhaps the same, or perhaps still just busy keeping hold of Freckles—was outwardly acknowledging, frisked and skipped away.

'Come here!' Jason ran at the horse, which pivoted on its rear legs and, with a joyous plunging motion and a whisk of its raggedy tail, dodged around him and took off past Freckles and Anna and Pancho and Junie, heading back the way they had come. Its hooves thudded on the dry trail and a screen of dust rose, and within it something shifted in the atmosphere, and Pancho and Freckles started into life. Beneath her Junie felt Pancho's nuggety hindquarters coil and then release as he made a regal, decisive about-face, pitching her askew. Freckles turned as well, and let out a squeal, his or her mane flying upwards, the whites of his or her eyes showing.

And they were galloping. The grass, the sky, the bare ribbon of trail, all blurred and shook. The thudding of hooves, Pancho's rhythmic snorts, Freckles's repeated squeals, Junie's jolting breaths—all merged into a wave that surged towards the opening in the fence, the raised tail and flashing hooves of Jason's horse, the distant silver cube of the shed.

'Ju-u-nie!' came Anna's voice. Junie managed to turn her head for a moment and caught sight of Freckles's sturdy, rocking-horse gallop, Freckles's flaring nostrils and rolling eyes, Freckles's whiskery lips, parted in a brown-toothed grin.

'Ju-u-NIE!'

She forced her gaze higher, and there was Anna, bouncing arrhythmically, helmet tipped forward. But her shoulders had dropped, and from her wide mouth—which was all Junie could see of her face—came laughter, jolting in bright, staccato bursts. Freckles squealed again, and Pancho gave an answering bray, and something undid itself in Junie's stomach, something broke open, and she also began, wildly, wrenchingly, to laugh.

Side by side they hurtled through the gateway and across the next paddock, stirrups colliding, teeth rattling, fingers velvety with horse-dirt tangled in reins and manes, their laughter flying like streamers. The ponies did not slow when they reached the yard; it was as if, right up to the very last moment, they feared it would be snatched away from them. Round the corner of the shed they whipped, and across the packed dirt to the far fence.

There was a sudden, gasping, stillness. The ponies stood as if rooted to the spot, as if they had never left in the first place, only the heaving of their sides giving them away. Pancho had halted so abruptly that Junie lost her stirrups and was launched forward onto his neck before slipping sideways to land on her feet beside him. She pressed her face into his mane and he gave an indifferent sigh.

Anna let out one last laugh—breathy and slow and full of satisfaction.

John was down at the beach when they got back, and then he was in the garden, hacking at Nan's rose bushes in his bathers, his back and shoulders shiny and deep red-brown, the mound of his tummy folding down on itself as he bent. Junie waited for Anna to run to him, to blab about the horse ride, Jason, the fly, the gallop—but she didn't. She lay on the concrete porch with her book, wearing a secret smile.

Dinner was Nan's stew: lumps of meat landmined with gristle, broth with its oily lace soaking into the mashed potato.

'So how was the ride?' John sipped from his can of beer, gave a soft, closed-mouthed burp. There were comb lines in his hair, and his skin was raw from sunburn and the shower.

Anna kept her eyes on her plate. 'Fine,' she said.

'How about you, Junie?' said John. 'Did you have fun?'

Junie put a forkful of mash into her mouth and let it dissolve. 'Yep.'

'Pretty ordinary set-up they've got there,' said Nan. 'Horses aren't much chop. I don't think we'll go back.'

They started talking about the garden, about the rosebushes.

Junie swirled more broth into her mash. Anna was looking at her. Anna's eyes shone and her lips pursed with a held-in smile, and there was a ballooning in Junie's chest, a hot, swift happiness, and she sat as still as she could, her own mouth twitching, her eyes on Anna's. *This, this, this,* she thought. *This, and nothing else.*

CRAZY BIRDS

They had not had their children yet. June was pregnant with the first, young and astonished, slowed to and mired in the rhythms of her own swelling. They were on the island, at the house that still felt like it belonged to Paul only. Where she might even find signs of other, past, women—a scented candle, a suspiciously unmasculine ornament, herbal tea—but the dark streams of envy and possessiveness ran, syrupy and remote, far beneath her then; she floated, impervious, well above.

They went to a party, not far away. They walked there, along the beach road, through night air oily with the smell of muttonbirds.

'They nest in the dunes, in burrows,' Paul said. 'And when the babies are big enough the parents fly off and leave them. They fly all the way to Alaska, can you believe it? And then a couple of weeks later the babies come out and fly there too.'

'To Alaska?'

'Yeah.'

'But how do they know the way?'

'They just know.' He pointed. 'Guess what they call that beach?'

'What?'

'Crazy Birds.'

A car came and they got up on the tussocky verge while it passed. She watched the headlights bump across the dune. She thought she could hear things, underground stirrings, soft cries.

The party was someone's fortieth, a friend of a friend of Paul's. The house was on a deep block, walled with old cypresses— tall, heavy-limbed, fragrant in the dark. There was a fire, and people sitting on logs. Inside the house a cluster of children lay before a television.

June drank mineral water. Paul drank beer. He introduced her to people, he sat with her; he treated her with great care and she took it as her due, sliding her hand in circles over her belly. The sky filled with the shapes of the muttonbirds coming in to land on the dunes, veering and flapping with hectic purpose.

'My family had a place on the island,' June said to an older woman. 'My grandmother. At Red Rocks—over the other side. I spent all my holidays there. By the time I was a teenager I thought it was the most boring place on earth. I was like, "I am *never* coming back." And then I met Paul, and he said, "I've got this house . . ."' She laughed.

'And now you'll be bringing *your* kids here,' said the woman.

'Yeah.'

But it didn't seem real—actual children, an actual baby— even when she felt the movements inside, solid and forceful. She couldn't get any kind of a grasp on the future—she was stuck in this, this heavy *now*.

It was not unpleasant. She had never been generous before, to herself, had never been kind. She had, in fact, been more or less unkind to her body, had fed it thoughtlessly, joylessly, had groomed it with a haste that was almost squeamish.

When she first met Paul, during one of their first weekends together, feeling the sting of possible cystitis, she began drinking glass after glass of water.

'Wait, wait.' Paul put his hand to her wrist as she glugged.

'It's a cure,' she said. 'You fill your bladder completely, and then drain it. Flushes out the infection.'

'Fair enough, but surely you don't have to slam it down like it's some kind of torture.'

She lowered the glass. Her stomach sloshed. She thought of the sex she'd had with others, before him. Nothing bad had happened, nothing truly debasing or shameful, but shame is what hid in her overfilled belly, at the falseness of these encounters, at her lack of actual pleasure, at the pretence, which she had held on to even when she was alone again. Sitting hungover in the kitchen of her flat, her robe undone, seeing herself from the outside as she smoked a cigarette that only made her feel sick—who was she acting for? Then, she didn't know, but later she would think it was perhaps for other women, for her friends at work, or her old uni friends. Women who were not lost, who knew how to have fun.

She is fifteen, lumpy and miserable. Lost, already. At Red Rocks, in the narrow dark strip of front garden.

Anna's too young to be getting into that sort of trouble . . . and Junie, what's happened? She's lost all her confidence.

Her grandmother's voice, accusing. Her grandmother and her father on the far side of the clothesline, screened by beach towels. Nan's hands appear, undoing the pegs.

John's voice is thick. *They're teenagers. You can't blame everything on me, Mum. On the divorce.*

She retreats, brushing against the geraniums that grow leggy and untended along the fence.

You think I wanted all this to happen? He's crying now, and she feels the familiar constriction, the weight.

There is the sound of a towel slipping off, flopping into the basket. *The marriage was a bad choice*, says Nan. *In the first place. I could've told you that.*

Whatever she was at that party—fat, slow, her nipples and veins and every bit of soft tissue sweetly and sharply hormonal—she was not lost. She was firmly anchored, there on the log with Paul's arm around her. She sipped her mineral water. Was it just the hormones that had done this, let kindness in? Later, with the first two children born, when she launches unexpectedly into a couple of years of good work, she will say that having kids saved her from herself. *I just didn't have time to indulge in my own neuroses any more.* This will be true—but it's also true that certain things don't go away, that certain things can and will lie dormant, biding their time.

The log became uncomfortable and she got up and walked around the garden, in the shelter of the cypresses. She inhaled their resin, her feet sinking into drifts of dead needles.

Nothing will grow under a cypress. Her grandmother's voice, its flat knowingness, unbreachable. *The marriage was a bad choice.* It wasn't the marriage Nan had meant—it was Helen, June's mother. Helen had been the bad choice. Nan was long dead, and Helen far away and not—whether good or bad, whether chosen or otherwise—really a mother any more, but June could feel it still, very deep, as if between her muscles, the innermost, unseen layers of tissue: wrongness, division, a tearing.

Eventually she wandered inside and stood shyly in the entrance to the roomful of children. Like someone visiting a zoo she took in their slim shoulders, their sprawled limbs, the softness of their hair. They gazed, steadfast, at the screen.

When she went out again Paul was coming towards her. 'I was looking for you,' he said. He put his arms around her and she felt his kiss on the top of her head.

She leaned into him, deliciously tired. 'Let's go.'

'Hey,' he said. 'Did you meet Cindy?'

'Cindy? I'm not sure . . .'

'That's her over there.' He indicated a woman on the far side of the fire—thin, long-haired, of indeterminate age. She sat leaning forward, looking into the flames, sipping from a glass.

'She's an old friend of Dave's,' said Paul. 'She needs some-where to crash and she's got her kid with her. Little—only three years old. She got a lift with someone and thought she'd sleep here, but the kid's tired and there aren't any spare beds.'

June will go back over this, years later, when jealousy floods her like a toxin. The way Paul spoke, his awkwardness. The infor-mation he gave—too much, too hastily delivered. When she can't see straight, when she is in fact mad with envy, she will think that of course he was nervous, of course he was uncomfortable, because he had slept with this Cindy, had perhaps slept with her only recently, not long before the two of them—Paul and June—came together. That he had probably not ended things properly, and this Cindy felt she still had some kind of claim. Because when June is in this poisoned state, the things she loves about Paul—his kindness, his gentleness—become weaknesses, ripe for abuse.

And later still, when the madness has gone, and—like all pain—become an abstract thing, shrunken and implausible, she will think that yes, perhaps Paul's nervousness, his discomfort, was because he had slept with Cindy at some stage, in the past. Which would have been fine. Or perhaps he and Cindy had never slept together and he was nervous because he was worried that she—June—might think they had, and be jealous.

But at the time she didn't even register his nervousness, if it did exist. At the time, she said, 'Yes, of course,' and leaned against him again as they walked towards Cindy, lifting his arm around her because it was late now and she was getting cold.

Cindy had a stroller and loaded the child—asleep already— into it. She stumbled as they went down the driveway.

Drunk, June thought, and a stiffness came into her. *How could you, with a kid?*

In the night, in the dark, she woke to a clear, thin call. Blurrily she wallowed from her side to her back, lifted her head from the pillow. A bird? From the dunes—lost or trapped somewhere in their yard, or on their roof. But it came again, resolved into a voice, human, youthful.

'Mu-um! Mummy!'

It was the child, Cindy's daughter, in the next room.

'Mum! Mum! Mum!' Sobbing. Then the crash of a door swinging open and the light thud of bare feet.

June hauled herself upright, elbowing Paul.

'Mum!' came the cry.

She put on the bedside lamp and got out of the bed, reaching for clothes.

'What's happening?' Paul blinked, rumpled, his bare chest flushed.

'She's up,' whispered June. 'The little girl.'

More wailing from the main room.

'But what about Cindy?'

She shook her head. 'I don't know. She must be still asleep.'

'I'll try to wake her,' he said, pulling on some shorts.

He went out first. June followed, buttoning her pyjama top. The child was standing by the couch, silent now, a shadowy figure beyond the spill of light from the bedroom.

'Misty?' Was that really her name? It seemed like a dream, them walking along the beach road, Cindy pushing the stroller, her skinny elbows stuck out, staggering slightly when they reached the corner. When they got to the house it had been Paul who lifted the sleeping child and carried her in. Cindy's face was white and sharp-boned under the porch light. She went to the railing and lit a cigarette. *She's a beautiful kid*, said June. *What's her name?* Cindy didn't turn around, spoke into the darkness, so low June wasn't sure she heard properly. *Misty.*

June stepped closer, moving slowly. 'Misty, it's okay.'

She could hear Paul in the other bedroom: 'Cindy? Hey, Cindy . . .'

She knelt. 'Hi, Misty, you don't know me but I'm a friend of your mum's.'

Paul came out. 'I can't wake her.' He switched on a lamp. 'She's okay,' he said. 'She's just really fast asleep. She was a bit . . . you know.'

June turned back to the child. 'You okay, Misty? Did you have a bad dream? It's all right. Why don't you hop back into bed with your mum?'

In the light the kid's eyes were huge. She had thick, dirty-blonde hair and freckles, and there was a bruise on one of her bare, pale shins. Her lips, her open mouth, looked very red. She was wearing a pink dress with stains and a picture on it of a rabbit in a pair of sunglasses.

'Come on,' said June, and held out her hand.

Misty took it.

Then June put her other hand on the seat of the couch to lever herself back up, brushing against Misty's dress and feeling the wet patch, and at the same time smelling the smell. 'Oh,' she said. 'Misty, did you have a wet bed, is that what woke you up? It's all right, come on, let's find you some dry clothes.'

Paul brought a clean t-shirt and June took Misty's wet dress and underpants off and slipped the t-shirt over her head. Misty went on staring, open-mouthed, but she didn't resist. Once the clean clothes were on she took hold of June's hand again.

'What do we do now?' whispered June to Paul.

'Shall we make you a bed on the couch here, Misty?' said Paul. 'Your bed mightn't be very nice to sleep in, if it's a bit wet.'

Misty stared.

Paul brought a blanket and a pillow and arranged them. 'There you go,' he said.

Misty tightened her grip on June's hand.

'Hop in, Misty,' said Paul.

Misty shook her head.

'We can leave the lamp on,' said June.

Misty put her free arm around June's leg.

June and Paul looked at each other.

'Do you want to sleep with us then?' said June. 'In our bed?'

Misty didn't answer, but when June took a step towards the bedroom she shuffled with her, not letting go.

*

They lay with the kid between them. It felt wrong. June switched off the bedside lamp but they'd left on the one in the main room and she could see Misty's open eyes shining in the dimness beside her.

Paul turned his back and might have been asleep, but as soon as there was a sound from the other room—rustling, and then Cindy's quiet call: 'Misty?'—he got up and went out. June heard him saying something about towels and then the opening and closing of the hallway cupboard.

Paul came in again. 'Come on, Misty,' he said. 'We've fixed up your bed so you can hop back in with your mum.'

Misty scrambled down and left the room, gliding silently in the oversized t-shirt.

June lay awake for what seemed like hours. The sky was beginning to lighten and the birds to call before she finally fell asleep, and the next time she woke it was late.

The house was quiet. The mattress from the second bedroom was out in the backyard, propped against a bush in the sun. In the laundry the washing machine whirred and rocked.

'Hello?' called June.

The second bedroom contained nothing but the bare-slatted bed base. In the main room the sunlight fell evenly on the timber floorboards, the shabby couch, the bookshelf and cobwebs and jars of shells and the paintings on the walls, all of which belonged to Paul, from before June's time.

The front gate opened and Paul came in, his hair in damp spines, his wetsuit a flapping skirt around his hips. Through the glass door she watched him strip the suit off and hose it and his surfboard down. The bend of his lean back, his brown arms.

In the kitchen she said, 'What happened to Cindy?'

He shrugged, propped against the bench in his towel. 'She must've left. Walked back round to Dave's, I reckon, to get a lift back to town.'

'So you didn't see her?'

He shook his head. 'I slept in, too.' He came closer, put his arms around her. 'But not as long as you did.'

'It took me ages to get back to sleep.'

He tried to kiss her but she moved out of his hold. There was anger in her, prudish and tight. She glanced out at the mattress, a glaring white slab against the green. 'Did she leave a note?'

'No. She was probably really embarrassed.'

She sliced some bread and put it in the toaster. 'How could you do that? Get drunk like that, with a kid? So drunk you couldn't even wake up when she needed you?'

'I think she's pretty good, usually. I don't know her that well, but from what Dave says she does it pretty tough, and . . . I mean, it must be hard, on your own. She probably didn't intend to get drunk. And it's not like she needed to drive or anything.'

June thought of the automatic, world-weary way Cindy had raised the glass to her lips, of Cindy's pale face under the porch light, the cigarette—and in her soft, ripe body there was no sympathy, only cold judgment.

For years Cindy was forgotten.

That summer went on. June advanced into the waves at the surf beach, her belly clenching with Braxton Hicks contractions. She struggled up the dune path, laughing and holding on to Paul.

The baby was born and everything shifted. They brought her to the beach house on weekends and tiptoed while she slept. They carried her in a sling and sheltered her little face from the sun, the wind, the spray; they stood close together looking down at her.

June's body retracted, dried out, took on a new form, narrower in some places, wider in others. It bore small silvery marks. Eventually it filled again, with hormones, fluids, and there was another child, and, later, a third.

Time sped up. The children grew. When the youngest was a baby June passed through the period of dreadful possessiveness. Whenever Paul was home she snapped at him. She held herself back all day, dampening the surges of irritation, the queasy anxiety, the pain in her body, the exhaustion. She forced her voice to be patient and gentle. She trudged home from picking up the oldest child from school with the baby crying in the pram and the others bickering. She had urges to hurt them. She went into rooms and closed doors behind her and wrenched at her own hair and let her face contort in agony. Sometimes she did this in front of the children and saw them become still and watchful. Once she did it in front of them and they took no notice, and that was when she resolved to do it only in private.

Certain pockets of calm would open, always when Paul wasn't around, and her love for him would swoop down on her as she lay feeding the baby on the couch, the toddler asleep and the oldest at school, and she would fill to bursting with the need to be near him, to let him know, to unblock the neglected channel between them. But then later, when the chaos closed over her again, she would forget—or not forget, but not be able to summon the sweetness again, to have the energy for it—and she would snarl at him from under the smothering mantle of her resentment, her fatigue, and her bewilderment, because she didn't quite understand how she had ended up where she was.

At night, when she couldn't get back to sleep after feeding the baby, she would go into the study and open Paul's box of personal things—old photos and worn paperback books with aeroplane boarding passes inside them. A couple of the books had inscriptions and were clearly gifts from lovers. She read them over and over, flayed herself with them. She searched the faces in the photographs—which showed Paul alone or with friends, other young men mostly, but also mixed groups—and was violently, caustically, envious of them all, male and female alike. She studied Paul's face—younger, fresher, in the richer tones of photographs taken in the 1970s and 80s—and ached at not having known him then, at not having been there with him, at not having had him all to herself, always.

Later, she will wonder if what she had been envious of wasn't Paul's having loved others, but Paul's former life in general—which she had chosen to see as free and diverse and bold, the opposite of hers. His former self stood grinning with surfboards by cars, white-hot under the sun, while hers sat in the shadowy kitchen, smoking, tarnished with shame and fakery.

When she does think of Cindy again, one day, she is unable to bring her into focus. Cindy remains a blurred figure, dark and unknowable. What June finds herself thinking of, with shock, is her own judgment—so clean, so categorical, so entirely and regretfully unworldly.

She realises that it wasn't only Cindy's lapse in parental responsibility that provoked in her such condemnation. It was more—it was Cindy's unhappy, bony face, the aura of dissatisfaction that clung to her, the unwillingness in her pointed elbows as she ploughed the stroller down the gravel driveway.

Had Cindy been drunk and happy, she realises, she—June—would have felt differently about her.

She sees herself: not yet a mother, not one at all, but thinking herself one. How, kneeling, speaking gently, helping Misty out of the wet clothes and into dry ones, she had, in part, been putting on a show for Paul, of being capable, motherly. A demonstration of how things would be when it was their turn, of the fact that they would *get it right*. She sees how the warm light under which this display was performed threw Cindy, insensible in the wet bed—flawed and unpalatably discontented, but surely, *surely*, deserving of compassion—into impenetrable darkness.

And she sees Misty, her white skin, her bruise, the redness of her mouth. How readily she took June's hand and followed her, how passively her small body accepted June's touch. She remembers this and groans aloud.

RED ROCKS BEACH

Here is his burrow, where he can listen, and he can have his fire, and smoke and drink. When the fire is really hot he gets a tightening of the skin on his face and the backs of his hands. He waits for it, and then he takes the first sip of cold beer, and this is true pleasure. True pleasure.

He sleeps, when the beer's finished. Stars show through the holes in his burrow roof. Waves shush him to sleep, and his fire sucks its flames back in and just glows enough for company.

Rabbit, rabbit.

Certain birds wake him. Wrens are best, sweet and polite, very close, so small they are just a flutter, soft brown or magic blue. Gulls, well, they're not subtle but they are cheery in the mornings, they celebrate, all in a gang, passing over, down to the beach for fishing. Plover are the worst. They start while it's still dark, angry faraway yelling and scolding, and once you've heard that all you can see in your mind are those crazy yellow eyes.

Rabbit, rabbit.

He waits for the sky to do its colours. Pink means time to get up.

He has a system of dunny markers, so he won't dig the same place twice.

Then down to the beach, which is all his in the pink morning. Little waves, little shells winking. Ah, this beach loves him, shines for him. The pink light cleans him and a string of gull voices ties itself around his shoulders and he is beautiful. Beautiful.

But now he has to go back, into his burrow, he has to thump his feet, run and dive.

Dive, rabbit.

And hide, squat behind his leaf wall, so still even though inside his heart is speeding. His eye to a peephole. If he keeps still, look, he is invisible, his eye actually takes on the colour of the leaves around it, his skin too, his face. No wonder they get such a fright when they see him, mottled brown and grey and the silver of paperbark trunks, and the dark green of ti-tree leaves.

It's a horse, on the beach. Girl on top. Smart horse, does a sideways jump, nostrils at him, shakes its flying hairs. It rolls its big eye, blows a trumpet breath. In the bushes, says the horse.

Rabbit.

Molly! says the girl, mean voice. She's smart too, she frowns and stares but all she can see is brown and green.

It's all right, Molly, says the girl, nice voice now. Come on.

This Molly! Her neck, so strong and bendy, her round marks like the sun dots that fall into his burrow, her legs that go so narrow before they hoof. She is lovely. Lovely! And she feels him loving her, she goes along nicely now, she puts her tail high for him.

Daylight. It's time. Mum is waiting and telly, but he can't. There's a feeling like needing the dunny, but it's in his brain. He hates when this happens. He whacks his hands on his thighs, come on, what is it, it's keeping him, it must be dealt with.

What happens, nowadays, as opposed to before

when he was a boy

when he wasn't brown and green
when he walked out bright
when he wore swimming shorts and walked out bright
his chest bare and normal skin
a boy!
What happens nowadays is things get stuck. It's mostly when
unusual things happen, like this
unusual thing
which was
rabbit, rabbit
something coming along
which was
on the beach
big and bendy, hooves and jumping
animal
Molly!
He very easily loses his thread. There are things he needs so
as to keep his mind in more or less working order, and they are
his burrow
his beer
his fire
the stars
his own pink morning beach
and then home to Mum and telly
Argh, what is it, this thing that's stuck? A shape in his mind,
wrapped up soft, he will need to squeeze it out.
But Mum and telly! He is waiting too long! He will get caught
here in his burrow when people come!
Breathe. Breathe. It's okay. This happens, it happens. He
knows what to do.
Hop, hop, rabbit.

Lie down on his soft floor. Put his hand to the white bones
of his fire, so it nearly hurts. Close his eyes and squeeze. Start
with one thing and try to follow, don't get tempted to go off
albino rabbit on the top of Red Rocks
actually a toy
someone left
with the stuffing coming out
where its ear was gone
and
No, that's wrong. Come on. Breathe. Start with
washed-up stingray
flipped on its back
pale
u-shaped thing, a mouth?
No, not that either. Slow down. Start again, what about
the Shell House and Mum bought him a box all covered on
the outside with shells
and inside there was felt, dark blue
for your treasures, she said
and then
it was lost
fell
from his bag
when he was riding
his bike
No. No! Shh. Calm. Breathe. Molly. Molly.
Molly! Yes, that is the start!
Molly's hooves, black in sand
Molly's sun dots
Molly's white hairs
furry ear cups, going front and back

Not quite it. Breathe, squeeze, he's close. It's not quite Molly, it's
the girl

girl

on top of Molly

dark hair, mean voice

he knows this girl

knew

this girl

when she wasn't big

when she wasn't sad

Ah, and it's all connected, see, because how does he know
this girl? From other times when he stayed too long, when he
got stuck in one of his burrows and had to creep and run and
dive with absolute caution, with the utmost care because

rabbit, rabbit

people

daytime people

big and pink

with bags and buckets and sticks

all bright colours

shoes

tromping through

They don't look. As a rule. As a rule, he is safe. But. Once
a boy, little, walking behind, he saw, round eyes and a jump
in the air, pink mouth and wet crying and legs running away.
And once a woman, quick stop and flat hand on her chest, then
walking off fast.

And so. The bones of his fire fluff into nothing. He lets his
hand fall. He has it now. Not Molly. Girl on Molly, and him
stuck in a burrow once or twice, or actually more times than

that, because what he saw, waiting, still, squatting green and
brown, was many things, different times, what he saw was

girl running down
little then
scissor legs
she belongs at the gumtree place
big garden
garden lady
old lady
always there
there when he was different
before
when he walked out bright
a boy

Garden lady on her steps, and him a boy on the fire track.
Here, she says. Here, Greg. Lemons, for your mum. Noisy white
bag, lemons inside shoot clean smells.

But he's gone off again. He's lost the shape. Just go back
quickly over it. Molly, that was it, and the girl on top. The

girl
little
garden lady's little girl
running
and him
brown hiding
girl running
down to the beach

Little girl with scissor legs, then she gets bigger, but always she
has another one, her own girl, always smaller, running behind.
When they are little they run close, hands holding, then they

get bigger and they run apart, one dark, one light. They get
bigger but

now

a time

of not

no girls

just garden lady

sad on the path

sad in her legs

sad in her soft shoes

And now big girl, back, but she's lost her own girl. And now
this is sad, and it's a bit like how Mum

lost

him

Mum still looks

she looks in him

she comes too close

she tries his eyes

his ears

his mouth

she talks like her boy might hear

but her boy is gone

and

he

wishes

he could bring him back

but

he

can't

he

doesn't

know

how

He gets up. His eyes are wet. The morning is gone now. Pink, beautiful, winking morning, gone away.

Time to creep

hop, hop, rabbit

along his paths of green and brown, with utmost care.

Down on the beach Molly left poo, a message for him. Golden, round, he feels it fall from her high tail, plop to the sand. Remember me, says the poo. Beautiful Molly! And that girl on top, so sad, sad knees, sad fingers holding Molly's reins. He sends his own message, sends it out with brainpower, along the track of Molly's hooves: Hold on, girl.

He makes sure he is properly brown and green, and then he lopes along his path.

MOLLY

Junie hates going to bed in that room, across from the other, empty, bed. She stays up late, watching TV with Nan, squashed into a corner of the couch, feet tucked under, hands drawn into the sleeves of her jumper. Nan's small bar heater glows red and gives off a singeing smell. In its light Nan's feet are brown and shapeless, crossed at the ankles, toenails reflecting orange-pink.

Nan finishes her whisky, gets up and slices an apple, passes Junie a piece. On the telly the green fields and hedges and narrow roads of *All Creatures*. One of the vets, drunk, gets ready to deliver a calf; he bends over a bucket to wash his hands and the soap goes flying. Then there is *Derrick*, the German detective with his leather jacket and creepy tinted glasses.

'It's the doctor,' says Nan. 'You watch.' And when it is, when Derrick and the police barge in and grab him and put on the handcuffs: 'I write the scripts, you know.'

Sadness at these in-jokes, these repetitions. Junie feels it in her lungs, like she can't get the breaths all the way down.

A strobe-flash of memory: sounds in the darkness and then the light blazing, everything flat and stark in their bedroom, the something's-wrong feeling of the middle of the night. Dad's big legs going past in pyjama pants, Dad's hair all sticking up. Anna's face against the pillow, the scrape of her breathing. Tears rolling out, one each side. *There was a tiger lying on my chest.* Dad with the puffer. *Only a dream. Here, sit up, big breath, ready?*

'Junie,' says Nan. 'Go to bed.' The telly is off, the heater cooling. Nan's fingers tap her shoulder, rest there for a moment. 'Go on. You've got an early start.'

She gets up, follows Nan through the kitchen.

In the second bedroom she passes Anna's bed without looking at it, falls into her own.

She has trained herself to wake early. The window an only-just-there rectangle; plover calls raking the darkness. She pulls on jeans that smell of dirt and animal. She walks blind to the toilet and her urine smells animal too, rich, like cut grass.

In socks she passes Nan's open doorway, pausing to check for the dry whisper of her breathing.

Shutting the back door quietly, bending for her boots, then away—past the clothesline, the geraniums, the letterbox and white-painted fence. She strides, silent, to the gate, and through.

The shining road, the sleeping houses. Moist, cool air on her face, sliding into her lungs. She pushes up the slope, feels the strength in her legs.

Cypresses at Mr Pierce's. Spider webs, fresh and taut. The gate's chain cold and heavy. The shed mouth is black; she'll have to feel for the bridle and saddle, and not think about spiders. At the back of the paddock, in the velvet shelter of the trees, there are legs, wisps of white, the turn of a head like gauze floating.

'Molly.' Taking out the apple.

The horse comes out of the dark, a magic trick, a developing Polaroid. Hooves, ears, nostrils, black-edged, as if soaked in ink; galaxies of dapples across her chest.

From the top of the hill she can see the pink sky, the wedge of sea through the break in the scrub. Black, pink, soft grey—new colours, like something just born. She feels so high on top of Molly. It used to feel like falling, but now it's more as if she could take off and fly down, skim the car park, the ti-tree, the sand messy with seaweed and rocks, the rising curves of waves. She nudges the horse down the slope, leans back into the one-two, one-two of their descent.

Junie Worth, seventeen years old, riding a horse in the dawn, down to the beach. What is everyone else doing, these September holidays?

In the last week of term Cassie Dean had stopped Junie outside the lockers to issue an unforeseen and inexplicable invitation, redolent of Extra chewing gum: *Come to Lorne, Junie? Tammie's coming, and Juliet, and Ricky and Spence; it's gunna be awesome.*

And there was Samantha Holmes, skinny, friendless, pink-rimmed nostrils and crooked teeth, coarse brown hair cut in a shelf of fringe, Junie's unacknowledged companion in maths methods and biol. Samantha the shy smiler and lender of pens. Her blush, her nervous hands: *If you don't have anything on in the holidays, maybe we could . . .*

Junie shook her head at Samantha. She shook her head at Cassie. She shook her head at Ms Howell, who called her back after chem. *Now, Junie, I understand things at home have been a bit—difficult. If you ever need to talk . . .*

She has splintered off. From them, and from what her life might have been.

They reach flat ground, the car park, and Molly's gait loosens, her neck lengthening as they enter the beach path, the dark passage through the ti-tree.

The beach is a moonscape, the sea metallic. Molly snorts and props at a pile of seaweed. This is intentional, Junie knows— high spirits—but a week ago such a stunt would have had her off balance, jaw tight, heart pounding. Now, she lets her back give, sways with the horse's little sideways jump. She clicks her tongue, sends a message with thighs and seat: *Enough of that.*

It had been Nan's idea, Molly. Nan knew Mr Pierce, who read the water meters, and also Mr Pierce's daughter, who worked at the supermarket. *He's bought another horse*, said Nan. *His wife's not happy about it. An Arab mare, lovely temperament, very quiet. He says would you like to ride her, keep her from getting too fat.*

Really?

Go on, it'll be good for you, get you out of the house.

But I haven't ridden for years.

What about that horse camp? With school?

Yeah, but . . .

It'll come back to you.

So, no supervision, nothing. She has never even met Mr Pierce.

That first morning, opening the gate, clumsily replacing the chain, she had a bubble in her chest that threatened to burst into fear, into failure. The camp, the camp—what could she remember? Her classmates' R.M. Williams and spotless jodhpurs and the shame of her own jeans and op-shop boots. The cabins, small, unheated; metal bunks with vinyl mattresses; Amelia Wright squealing at a centipede. What about the actual horses? Riding? Lessons? All Junie could dredge up was one long, plodding trail ride, with Amelia Wright complaining of a broken fingernail, and the dim interior of a large shed in which a woman—tracksuit, dirty sneakers, red hands and a scowl—brusquely applied straps and fastenings to a long-suffering knock-kneed bay, and then, pointing to the animal's shoulder, said, *That there's the intercostal nerve centre.*

She had nothing, really, no knowledge. She was on her own.

But then Molly herself, her patience as Junie fumbled with saddlecloth and buckles, her placid acceptance of the bit. And then, when they were finally out on the road and she'd clambered up and got everything arranged, armpits and back prickling with sweat, the sudden, unexpected, arrival of instructions. Not from the horse camp, or from an earlier, dusty, sun-blasted visit to Macca's Trail Rides here on the island, which now seemed like ancient history, and which in any case her memory abruptly withdrew from, like a finger put to hot metal, because of Anna. (Anna on that galloping pony, helmet tipped forward, red laughing mouth.) These instructions came from somewhere even further back; from a long-neglected part of her mind. Complete sentences, she saw them, floating, black on white, in the blockish, serif print of childhood library books. *A straight line should run from the rider's heel to ear, through hip and shoulder. Rein length depends on gait and activity. Imagine a piece of elastic stretching from the bit to the rider's elbow.* She clung to these, those first few rides, rigidly and joylessly, girded herself with rules and invisible lines, and returned to Nan's sore and exhausted, and full of a kind of tense triumph.

The pleasure, the strength, in meeting Nan's *How'd you go?* with an equally off-handed *Fine.*

It was time that showed her what else was to be had, that thawed her, woke her up to the beach, the dawn, the secret wildness of it. The piles of rocks, their tide-smoothed edges. The carved channel where Saltwater Creek met the sea, the cleanness of its low, vertical sand walls. Molly's snorts and head-tosses, her mane flicking like seaweed, like the froth of waves, the plunging of her hooves.

She walks back in the glare, ravenous, unshowered, needing the toilet. The sky still white, the air not yet warm. The flat damp grass, the lemon tree, the vegetable garden rioting behind its fence. She is tired, and empty, and this is how she needs to be. But still, before she can get inside and into the bath-room—*Anna!* shouts the sky, the lemons, the ants rushing on branches. *Anna! Anna! Anna!*

Nan and Mrs White from next door in the shade of the mirror bush, one each side of the fence, low voices. Junie behind the compost heap, kneeling, hidden.

Nan: *You try to think of explanations. She's never been an easy kid. Always sick. Prone to asthma, things like that. Trouble sleeping. Bites her nails. But Rob was like that, my first son. You never saw a boy so worried about everything. It was the war, I think, not that he remembered, but he'd have heard us talking about it. If a plane flew over he always came inside. Didn't say anything, just came in and stood beside me, waiting for it to pass.*

Mrs White: *Yes, but he turned out all right, didn't he? Rob?*

Nan (impatiently): *Well, maybe he did, Rhoda, but do we really know? We just sent them off to boarding school, who knows what happened to them, if they were all right or not?*

Mrs White: *Yes, but look at him now, he's—*

Nan: *He told me he hated it. He came home for his first holi-days and didn't say a word, and then when I drove him back for second term, he just said it quietly, as we pulled up to the gates.*

I hate it here, Mum. *Just like that, sad little voice. He knew it wouldn't change anything.*

Mrs White: *Poor boy. But he came good, didn't he?*

Nan: *I think the difference is, with kids these days, kids like Anna, well they just don't know where they stand. They've got these parents saying,* All we want is for you to be happy. *Happy! We never worried about happiness, we just got on with it. Rob wasn't happy, was he, but yes, he got on with life. And John, well, he was happy enough, far as I knew, and now look what a mess he's made of things.*

Mrs White and Junie on the fire track. Junie head down, half-turned for the gate.

Mrs White: *Mr White and I are thinking of your family, dear. And praying, although your grandmother doesn't approve of that!*

Junie (mumbling): *Thanks.*

Mrs White: *She'll come good, don't you worry.*

Junie: *Thanks.*

Mrs White: *And Lois—your gran—tells me that Anna's stayed back these holidays, at home, with Mum?*

Junie: *Yep.*

Mrs White: *Pardon, dear?*

Junie: *Yes, that's right.*

Mrs White: *Well, that's nice, isn't it. For her to have that time. That attention. That's probably the best thing for her.*

Anna crying in the night. Anna's asthma. Anna rocking her head side to side on the pillow after lights-out. *What are you doing? Stop it!* Anna's bitten fingernails, her cuticles red and oozing. Anna's blinking, her tapping, her throat-clearing, the pink spot of scalp where she'd pulled hair out. *Stop! But I can't help it!* Anna on the whizzy-dizzy at the park, seven years old, head tipped back, laugh spiralling into an animal bleat, leaning out and further out, the flick of her unseeing gaze. Letting go, hitting the gravel and skidding, the hollow at the base of her throat, the spurt of yellow vomit. Anna on the pony, her wild grin, her laugh, her hidden eyes. Anna at twelve, smoking cigarettes at the tram stop. Anna at fifteen, smoking on the roof at Mum's, coming back in through the skylight, school dress catching to show cuts on her thighs in tight rows, fresh ones scabbed and dark, older ones pink, like raised texta marks. Anna seen by Tammie Markos at Flinders Street Station with some guys, older, drinking from a hipflask. Anna at Dad's, shouting: *Shut up, shut up, shut up!* A wineglass exploding against the skirting board.

Anna will be all right. This is what Dad said, in the car, driving back to the flat, which is where Junie lives now, with him, where she sleeps alone in another room with two beds, meant for two sisters.

Anna won't go to Dad's. Anna keeps making new rules for herself.

She'll be all right. Looking away. The mad tick of the indicator.

And again, after parking in the sunless yard at the back of the flats, on top of the big number six, faded white inside its faded white rectangle. Pittosporum lunging from the fence line, indentations in their lower foliage from the bonnets of the cars. Putting his hand on Junie's knee. *She'll be all right.*

But how could he know?

LOIS

Awake, bed . . . Damn, the thing, the—the—strabe. Stran. Toke.
She was out in the spar, walking the plants, and

She was in the garn, knees wet, she dropped the horn. The slobe

it dropped and wet her. She was spanning up she thought but
no, sideways and something digging. Stickins. Cranchels

Awake, bed, hobe—home. Window-top, door. Someone there.
A close voice: 'Mum?'

※

A stoke

in the granden

she dropped the drove and it wet her knees

she was sideways in the bushes and cranches stuck in

⁂

Words are harb

worbs take worb

too mush worb

So tire. Rest, close her gars.

⁂

Words come. Quite easily, on their own, if she lets them. It's the trying that breaks them, makes it worse.

Here she is again. Awake. Dark now, someone there though, beside her, too high to see. Only that small opening, a slibe. Slice. *I'm here, hello?*

⁂

Light again. She's fairly sure she can't speak.

She is awake though, can't they see? Tiptoeing about, ridiculous. She's here, here! In the bed, awake and hearing. Seeing too, though only a clinch. A—bit. Only a bit. Top of window, doorway.

Someone bends in. A woman, a stranger. 'Just going to turn you over now, Mrs Worth, that's it . . .' The window goes, arcs away, now it's the dresser, the photos in their frames.

74

'Can she hear us, do you think?'

'It's possible, yes. Talk to her. Just try. It might feel odd at first but it'll get easier.'

⁂

Someone near her feet, heavy hand through the blanket. Someone crying. It's Rob. Or John. One of her boys. Big now, though; a man.

'Mum, I don't know if you can hear me. It's Rob. Everyone's here. And a nurse, she's the one who's been turning you over.'

⁂

A stroke. She knew—off to her left the air swung like curtains and her arm went and the hose fell and she was sideways in the correa and there were oval things, beautiful with veins hairs silver-green, but the word blew away, *Leith, feiths,* and she went after it, thump thump, grab and grab, into the dark

Job. Rob. Rob? John? I'm here. But no answer so yes, the words mustn't be

Through her slice are the pictures in the frames, Johnny in the Austin, grinning out the window, and little Rob with the dogs, the kelpie and the other one, the white bitser, what was her name, and there had been another dog Rob used for rabbiting and there's a rabbit stew now in that big pot with the wrong lid never fit properly and in the kitchen at Churchill she wrings out the dishrag and hangs it on the back of the door and one of the boys calls, *Did you know, Mum, I've still got every marble I ever won, a hundred and five marbles*, and outside the crabapple tree shakes its branches, the fruit bright and hard, mean little things, but then they foam pulpy in the pot, toffee smell and the tea-spoon test the chilled saucer the wrinkling skin and oh tipping into jars the clear red liquid, *pure*, that's the word, breathing the steam sweet and tart

⟡

'Hi Nan. It's me, Junie.' Rustling, a freshness—leaves, grass, has she been out then, on the horse? But that was before, she's getting mixed up, Junie's grown now. Grown, off and away, Junie and, oh God she's tilting, she can't get it straight, the other girl, the one they lost, what was her name?

She can't speak. She can't move. Listening is tiring, and peering out all the time. She lets the slice close for a while, and another vista opens, wider, brighter. She shrinks and flies into it. Running down the hill to school with Mary Lyon. New socks, she will keep them white forever.

She makes a sponge cake, eggs flour sugar she could do it with her eyes closed, the electric mixer groans, it smells like burning if she turns it up too much.

Frank is dead, coming home from the Cowes RSL, drove into a pole. Mal Jennings at the door in his police uniform, taking off his hat like in a film.

Churchill State School, third grade, five fives are twenty-five, six fives are thirty, banging out the blackboard dusters with

Gladys Martin and there at the window is Billy Harding, *Lo-is and Gla-dys, yer lunch's full of mag-gots*, chalk-dry fingers, turn to the empty yard, *Just ignore him, Gladys, just pretend he's not there.* Miss Eldon with legs that go straight down, no ankles, brown stockings. *Seven eights are?* Straining upwards until her shoulder cracks, waggling her fingers, me, me, me! Miss Eldon scans. *Anyone? Anyone? Oh, all right then—Lois.* At lunch Billy Harding pinches Gladys on the arm but Gladys doesn't ignore him, she does a show-off yelp like a fat little pig and then smiles privately and Billy grins too, running like a madman across the yard although he has nowhere in particular to go. So now she says, *Please don't sit with me, Gladys, I'd rather be alone*, and she chews her sandwich with dignity and doesn't think of maggots, she drinks her milk, she smooths her dress, she tugs cardigan cuffs over frayed sleeves, she says her eight times table in her head. She knows what makes Miss Eldon hate her, what makes everyone hate her, and oh, she has lost Gladys now, her only friend, but when Gladys comes back with half a crumbly shortbread, saying, *Look, your favourite*, she stares just past her soft nice shoulder. *No thank you.* Later she'll cry but not now. She knows why they hate her, everyone except Gladys. Ike, they call her, Lois Ike Green, and Ike is for I Know Everything. But she cannot stop, she will not, the more Miss Eldon ignores her the higher her hand goes.

Frank: *The trouble with you, Lois, is that you always have to be right.*
  Lois: *But I am right.*
  Frank: *Generally speaking, yes, you are. But you don't need to let everyone know all the time.*

Well, she was right. She was right about that damn Helen. But yes, Frank, perhaps she should've kept it to herself. Is that what

it means, then, to be a mother? To suppress your own intelligence, to allow them their mistakes, to say, *Of course you should,
you just go ahead, yes, that's a good idea.* And then later, when
they come, angry, saying, *Why didn't you warn us, isn't that your
job*, then what? Well, then there's no other option but to go on
with the charade. *Oh dear, what a shame, I'm so sorry, I had no
idea it would turn out like that.* So you can't win; you're either
a know-it-all or an idiot.

Her father's voice now: *Nobody likes a know-it-all.*

And her mother is in the kitchen with Aunty Kit, playing cards
and smoking, and probably drinking whisky too, but her mother
sneaks into the drawing room to pour it so the bottle's not on
the table, and so it must be a Friday evening and her father's
at the RSL, and Ruby's out with Kelvin Harris and she's in her
room reading but then she sneaks into the corridor to listen
and her mother says, *I do worry about Lo, it's as if she goes out of
her way to put people off.* And Aunty Kit says, *Oh, perhaps she'll
mellow*, and her mother hisses in smoke and says, *I doubt it*, and
Aunty Kit says, *Gin!* And her mother says, *Darn you*, and then,
At least I've got Ruby.

❧

They are there still. She notices sometimes the feeling of someone
beside her, or of a hand holding hers, or touching her arm or leg.
That feels nice, she'd like to say, or, *Thank you*, but the phrases
dissolve. The nurse descends from time to time, and the room
lightens and darkens, although it's not as easy to tell, her little
slice seems to have shrunk and blurred, an uncleaned window

with the shade half-down. But she doesn't mind. She wishes she could let them know, reassure them, because they're upset, that much is clear. *I'm all right*, she wants to say. *I'm fine, really*, but again the words are barely formed before they're gone, clouds of breath on a cold morning.

Bitsy, she was called, the white dog. Bitsy the bitser.

And no one would dance with her at the Leaving dance, and it wasn't because of her dress, which had been Ruby's, which their mother took down as much as she could but which pinched under the arms and, once heated by her skin, gave off the smell of Ruby's stale sweat. Nobody spoke to her as she stood alone with her elbows in trying not to let the smell out, her feet hurting in shoes that had also been Ruby's, marked inside with the prints of Ruby's toes in grey. Ruby had danced, of course, Ruby had danced until she sweated, until her toes made marks in her shoes. Ruby wasn't a know-it-all, people liked her and now she worked at Bilson's and spent her money on Nice Things and did her nails of an evening with a little pot of special cream and an orange stick and said, *Come on, Lolly, let me do yours*, and why why why when she could sit in front of the fire and put her cold hand in Ruby's warm one and have Ruby lean in close with her sweet breath would she choose to shake her head and go into her room and close the door? But this is what she does, Lois Ike Green, who nobody will dance with.

On the other side of the dance floor Gwen Barker and Phyllis Neville are whispering and smirking and giving her looks and she pretends not to see, she pretends to be watching the dancers plod and wobble, or glide, in the case of Dianne Kelly. She even nods her head to the music, a bit but not too much, as if she doesn't mind it although it's not her favourite song, her favourite would be something much more sophisticated, which nobody here would even know of. And then there is someone at her elbow and a smell of lavender and a soft fat hand on her arm and Gladys Martin says, *Hello, Lois, I just thought I'd come to say hello and I think you look lovely in that dress*, and she turns and poor Gladys is in something ludicrous with purple flowers, like an armchair, and Gladys's nose is shiny and her little smile trembles. And she wants to say, *Gladys, I'm sorry I've been so mean, ever since third grade I've been mean to you and I have no excuse, I suppose I'm just a mean person*, but then the music stops and Mr Thomas is up on the stage, calling out in his headmaster's voice, *Ladies and gentlemen*, and Gladys whispers, *I'd better run, I'm helping give out the prizes*. And Gladys's hand lets go but she grabs it and pulls and feels her eyes stinging with tears and hears her own whisper hot and fierce: *Gladys, you are a good person*.

And Frank! Who she took for granted for so long, his freckly dullness, his determination. *Well, Lois Green, you'd better be ready on Friday evening because you're coming with me to the pictures, like it or not.* She was rude to him, she was dismissive, from the beginning there was a weight in her heart that said, Of course this is all you get, Lois, a trainee accountant with ginger hair.

Frank coming for dinner, a Churchill winter, smoky, dark. She doesn't change her dress and when her mother says, *Put out the good tablecloth*, she mutters, *What for?* Frank combed and tidy, the rims of his ears pink. Cutlery instead of conversation, the four of them knifing and forking as if their lives depended on it. Frank, at last, bravely: *This is delicious, Mrs Green.* Her father picking up his chop bone to gnaw, her mother inhaling through her nose, her father putting the bone down again. Afterwards her mother produces a trifle and the cut-glass dishes and Frank says, *Mrs Green, you didn't have to go to so much trouble*, and her mother says, *Oh, no trouble*, but makes a performance of the serving under the hanging lamp, passes out the dishes like a sacrament. And after that, a glass of sherry in the sitting room, her father at the fire, clanging a good deal longer than necessary with tongs and poker. Frank sits beside her on the couch and she stiffens like a dog. She wants to shout, *I'm not sure I even like him, can we all just wait a moment, please!* Her mother says to the air, *Ruby gave me the recipe for that trifle. Calls for a six-egg custard, very rich.* Frank says, *Oh.* His fingers are spread on his knees, there are freckles even on the knuckles. *Do you know Kelvin Harris?* says her mother. *No*, says Frank. *Ruby's husband*, says her mother, *he's an architect. Draftsman*, says her father. Her mother pretends not to hear, sips her sherry. *They've bought a place out on Mackeys Road, and they're going to make improvements, Kelvin's already drawn up the plans.* Her father goes out the back to get more wood and then someone knocks at the front door and her mother says, *That'll be Edna with the pattern for Ruby*, and rushes to answer it, and she turns to Frank and a horrible simpering voice comes out of her and says, *That'll be Edna. Don't you know Kelvin Harris? He's an architect*, and then there's a catch in her throat and she thinks, Shut up, Lois, you fool. But Frank smiles gently and she notices for the first time how nice his teeth are. With one finger he touches the back of her hand.

Oh, she's harboured some terrible thoughts. That Helen, she couldn't stand her; fast they used to call girls like her, and fast she was, whizzed right by them all and John under her thumb like that, a pushover, weak, no wonder she left him. She's thought it a shame those two daughters were ever born. She's thought John did it on purpose, finding exactly the wrong sort of woman and marrying her, she's thought he did it to spite her. When the girl was lost she thought they both deserved it, that it was their comeuppance. That's what happens, Helen, when you put yourself first, she thought. That's what happens, John, when you go in for that sort of a marriage. Terrible thoughts; good thing she kept them private.

But she was jealous, really that was it. What she would have given, to have been allowed Helen's audacity. To have been allowed to put her brain to use. That little smile Helen would have on at the dinner table, what was that smile saying? I'm better than you, Lois? With my degrees and my honours and my *career*? And I've got your son and he loves me and he doesn't even *like* you? No. No. Helen didn't care enough about her to even bother to gloat. Perhaps it was a smile of pity, which would have been worse. Perhaps it had no meaning, was just a smug expression, a habit, like her own face that all her life she's caught in mirrors with that jaw and those frowning eyes, a face that says, *Life has disappointed me.*

She was jealous of Helen but she was jealous, too, of the love between Helen and John, that early love, you couldn't miss it, it was a passion really, a love like a glittering sea.

One day, before they moved to the island but well after the boys had gone, it was winter, grey and sharp, and Bitsy hadn't been at the door in the morning but she'd been busy making biscuits for the library volunteers and then when she did go out she found her dead in the dog yard, cold and stiff by the water dish, and she hadn't liked Bitsy, who chewed things and was smelly even for a dog, and she was not afraid of a dead thing, God knows how many pets' graves she'd dug over the years, and how many chickens disposed of, but she began to shake like mad, her teeth chattering. Her knees gave and she sat on the wet grass. She might have sat there all day if Stan Harding hadn't come with the coal and seen her and he must've gone and fetched Frank, not that she was paying any attention, she'd completely dropped her bundle, it's like empty space to think of it now, she didn't even feel the cold. But then Frank was there and she was inside and he had her changed into dry clothes and in front of the fire, and he just sat with her and held her hands, and none of this she remembers properly, just a sort of coming-to and him there and her bleating like a pathetic little goat, *Poor Bitsy! Poor Bitsy!* And then after a while, *Nobody loved her and she died all alone.* And then eventually she gripped Frank's hands and stared right into his eyes and said, *The boys will never come back. They hate me. All they see is a mean old woman.* And Frank didn't speak, but he looked at her. He saw her, and he stayed where he was, not letting go.

Frank died and left her on the island, which was always his place. She made the best of it, and she did love it, she loves it now, the bright summers, gold and blue and the red of the rocks, and then the breezes sweeping in of an evening, and her garden, her roses, walking down the slope of lawn, the heavy petals, the perfume thick and warm, you could swoon breathing it. And the lemon-scented gums stirring overhead at night as she lay, as she lies now. She has loved the island, but it's Churchill she thinks of, she flies over it, the dark hills, the houses and damp gardens, the eaten-out valley behind, the smokestacks. There is her house, hers and Frank's, with the back verandah they had built in when Rob needed his own room, the crabapple tree and the woodpile, the incinerator, the dogs, she can see them running, and there's little John running too, around the house. And he vaults the front fence like a gymnast, he rises to meet her and she sees his falling-down socks, his knees red with cold, his darling face, he wants to tell her something, he's bursting with it, and all she has to do is listen but she can't hear him, his little voice darts away and now he's falling back, getting left behind and she can't turn around, she's flying on along the row of shops that are teeth to the road's tongue and down to the other end of town where, before the railway line curves out and away between hills, there is a low flat place and God knows what became of it, a supermarket most likely with a car park and fat people waddling to and fro, but it's not yet and it's not Greyson's wrecking yard yet either, with its rusted car skeletons, where Billy Harding went to work in his blue singlet, the muscles popping up on his scrawny arms and the stubble on his face like smudged dirt, because even when he was forty and a father of six he still managed to look like a ratbag kid. The cindery sky has wound itself back and back and taken the land with it and on that swampy flat where the houses were smaller and meaner and had yards speckled with rubbish and too many children, there is the house of her childhood, the tidiest one, and there is the outhouse and the chicken run and the passionfruit vine, and now she is swooping down and the chimney throws smoke at her and the fence flashes white and the letterbox, and now she is on the front steps and the sunlight stops at the fourth step up and if you sit at the right place you can split into two halves, a front that is bright and a back that is shadowy. And there is her father, his long legs, his hands in his pockets, he is walking up the path and he makes the steps creak and then he turns and down he comes beside her, enormous. He sighs and rests his wrists on his knees and she can see the black hairs on the backs of his fingers. *What do you know, Lo?* he says, and she takes hold of the material of his pants leg, and she looks up and sees his face lit but the back of his head in shadow and right then she does know something, but it's not something you can say, it's something you can only sense, like the coolness of a body of water—his mind, inside, a private mechanism that, like her own, like that of every person who exists in the world and ever has and ever will, speaks its own secret language.

In the Churchill Public Library a man came in drunk. She didn't know him. Army uniform, that Changi look, skinny, ruined. Came straight to the desk and took her hand, his fingers shaking, his lips hot on her knuckles. *Dianne Kelly*, he said, *you were the prettiest girl in Churchill.* A tear landed on her thumb. *If I had my time again I'd marry you quick before anyone else got a chance.*

Dianne Kelly! Her black hair, her green eyes, the collars of her blouses perfect, a swan of a girl. They didn't stay, girls like Dianne Kelly, didn't marry a ginger accountant and work at the library.

She didn't say, *I'm not Dianne Kelly.* She didn't say, *Dianne Kelly swanned off to Melbourne, married a doctor, left us all behind.* She didn't say, *We don't get our time again so might as well make the best of what you've got.* She didn't say anything; she raised her other hand and touched his hair, his ear, his cheek.

APPLEY AVENUE

Sun May 17th 1998

Arrived at Monica's. Bloody freezing. House is still a shitbox, don't know how she doesn't have major depression. (Perhaps she does?) Greg's room like a cell, he sleeps on a camping mat. Seem to recall a reason for this: he rips up mattresses. Will keep the door shut so I don't have to see.

M's room's okay, although reeks of old maid. Nice view of garden. I think that's all she's got.

No sign of cat. Put food out.

Called Ally, no answer. Didn't leave a message. Drank most of a bottle of wine then called again. Many times. Still no answer. I MUST STOP DOING THIS, THE WHOLE POINT OF THIS WEEK AT MONICA'S IS TO GET OVER ALLY.

Mon May 18th

Appley Avenue, sounds so pretty, like there should be apple trees, blossoms, but it's big dark cypresses, overgrown gardens, twisty ti-tree. Don't remember it being so dark. Guess I've never been here when it's not summer. Even the beach seems gloomy, grey,

grey, grey, and brutal wind. Got paints out but no energy, did a few sketches. Did not see one person.

M rang. Greg needs eight teeth out! Root canal and some other procedure involving bone, didn't catch details. M crying, 'All my fault, I should have done more, but so hard just getting him to eat and wear proper clothes, let alone clean his teeth for him,' etc. etc. My heart goes out to her, what a life. I should help more. Aaah! Don't need any extra bad feelings right now.

Going to paint, fuck it.

(Later)

Three watercolours of Red Rocks, not bad. Only saw two other people, one fishing, one walking. Tomorrow I'd better go into Cowes. Stupid name for a town when you say it out loud, moo, but quite pretty written down, a pleasing shape.

Cat showed up, good, so I could call M to say all is well and I'm looking after her. Him? Can't remember.

Don't feel like eating anything other than cheese and biscuits, and drinking WINE. But M wittering at me over phone to harvest vegies from her cornucopia, 'pick the beans while they're tender, silverbeet's full of iron,' blah blah, so okay I will. She uses seaweed for fertiliser. Stinks.

Tues May 19th

Didn't try to call Ally last night so why do I not feel any better today? Went for walk on beach, saw one person, a girl. Wonder what she's doing here. Young, early twenties? Looks a wreck, I have to say, probably even worse than I do, thought we might exchange smiles of fellow isolates but she wouldn't look at me.

Gearing up to go to moo-Cowes, better call M first.

(Later)

Missed M, tried a few times, idiot at motel reception couldn't say if they were actually in room or not. Visions of poor M trying to contain G. She was worried about taking him out of familiar environment. But she did get extra meds to 'calm' him, i.e. stupefy. Teeth must be seriously bad to warrant all this, trip to Melb, paying for motel. She must be as broke as I am.

Poor, poor M. What would Mum think? 'You make your own luck.' Yeah, Mum, but you didn't have a kid like Greg. Your two kids are just fuck-ups in the regular sense of the word. Actually, M isn't a fuck-up, she's just had her life hijacked by G and his illness. So that leaves me and what excuse do I have?

Wed May 20th

M rang last night. They've done some of the stuff to G but it's more complicated than they thought, they've booked him in for 'priority surgery' but prob won't happen till Fri. She says he's quite settled at motel so they'll stay there. I asked about money and she said it's okay, she has quite good savings and she's never spent her half of what Mum left us. She sounded quite chipper, considering, maybe she's enjoying the change of scene. Maybe the motel room has a good heater. Writes me, wearing two jumpers, scarf and sitting in bed with electric blanket. Cat has decided it likes me now electric blanket is on.

Big relief, actually, that M okay for money. Been feeling bad I didn't offer her my place to stay in Melb. But she knows it's a studio. Where would G sleep? And what if he did something to my paintings?

(Later)

Should I regret spending Mum's money on trip to Europe with Ally? Probably. But fuck it was beautiful, fuck she was beautiful, it was like everything was a hundred times more glorious when I looked at it, then her, then it. That painting I did of her in our room in Paris will never be a great painting but it will always be a favourite.

This too shall pass, I know. Wallowing is a privilege, I know this too. M has never wallowed in her life, no time for it.

Apart from G's room with camping mat and paint chipped (picked?) off walls and no curtains or anything, this is the most orderly house I've ever been in. Poor as all get out, but never seen a house so clean and tidy. Reckon M cleans the bathroom every day. Stove has not one mark on it, like never used. Pot plants drooping, have I watered them too much?

There is a sunset, I'm going for a walk.

(Later)

A development. Sitting on beach, not too cold and wind dropped for once so got out pastels and sketchbook. Deep in work, eventually realise someone standing behind me. The sad girl walker. She says, 'Wow, you're good.' Then she says, 'Really good.' I look at her, she's pissed. Swaying on her feet. She kneels down beside me, I can smell the booze on her. 'I'm a painter,' she says. 'Yeah?' I say. Feel a strong sense of being the responsible adult (new experience). She's in a bad way, slurring her words and leaning all over me.

She says she's staying at her grandma's house, grandma dead, had a stroke three months ago. 'I've been coming here my whole life. But it's different now.'

I don't say anything, keep drawing. Feel kind of nervous. She seems v volatile. Not in a threatening way. She seems *raw*.

She does a big sway, says, 'I'd better go.' I help her up. Skinny little arms. I touch her hand and it's freezing.

I ask who's with her at her grandma's house and she says no one. She says she's 'having a break' from her boyfriend. Then she says, 'Actually, we're splitting up.'

I say, 'Yeah?' But I don't tell her about Ally. Why not? Don't know. Instinct. Respect? I've never been the competitive type and she's clearly way worse off than I am. I've done early-twenties break-ups and what I'm going through now is not a patch on one of those. Poor kid.

I help her up to the track. Her grandma's place backs on to it, same as M's, but she's down the road end, near the car park. I ask if she needs me to come up to the house with her but she says no.

Thurs May 21st
Went for another walk this eve. Windy this time, v cold. No sign of girl. I even loitered on track near steps up to her place. Could see a light on.

Spoke with M. Everything okay, surgery tmrw. Reckons she'll be back w G on Monday, says I'm welcome to stay longer. Maybe I will, for a day or two, give M a break. Haven't done that for a long time now, feel bad. Fucking Ally, bewitched me for five years, made me forget my poor sister.

Started three more watercolours today. V happy with one in particular.

Fri May 22nd
Went into Cow-town this morn. On impulse stopped at girl's house and knocked on door, thought I'd ask if she needed

anything but no answer. Her car there, little rust bucket, even worse than mine. Curtains not drawn and light left on in kitchen. Wasn't snooping but did see table with paints laid out, cheap brand, and she's working on paper, must be flat broke. I remember those days.

Called Meredith and told her I'm doing some watercolours if she wants to book a show later in the year. She sounded chuffed; 'Oh, Lindsay, I'm so pleased,' in her fake English accent. Good old Meredith, she's put up with me when others wouldn't. Felt quite jolly, went down to beach and started two more paintings.

(Later)
M rang, all went well. A day's rest at motel then they're driving back Sun if G okay by then.

(Later)
Restless.

I WILL NOT CALL ALLY.

Why did I buy this nice shiraz? And this unfiltered grenache? And this brie? Down to $170 in bank. If only my income could keep up with my middle-aged tastes.

Lonely!

Sat May 23rd
Hungover. Monster bruise on shin.

What was I thinking? Forty-something semi-successful (i.e. dirt poor) lezzo artist drinks a bottle of wine then staggers along poorly lit track to house of recently deceased old lady to ask lady's granddaughter who is almost total stranger if she'd like some brie. And trips on stairs on way.

Truth is I don't know what I was thinking. I don't think it was horniness, or attempt to fill an Ally-shaped hole. Restless, yes. Lonely, yes. But not horny. Not for that poor kid.

She let me in. I saw her work, her paintings, before she cleared them from the table. I said nothing because I didn't want to scare her, but they're very good.

We drank the shiraz. We ate some brie. We smoked my rollies and listened to Sonic Youth on her grandma's tape deck. Eventually, after enough wine, we sketched each other. Nothing sexual, not at all. She's good, an exceptionally good artist. It was fun, it was what I needed, to get out of my own brain. And maybe the same for her. Hard to tell though.

But then she brought out the brandy. And things got blurry. Not sexual! (Why do I keep saying this? Because there were vibes? Were there vibes? Two-way vibes, or maybe just my usual non-specific sad middle-aged vibes at the sight of youth, the excruciating, ungrateful beauty of youth, which I get all the time, over anyone, female or male, which I even got over the teenaged boy with the mullet at the supermarket in Cowes yesterday. Or is it because I didn't tell her I'm gay, because I didn't want to scare her, to spoil the mood? And that feels weird, to lie by omission, but also I know that if I told her she'd probably freak out and it would be awful because no encounter in which the words 'I'm not hitting on you' are uttered ever goes well.)

Aaah! Whatever, things got blurry in a completely non-sexual way. And she started to talk.

Sitting at the table, room full of grandma stuff, row of photos on a shelf above her head, I could see her up there, young and gawky, school uniform.

There are blanks in my memory. Maybe I wasn't paying attention, but I thought she was talking about her boyfriend, the break-up. In fact, she was, because she said, 'We speak on the phone and it's the same thing every time, he says, "Why can't you be happy?" and I say, "I don't know." And then he says, "Is it me?" and I say, "No!" And he says, "What is it then?"' etc. etc. and then suddenly she's got her head down on the table and she's not talking about him any more, she's saying, 'I hated her. Not all the time, but still, I did. I thought she was a brat, that she just wanted attention. I hated that she still loved Mum. I hated her for choosing Mum over me. And now she's gone and I can't stop thinking if I'd been different, if I'd been nice to her . . .'

She said other things, but that's all I can remember, and then right in the middle of this head-on-the-table speech she jumped up and said, 'Thanks for the wine, you have to go now,' and next thing I'm out on the lawn, groping my way down the steps and back here in the dark.

(Later)
I thought it was the grandma she was talking about. 'Now she's gone.' But then what about the stuff about being a brat, wanting attention? Can a grandma be a brat?

Sun May 24th
The girl has left. Her car wasn't there when I walked past last night, and not there today. All the curtains closed, lights off. Gate locked with padlock.

Poor kid. Feel quite shaken up.

Beautiful, mild day. Sitting out in garden, listening for M's car.

In a week I will be 42 years old. Realise with a shock that *I am actually going to be okay.* Thinking of that girl, what I could have said to her, about art and pain and work and salvation, what lessons I could have passed down, worldly wise guru that

I am. But who listens, at her age? Some things can't be known until later.

In the boot of my car are my new paintings, ready to show Meredith. Also in there are the sketches from Friday night—both sets. Funny, she looked so sad to me, the whole time, from when I first saw her on the beach to when she jumped up and ran out of the room at the end, but in my sketches she doesn't look sad. She looks smart and tough. In one she holds a cassette, cigarette between her lips, and she is slyly smiling. And how do I look, in her sketches? With my little crow's-feet, my knobbly nose? I look—ha—I look *kind*. Gentle, and kind. That's a surprise.

Sun on my face, breathing the tang of M's seaweed garden beds—I am having a moment of hope, sweet hope, and am glad no one's here to see my foolish grin and a couple of tears sneaking out. The tears are for her, I think, the girl. I hope she makes it, gets over whatever it is she needs to get over—to do with that person who is gone, the brat. And maybe I'm crying for M a bit, too, for her garden, her work of art, her salvation, which she has gone about making so quietly, so privately, that it puts me to shame.

I will stay for a while, if M will have me. Give her a hand. Spend some time with G. Maybe I am kind. Kinder than I thought I was, anyway.

PART TWO

IN TOWN

PAINTINGS, 2005

NO ROOM AND CURVES
by June Worth
All paintings oil on canvas.

Sex Is a Mind Game
Thickly daubed paint, white and flesh tones on a deep blue background, small amounts of crimson, pink and yellow in details. Execution is rough; the painting is almost primitive in style. A room, a window, a bed, sheets falling towards the floor. On the bed two naked figures—a woman with shoulder-length dark hair, and a man with shorter, fairer hair. They are in a sexual embrace; both faces have broad smiles; the woman covers her eyes with one hand. On the floor at the far end of the room lie a pair of scissors and some cut-up pieces of fabric, pink and red lace-trimmed satin.

Lingerie
On a dark background, brownish-red, a pair of lace underpants floats, skimpy, crotchless. The underpants are a salmon pink colour, rendered in chunky paint; the effect is almost skin-like.

The slit in the crotch of the underpants is angled to face the viewer, the lace at its edges looks like teeth against the very deep red that shows through.

Anna

A bathroom, brightly lit by a beam of sunlight from a window. The walls are pale green, paint applied thickly and unevenly. There is nothing in the room but a showerhead, reaching in from one side, crudely rendered. Paint is dabbed and streaked in luminous white, pale green, yellow and grey to create a cascade of water filling most of the space below the showerhead. Behind these dabs and streaks there is a whitish-pink shape, featureless, ghostly, recognisable as human only by the thin arm that protrudes from one side of the veil of water, holding a cake of soap.

No Room

This painting is more detailed, with finer, less textured application of paint. An interior with a window, sofa and television. The light is greenish; through the window a dartboard is visible, hung on a brick wall. Two girls, perhaps in their early teens, one fair, one dark, kneel, watching the television, their backs turned. Most of the room is taken up by an enormous woman—a giant—who lies on the sofa, but overflows so that one of her legs stretches over the heads of the girls, like an archway. She wears only red lace lingerie, bra and skimpy underpants. She is not fat, just oversized, out of proportion with her surroundings. She smiles gently, staring into space. Underneath the woman, between her body and the sofa cushions, is a dark area, in which another figure lies, very shadowy and with a barely discernible face. Hairy dark arms, inhumanly long, emerge from this figure to reach around the woman; they end in long-fingered hands, one resting on the woman's breast, the other disappearing into her underpants.

No Room 2

The giant woman from the other painting lies on the floor of the same room. She is naked in this painting, and even bigger—she has grown so big that the sofa has been pushed by her body into one corner, the television into another. The woman's face is averted; her hands reach between her own legs in a self-pleasuring action. Pressed against one wall by the enormous woman's bent knee is the dark-haired girl. Her face is grim, her eyes closed. She wears a pair of shorts but no top; her arms are lowered and the side of one small breast is visible, flattened against the wall.

Curves

A dark background, thick slabs of paint, deep purples, reds and browns—nightmarish colours. From the left-hand top corner of the canvas descends a flesh-coloured shape, a large, soft semi-circle, suggestive of a body part—breast or buttock. Near the left-hand edge of the canvas the flesh colour darkens, and is bisected by a line. Here also is a cluster of squiggly dark lines—pubic hair? The colours of this flesh vary greatly—parts are a very pale pink, others bright pinkish-purple, others grey and pale brown. The 'flesh', if it is such, has an almost map-like quality. There are small brown dots and light marks, which could be freckles, moles and scars.

Curves 2

The same bathroom as in *Anna*, but this time rendered with more detail, the paint applied less thickly. There is no falling water this time. The dark-haired adolescent girl stands under

the dry showerhead with a towel around her waist. Her breasts
are small, the nipples coloured very brightly, and they have an
upwards perk to them—the girl looks down, frowning, and it
is as if the breasts are a second set of eyes, gazing back up.

Curves 3
A very pale blue background, like a sky. Two figures in the middle
of the canvas—teenaged girls in school uniforms. They appear
to stand between the viewer and the sun: their figures are very
dark, details such as the buttons on their dresses almost too much
in shadow to make out, and, due to the backlighting, they each
have two silhouettes, those of their dresses and those of their
bodies underneath. A very close inspection reveals that there
are in fact three silhouettes: the dresses, which are see-through;
the girls' adolescent bodies with their slight curves of hips and
breasts, which are dark but not completely black; and then an
innermost silhouette showing smaller, thinner bodies inside the
adolescent ones—the girls' prepubescent bodies, totally opaque.

GOLD STREET

The boyfriend's house was small, stuck in between two other houses, stuck right up against them so that they shared walls. And this was in the middle of a whole row of such houses. A terrace, Helen said it was called, the row, and the houses were terrace houses.

The front gardens had walls too, dividing them, and some of the walls, if the houses were painted different colours, had a line right in the middle of the top of the wall, where the colour changed. Sometimes one side was fresh and new, and the other flaking, worn. The boyfriend's house was flaking all over; weeds grew up out of the cracks in his side of the wall.

Once you were in, there was a feeling of being trapped. The hallway was narrow and dark, with dark brown carpet, and all it had was doors down one side, no windows. You had to get down that long tunnel and into the back room before you saw any light—and then it was green light, thick, because outside the windows of the back room was a roof made of heavy corrugated plastic, pale green. This room had a couch and a television, and half of it opened into a very small kitchen, dark brown tiles, yellow laminex. Beyond the kitchen was the bathroom, which had the same colours.

Pretty much the only good thing about the boyfriend's house was that they might get better food—watermelon, strawberries, blue cheese, chocolate—special-occasion food, because almost everything seemed to be a special occasion now, if Helen was involved.

They might get to watch a video, although the choices were limited. There was *High Society*, which was Junie's favourite, but Anna didn't like the romance. There was a David Attenborough film about lions hunting wildebeest and zebras and other herd animals that came to drink at a waterhole. Anna was scared of that one, and in fact Junie was too, and relieved not to have to admit it—the rolling eyes of the prey when the lions sprang and clung and brought them down; the twisting necks, the way they slowly, uselessly, kept trying to get up again, even with half their skin torn off. Then there was *Dot and the Kangaroo*, a cartoon, which was Anna's favourite, of course, bouncy and boring. And the only other one was a film of *Carmen*, the opera.

Inside the television cabinet were other videos, not meant for children. Junie and Anna would look at the covers of these sometimes, while the grown-ups were not around. They didn't seem very interesting, the titles usually in other languages, and most appearing to be set in the olden days. There were a few with people kissing on the cover, the women in revealing outfits, black and lacy. If Anna hadn't been there Junie probably would have tried to watch one of those.

That was it for the good things. There was a dartboard outside, under the green plastic roof, which might have been good if there was anyone to play with other than Anna, but proved quickly to also be boring, and even problematic, as it caused fights.

The bad things were the smell, which was like the one in the shed at Nan's where there was mouse poo and old blankets, and which was worse the closer you got to the carpet; the boredom; the boyfriend's bed in the front room, which you had to try not to look in at as you went past; Helen laughing in her new laugh at the boyfriend's jokes; Helen touching the boyfriend all the time and then trying to touch you; Helen making groaning sounds as she tasted a bit of food the boyfriend had put into her mouth for her like she was a baby or there was something wrong with her hands; Helen and the boyfriend drinking from enormous wineglasses, sloshing the wine around and making a big deal of sniffing it; the bathroom, with the boyfriend's things in it, which were all slimy colours, dark green and black, and in which it was impossible not to imagine the boyfriend naked; Anna climbing onto Helen's lap all the time like she was still a kid; Anna hugging the boyfriend hello and goodbye like she actually knew him; having to agree with Anna about the choice of video; fighting with Anna over the dartboard; Anna never just sitting to watch the TV like a normal person but always having to balance on one arm of the couch so that when she slipped and fell she'd kick you by accident, or lie on her back on the floor with her legs up, again accidentally kicking you, twisted round with her head in a position that looked so uncomfortable it was just plain annoying. This last one happened at home, too, but at least there you could go to your room and draw.

They watched *Carmen* the most. That Carmen! Her flashing eyes, her curly black hair, the way she jumped up on the table, swirling her skirts—Junie couldn't look away. The men were forgettable, poncing about in uniforms, straining at the notes when they sang. But she was effortless, quick and light, swishing away whenever one of them tried to kiss her. And then the shock of her death, the fast knife, the blood, her body in the dust. Anna couldn't watch that bit, and rolled on the floor with her eyes covered, but Junie was transfixed. This wasn't like the poor zebras and the lions that had to eat, to feed their cubs; this wasn't the violence of nature, necessary, excusable. This, no doubt about it, was punishment.

The phase of visiting the boyfriend at his house was a short one; before long he would move in at Avoca Street, bringing his slime-coloured toiletries with him and imbuing Helen's bed with his smell, which, although not as bad as that of the brown carpet, was still unpleasant.

It must have been on one of the last of these visits that the worst fight over the dartboard happened. It had been raining, but then it had stopped, and Junie—bored, bored, always bored—had gone outside and was standing alone on the wet bricks with the rusty darts bunched, heavy, in her left hand, when Anna came leaping out, letting the door slam behind her.

'Can I play?' said Anna.

'No,' said Junie. 'I've already started. You can have a turn after me.'

'But you haven't started.' Anna tiptoed along a row of bricks, then turned and tiptoed back again. 'You haven't even thrown the first one.'

Junie didn't answer. She selected a dart, a green one, and aimed.

'Junie! I want to be in the game! Let me play! You haven't even started!' Anna twirled and skipped closer. 'Please!' She made gestures of appeal with her arms.

'Too late. And you're too annoying, you don't play properly. You don't *try*.'

But Anna stepped between Junie and the board. Anna planted her feet and stuck her hands on her hips.

Junie didn't lower the dart. 'Move,' she said, 'or I'll throw it, and you'll be in the way.'

Anna stood firm.

'Move,' said Junie, her voice calm and mean. 'Or you might get hit.'

Anna's nostrils flared. She had pulled in her lips so her mouth was a colourless line. Her breaths were loud and defiant. But when Junie drew back the hand with the dart she cowered and wailed, 'Mu-*um*!'

They waited. No reply.

'Mu-*um*!' called Anna again. 'Junie won't let me have a turn at the dartboard!'

'Junie,' came Helen's voice from inside the house, 'sharing, please.' It wasn't her real voice; it was the one she used to tell them off when the boyfriend was around—friendly and reasonable, but with a finality to it, as if Anna and Junie knew what to do really, were good girls, but just needed this one little reminder. At home, without the boyfriend there, she might yell, 'Oh God, you kids, just stop it,' or, more likely, not respond at all, but close a door between herself and them.

A few things happened then, all at once. Junie again drew back her right hand, although she didn't intend to actually throw the dart; Anna made a grab for the bunch of darts in Junie's left hand; Anna slipped on the wet bricks and went down, hard, slamming into Junie's legs; the handful of darts fell on top of Anna.

Silence, then screaming, and Helen came rushing out.

Anna lay on the bricks. Her knees were bleeding where she'd landed on them. The darts were scattered around, a couple on top of her, but none actually sticking in. It looked a lot worse than it was.

Junie stepped back. She knew what was coming. There was no point in trying to explain.

It was a typical Anna performance. Shrieking, running around, wriggling out of Helen's grasp, refusing comfort or to have her knees wiped with wetted sheets of paper towel. Helen chasing after her, in and out of the house, saying in a crooning voice that became less crooning as the chase went on, 'Anna, Anna, it's all right, darling. Settle down, settle down.'

Eventually Anna allowed herself to be caught, and stood bawling into Helen's chest, then treated everyone to a little escape attempt, then did a bit more bawling, followed by loud breathing and hiccups. And for the rest of the evening she would not get off Helen, but had to sit all over her, legs dangling ridiculously, face in Helen's neck, fingers in Helen's hair.

Later that night, back at Avoca Street, Junie sat hidden on the stairs and listened to Helen speaking on the phone in the kitchen. It was a friend—Junie could tell by the voice Helen was using, and also because Helen mentioned book club, and how she kept eating cheese even though she was supposed to be on a diet. From where Junie was she could see the bottom half of Helen in the kitchen armchair, her crossed legs, her hand playing with the coils of the phone cord.

'The girls are good,' said Helen. 'They're coping really well.'

Junie listened harder.

'We did have a scene today though,' Helen went on. 'At Phil's. Junie did one of her stealth attacks, God knows what exactly, but Anna fell and hurt her knees, blood everywhere.' She said the word *fell* as if it was in quotation marks.

Junie leaned forward on the step, licked the skin of her own knee. There was a certain glory in being judged incorrectly. She opened herself to it, to its cold, lonely pleasure.

'. . . very clingy, afterwards,' Helen was saying. 'Poor Phil, he'd made this delicious curry and I had to eat it with this child stuck to me.'

A pause, while she listened.

Then, laughing, 'Yes, yes, but you know what it is, Shanti?' Her hand slapped down on the edge of the telephone table and she gave a theatrical sigh. 'It's a punishment.'

Junie went back up and got into bed. She must have missed something. What was the punishment, and who was giving and receiving it? Was Helen going to punish her, Junie? But Helen had never been into punishments—that was John, although he called them consequences.

Junie didn't understand what Helen had meant until many years later, until she was an adult, with her own children. She was picking one of them up from child care and as she went in the gate another woman came out, carrying a struggling, red-faced, wailing toddler.

'My punishment,' said the woman to Junie, with a wry smile.

Junie, or June as she was by then, stood in the tanbark of the child-care centre's front yard and remembered sitting on the stairs, remembered Helen's overheard sigh and her pronouncement. Now she saw. Anna punishing Helen, that was what Helen had meant—Anna, with her tantrum, had been punishing Helen for the boyfriend, the end of the marriage, the end of their family.

She remembered Anna's distress, its theatricality, what it demanded of Helen, and the entitlement of that demand. How close together the two of them came, afterwards, their bodies in the chair, Anna's cheek to Helen's.

June remembered the video, the long, deep notes of the music in the death scene, so grave, so formal. How, once he had stabbed her, the man at last held Carmen close, and sobbed.

AVOCA STREET

After school Junie caught the tram to Avoca Street. This was not usual, because now she was living with John, at his flat. She had to, to get through year twelve.

Today was because they'd asked her, Helen and John. They had to go to the school for a meeting with the teachers, about Anna, and they didn't want her left alone for too long— Anna. Anna, Anna, Anna.

She'd seen Anna at the school stop, pretending Junie wasn't there, getting on the tram by the other door. *This is stupid*, thought Junie. She shuffled down the aisle, plonked next to her sister.

'Hi.'

'Hi.'

'I'm coming home with you, did you know?'

'No. Yes.'

Anna sat low, bag on lap, knees knocking as the tram swayed. The top half of the window was open; in a whirl of plane tree pollen they overtook a pack of Christian Brothers boys, blue blazers, yelling mouths. Anna's raw fingers worked at a scab on her arm.

*

They started off walking together, from the Avoca Street stop, but Anna was slow. She was doing it on purpose; she dragged each foot with a scrape, staring down as if the scraping feet were not hers, hair in her face.

'Come on,' said Junie, and then, 'Come on, Anna,' but Anna kept scraping along and it was so annoying that Junie sped up and left her behind.

At the house, in the fridge, Junie found cold potatoes and slices of cold lamb, grey with edgings of hard white fat. She took a potato and flopped into the big corner armchair, pulled her feet up. Inside her head, Helen's voice: *Shoes off, please.* Junie kept them on. Through the window she watched Anna enter the yard and go to the back fence to smoke. Up and down Anna walked, ginger-bright against the wisteria, then she turned towards the house and kicked first one leg and then the other, and her shoes flew across the lawn.

Junie finished the potato, licked her fingers, wiped them on her skirt. She thought about Molly the horse, about the beach, the island. It was a secret, it did not cross into her life of year twelve, of study periods, of common assessment tasks, entry scores and preferences, plans for schoolies and parties, parties, parties. Everywhere you looked groups of girls were jumping and squealing. Changes were coming and she, Junie, was not excited, was not keen, was not ready.

Outside Anna stalked the grass in her white socks, puffing with vigour. Junie rearranged herself in the chair and sank into a vaguely assembled fantasy of living alone, somehow, on the island. Blue-skied days. Riding Molly, swimming. Maybe she worked for a farmer, or maybe she worked at the library in Cowes, pushing the trolley, slotting books into the shelves. She had a car, a ute; she drove with the window open and her elbow out. A boy, yes, there was one, but he wasn't gross, was a man in fact, mature, like her, maybe he was a surfer, and they met in the evenings, they had a bed with trailing sheets under an open window, white curtains blowing in . . .

Anna thumped through, slinging her bag and shoes into a corner. In the next room the television started up. Junie got out of the chair and went to the doorway.

'Don't you have homework?'

'Don't you?' Anna was huddled at one end of the couch. The blind was drawn, the room dim. She was watching *Ocean Girl*, gnawing at her thumb, jiggling one knee.

'Always.' Junie perched on the arm of the couch, the other end from Anna.

On the screen, to the sound of ominously stabbing keyboards, Ocean Girl was discovering blue barrels of toxic waste on the bottom of the sea.

Anna took a sudden, gasping breath. 'Shit,' she whispered.

'What?'

'Nothing. I just sometimes can't breathe properly.' She did a few more deep breaths, hand to chest.

Drama queen. Junie got up again. 'Maybe you should stop smoking.'

'It's not that.'

'Well, what is it then? Asthma?' Junie went to the window and tugged the cord and the blind went ripping upwards, filling the room with white light.

'Hey!' Anna flung herself around. 'I can't see the telly with the blind up!'

'It's depressing, sitting in the dark,' said Junie. 'Plus, it stinks in here.' She shoved the window open. 'Plus, that show is rubbish, it's for kids.'

'*Plus*, why don't you fuck off, Junie? Just go back to Dad's. Go and do some homework. Go and draw your stupid horses.'

On the TV, Ocean Girl's friend the whale was heaving himself about at surface level, making long wet huffing sounds and waving a stippled flipper.

Junie walked out, muttering, 'If you're having trouble breathing you should see a doctor.'

'I have,' muttered Anna, getting up to close the blind.

On the kitchen floor, under the telephone table, lay a piece of paper with Helen's writing on it. Junie picked it up.

AGREEMENT
If clothes not in dirty clothes basket they won't get washed.
Mon, Wed, Anna cooks dinner.
All other nights Mum, apart from Fri—takeaway!
Homework before TV.
Saturday morning housework, do together.
Be honest with each other. Respect!

She let it fall, slid it with her foot back into its forgotten place. From her schoolbag she took her maths homework and spread it out on the table. Sat down. Got up. Walked three times around the table, then to the window. Then she went upstairs.

Her room was just the same. Dustier. She hadn't taken much to John's, apart from clothes, because it was only meant to be a temporary thing. Her wall of horses looked sad, crumpled. She tried to fix some drawings that had come unstuck. Then she went back out of the room, climbed onto the bannister at the top of the stairs, opened the skylight window, pulled herself up and scrambled out onto the roof.

She wriggled across to where she could lean against the chimney. The tiles lapped down, some rich brown-red, others with a lace of grey stuff—lichen or something. Yellow patches on the lawn below made Junie think of ringworm. Anna had been busy: the gutter held a drift of cigarette butts.

A disturbance at the skylight. Anna's hands appeared, then her head and shoulders, her face—sun-blinded, fiercely pale. She collected herself and scooted across to Junie. Reached into the pocket of her school dress, took out a joint, offered it, but then pulled it back again.

'One rule,' she said. 'We can only say nice things to each other.'

'Okay.' Junie moved over to make room. 'We'll smoke in silence then.'

'Ha ha.'

Anna lit the joint and they handed it back and forth. What felt like a long time passed. Junie sank into the tiles, the chimney at her back. The heat from the sun ran up one side of her head and then down the other, then settled, buzzing, in her ears. A breeze slid incredibly slowly over her shins.

'I don't even like it at Dad's,' she said eventually. 'He's like a robot. The same things, every day. The same food, the same jokes, the same stories. He just loves repetition. He thrives on it. Thrives. Thr-i-i-i-ves. That's a really strange word when you think about it.' Her eyes had been closed; she opened them, the yard below rippled, and she closed them again. 'And then he has two glasses of wine with dinner and gets all sad.'

'Why'd you go and live with him then?'

Anna's voice sounded very close. And was that Anna's breath Junie could feel, on her cheek? She reopened her eyes, just for a moment. No, Anna's head was turned away; she was looking off over the neighbours' yards.

'It's not you,' said Junie. 'Not your . . . stuff, I mean. Your problems.'

'What is it then?'

'Mum.'

'What about Mum?'

'I don't know, she just really annoys me. I mean, she wrecked everything, our whole family, and she takes no responsibility. She's so *positive* all the time. Everything she does is an act. She's all, *Isn't life great? Let's drink wine, have you met my new boyfriend?*'

Anna laughed.

Junie tried opening her eyes again, but it was still no good.

Anna sighed. 'I actually miss you.'

'Really? You have a funny way of showing it.'

'I'm sorry. I don't know what's wrong with me.'

'That's okay. I'm sorry too, for being a bitch. And I miss you too.'

'I miss myself.'

They laughed. Their laughter spooled out and out. A bird came whirring past; Junie felt its wingbeats. 'I miss everything,' she said.

'Me too.'

'Where'd you get that joint?'

'That's for me to know and for you to find out.'

'From Hamish Kennedy?'

'No way! He doesn't even have drugs, he just pretends.'

'I wouldn't have a clue how to get pot.'

'It's not that hard.'

'We should go back down, before they get home.' Junie forced herself to open her eyes and keep them open until things stopped rippling.

'Have you had sex?'

'Anna! No. Have you?'

'No.'

They inched back to the skylight. Anna went first, so Junie didn't see, like she had that other time, if her skirt went up, if there were cuts on her thighs. The thought was as bad though; it gave her a choking feeling.

'So does she have a boyfriend at the moment?'

'Who?' Anna leaned her elbows on the bannister and pushed one knee between its slats.

'Who do you think? Mum.'

'Oh, her. I don't know. I don't think so.'

'What do you mean, you don't think so?' Junie sat down on the top step. 'Is there a man, you know, that she brings home and sleeps in her bed with?'

'Not that I've noticed. She does have people over, for dinner and stuff, and some of them are men. But I don't think any of them are, you know . . .'

'They probably are. She'd fuck anything that moved. She's probably fucking them all.'

Anna gave a gasp. 'Oh no.'

'What?'

'Shit! Shit!' She was swaying back and forth, hands braced on the bannister.

Junie stumbled to her feet. 'What? What is it? Is it the breathing thing again?'

Anna's head had fallen forward, her hair a red-gold mess. Her shoulders shook.

Junie put her hand over one of her sister's. 'Stay calm,' she said. 'Just take deep, slow breaths.'

Anna made a noise. She threw back her head; her face was flushed, and tears glittered at the corners of her eyes. She was laughing. 'It's not that,' she said. 'It's my knee. My knee's stuck.'

They both looked down at it, pink and smooth, its sides compressed by the timber slats.

Grunting, Anna worked it free.

'Oh God.' Junie collapsed back onto the step. 'You are such an idiot.'

John stood in the middle of the kitchen with his hands in his pockets while Helen marched around in her heels, taking things from the fridge to the bench.

'We agreed to continue the discussion another time,' said Helen.

'But,' said John, 'I just—'

'Another time. Hello, girls!' She put down a bowl, kissed Anna, then walked to Junie, arms outstretched. 'Junie! It's so good to see you!'

'Hi, Mum.'

Being hugged by Helen was like being tackled. Junie pulled away. 'Okay, okay,' she said.

'Sorry!' Helen stood with her hands on Junie's shoulders, her smile so wide Junie could see molars. 'How's things? How's that biol CAT going?'

'It's fine. I've nearly finished.'

'And the maths thing, the what's-it-called?'

'It's done. I told you that.' Junie extracted herself and fell into the armchair.

'Did you?'

'Yes. I told you all this last night, on the phone.' She pulled her feet up.

'Shoes off, please.' Helen went back to the bench. 'Just leftovers for dinner, okay, Annie-pie?'

'Don't call me that,' said Anna from a tipped-back kitchen chair, but she sounded pleased.

Helen began to tear apart a lettuce. 'Sorry. John, Junie—why don't you stay?'

'Oh,' said John, taking his hands from his pockets, 'well, that might be—'

'No thanks,' said Junie, getting up. 'I have heaps of home-work to do.'

'Oh, come on,' said Helen. 'Just a quick dinner, it'll take half an hour. Glass of wine, John?'

'No!' Junie swept her schoolbooks from the table and shoved them into her bag. 'I have so much to do, Mum. I've got this CAT due next week, and I'm behind in maths, and there's a prac-tice exam for chem on Friday.' She thrust one arm through the bag's strap and hoisted it to her shoulder. 'And I've got a head-ache.' This was true—there was a gritty feeling behind her eyes.

Helen had turned from the bench. 'Oh, okay then. I under-stand. Poor Junie, I didn't know you were under so much pressure.' She came closer, but Junie sidestepped her, adjusting her bag.

From out of the headache a mean impulse sprang. 'Anyway,' said Junie, 'isn't it Anna's turn to cook?'

'What?' said Anna.

'It's Wednesday,' said Junie. 'I thought Anna cooked dinner on Wednesday nights. I saw it, on your agreement.' She went to the telephone table and slid out the piece of paper. From the corner of her eye she could see Anna glaring at her.

'Yep,' said Junie. 'Wednesday, Anna cooks. Also Monday. What did you cook on Monday, Anna?'

Anna flew from the chair, sending it crashing. Her face was white, her fists clenched. 'I just don't get you!' she shrieked. 'What were you being all nice to me for? Why would you do that when you obviously hate me? Just fuck off, Junie, you fucking bitch. You cunt!' She ran to the stairs and up them, and the slam of her bedroom door rattled the windows.

'Anna!' John started across the room, but Helen blocked him.

'Don't,' she said. 'It'll just make things worse.'

'But she can't get away with that,' said John.

'I'll talk to her later,' said Helen. 'She's tired. She hasn't been sleeping well. It works better if you give her a chance to cool off.'

There was a pause, during which something happened to Helen's face. She dropped her gaze and her mouth and the skin over her cheekbones sagged. But then there was an adjustment, and when she lifted her chin the stretched beam of her smile had returned. She rolled her eyes. 'Teenagers, hey?'

'Can we go?' said Junie to John. 'Please?'

At the flat Junie had a desk in the bedroom. It only just fitted, and was in fact wedged between the wall and the foot of the spare bed, the bed that had been Anna's, which now held piles of Junie's clothes and books.

She put on the desk lamp, got her maths stuff out of her bag, and worked for a while in a half-hearted way, every now and then stopping to draw a horse on a spare bit of paper.

In the kitchen, John sang, *'Strangers in the night, dah-dah-de-dah-dah . . .'*

It was dark outside now, and getting cold. Junie took off her school dress and put on tracksuit pants, Explorer socks and a jumper. Taking her maths book she went into the main room, where the gas heater was.

John was at the bench, slicing something. Chops spat in the pan. 'Dinner's nearly ready,' he said, and then, at the *click-click-whump* of the heater: 'Put a jumper on, if you're cold.'

'I have.' Junie lay down with the open book. On the carpet nearby was a stain, faint reddish-purple, a long oval shape, and on the skirting board there were a couple of deep red splatters. This was from a glass of wine Anna threw during an argument, the last time she had come to John's.

They ate at the little round table, with the TV on, for the news. Jeff Kennett gave a speech and John said, 'What a goon.'

Afterwards Junie washed up in the tiny sink, and John stayed at the table with his second glass of wine and the cryptic crossword. Every now and then he sat back and spoke.

'It might've been nice if we'd stayed for dinner. I would've liked the chance to spend some time with Anna.'

Junie scrubbed at burnt chop fat with steel wool, her fingers red in the hot water.

'It's very hurtful to me that she doesn't want to come here any more. My own daughter!'

Junie lifted the pan and angled it to get its other half into the sink.

'I've said that before, haven't I? Ha ha, sorry, Junie, I'm like a broken record.'

Junie sloshed and scrubbed.

'But I just can't help it. I'm very upset about it. I don't understand why she doesn't want to see me.'

Junie lifted the pan, balanced it on top of the sink and ran clean water into it.

'I mean, I don't expect you girls to be angry with Helen for what she did. I think it's important you know what she did, and that's why I've told you about it. But I don't expect you to be angry.'

Junie tipped the pan out and put it in the draining rack.

'I just can't really see how it is that I've become the villain here. You know, I *cared* for you kids, when you were little. More than Helen did. You wouldn't catch Helen getting up in the night for a kid with nightmares, with asthma.'

Junie wiped the bench.

'You don't mind me talking like this, do you, Junie?'

Junie shook her head. Anna minded—that was why Anna wasn't there. (The flying glass, projecting a red tongue of liquid, its round, bursting shatter, Anna shouting: *Shut up, shut up, shut up!*) And Junie used to mind, but not any more, not now. When John spoke like this it gave her something, an importance, and she didn't know yet that it was the wrong kind.

BODIES

Helen in a dress with small flowers, blue on yellow. A long dress, her legs under it are bare, are nice, are sturdy. Junie loves these legs. Hidden beneath this flower dress is a cotton bra and cotton undies, plain and white. When Helen lifts Junie up Helen's hip is a seat, pressing firm into the split of Junie's legs. Helen's arm is strong at Junie's back, her fingers wrap around Junie's thigh. Helen holds Junie and Junie fits onto Helen.

This is when Junie is small. Before things changed. Or before Junie changed, in the way she saw things.

Helen in the bath at Avoca Street. Her body is lush, is greedy, is shameless. Opening in the water, taking up all the space, hair and lips and flesh. Junie hates this body. Junie doesn't want to see it but it's always there, a hungry soft monster wanting sex. This is when Junie is older. When she can't not see things.

Helen has creams she rubs into her body, she has make-up and stockings and lacy red underwear and condoms and lube in drawers. If you go into her room you can find them, all you have to do is slide out the drawers and look. She doesn't hide things properly.

Helen crying is monstrous. Pink and wet. Loud. Everyone has to know about it. Sometimes she says it is happy crying, but that is no better to have to watch.

Sex should be private, but Helen's body doesn't keep it private. Sex oozes out of Helen, it waves at people, it has no shame. Or does it? Or is it just that Junie sees the sex and only the sex, even imagines it when it's not there?

Teenagers at the island, on the beach. Girls with fluoro bikinis, brown skin. Painted fingernails. They arrive with men, in panel vans. They drink UDLs and wrestle with the men in the water. A man snatches at a girl's bikini top and pulls it off. Shrieking. Bobbing white breasts, slapping waves. Junie hides in the ti-tree and watches. Dune grass tickles her bare thighs. Something throbs in the thin, hot air, over the brown bodies wrestling in the greenish water, over the yellow sand, over the spiny grass and into Junie. An ache between her legs, a swelling feeling.

When the panel van girls and their men get too loud, when there is too much wrestling, when the bikini tops come off, Nan makes Junie and Anna go back to the house. Junie, then, is often difficult, sullen. The swelling has gone and she feels restless and hollow. This is when she is twelve, thirteen, and everything has changed and she wishes it hadn't.

Anna in the bath, at the island. Flat chest, little indent where her ribs meet under her breastbone. White lines, the ghost of her bathing suit. Remains of zinc cream smudged over freckles. Blue veins around her flat child's nipples. Skinny arms, skinny legs. This body hardly takes up any space. This body is simple and blameless. Junie wants this body. She wants to take it from Anna and have it for herself.

*

Junie in the shower. Soft new flesh. She digs her fingers into her thighs. She hits her woman's flesh, kneads it, punishes it. She hates this body. It is disgusting.

But also Junie's body is sexy. In mirrors it plumps, it runs in smooth lines, it dips into hollows and erupts in nipples and hairs, provocative, tender, surprising. Junie admires this body, but she is afraid of it.

This body, disgusting and sexy, is now separate from Junie, from her true self.

This is when Junie is twelve, thirteen, fourteen. Fifteen, sixteen . . . all the way to her mid-twenties, to Paul, and children.

Anna climbing through the skylight. Long pale legs, tendons jutting at the backs of her knees. Up high, where her school dress lifts, red marks like braille. Under her school dress are breasts and hair that Junie has not seen, not since there was less of them, not since Anna started locking the bathroom door.

Anna in the shower, at Avoca Street. This is before the skylight, before the locking of the bathroom door. A haze of steam. Falling silver water in morning sun. Shoulders, thighs, firm flesh brightly flushed, the slightest of swellings under puffs of nipples, nascent scraggle of blonde-pink pubes. Head down, not hearing the door open. Greenish hair flattened, wet and shining.

Junie doesn't want to see this body. Junie grabs her tooth-brush and the toothpaste and runs downstairs and cleans her teeth at the kitchen sink. Junie doesn't hate this body but she is repulsed by it, by its softness, its vulnerability. She pities it. A sucking hole of unwelcome pity opens in her.

*

Anna, fourteen, cuddling with Helen on the couch at Avoca Street. Anna's face in Helen's neck. Anna's fingers in Helen's hair. Anna's too-long legs trying to get onto Helen's lap.

Helen's head tipped back, Helen's eyes closed. Helen's face peaceful. Helen's fingertips trailing up and down Anna's bare arm.

Junie goes outside. She slams the door on them.

Junie having sex. To do this she melts herself with booze. Her brain melts into her body, and then her body-brain melts into the other person. When she comes there are no thoughts whatsoever, she always has her eyes closed and she sees space, crackling, white and empty.

This is when Junie is eighteen, nineteen, twenty.

June pregnant. This body is urgent and full and sore. This body takes over. It does not require melting. It wants things, sharply, strongly. June is relieved and dazed. When she has sex in this body she feels monstrous, and fearful. She laughs during sex, helplessly, and Paul laughs too.

Would she say this is her true self, this brain in this body? No, she would not. The true self, or the idea of the true self, will always belong to the time before Helen began to ooze sex, before the panel van girls, before Junie's hateful, disgusting-sexy body and Anna's pitiful, defenceless, pubescent one. But of course that isn't June's true self either, the child self, the innocent. That particular self is just a part of her that—because she felt it was smothered by Helen's sexuality and John's sadness; because she didn't get the chance to leave it behind, to outgrow it—June can't stop mourning.

AVOCA PARK

Every few years there was a whole-school photograph, an epic event involving a temporary scaffold and raked benches and the assemblage of every kid in the school, from year seven through to year twelve—hundreds and hundreds of them. Out to the oval and up they went, in raucous, elbowing blue-and-yellow rows, half-wild with hormones and a sense of escape, leaving behind classrooms that resembled evacuated disaster zones with their splayed books and dropped pencils and crookedly abandoned chairs.

It seemed always to be windy. In the background the school buildings spread their grey arms, flew their flags. The vice-principal, suit coat flapping, sent threats through a megaphone to a deaf wall of chatter. There was usually some stunt, or mishap: mysterious hand gestures appearing suddenly on the photographer's count of three; an attack of vertigo forcing a senior to sit, cross-legged and shamefully enormous, on the grass down the front with the year sevens.

The morning after one of these, Ryan found his mother at the kitchen table, filling in the order form.

'What're you doing?' he said. 'It costs thirty-five dollars.'

She didn't respond, but went on forming careful letters inside the boxes.

Ryan went to the fridge. On its door was the letter confirming his scholarship, which his mother still refused to take down, even after six years. The paper was flyspecked now but still thick, the school crest in dull gold. He took out the milk and leaned on the door to close it.

'Mum? We can't afford it.'

Without looking up she said, 'It's your last year. We can afford it. And don't drink from the carton.' She folded the bills, twenty, ten and five, inside the form and put the form into an envelope. She held it out to Ryan and the pink light caught the sleeve of her terry-towelling robe, its fringe of loose threads like the legs of spiders, the roots of tiny plants.

Junie Worth's younger sister Anna was at the tram stop. Smoking, at eight-fifteen am. Thighs skinny and goose-pimpled below her miniscule skirt. Ryan semi-looked, and thought of Melanie Geare, the brown of her legs as she went up the stairs to the assembly hall. The time he went to his locker late, after training, and Melanie was there, just her and her legs, and she smiled at him.

The tram came and all the office workers got on, and then Ryan. Anna Worth left it until the very last moment, swinging in as they took off, one hand on the rail, one foot on the mounting board, flicking her cigarette away. The dark road flying past her shoes, her narrow white shins.

Worthless, they called her. Kids said she'd give you a blow job for five bucks. That she'd sell you speed, or acid, good quality. 'Hey, Worthless,' guys would yell, 'what're ya worth today?' And Anna would walk past, a half-smile on her face, like she was thinking of a different joke, a better one.

As far as Ryan knew, she didn't actually do any of the things people said she did. A lot of bullshit rumours went around the school. But she did smoke at the tram stop at eight-fifteen in the morning like it was some kind of a performance, and she did jump on the tram that way, with her bitten nails and tiny skirt, dark circles under her eyes.

What was it with kids like Anna, who had to advertise their awkwardness, their ill-fittingness, wear it like it was fluorescent? Surely this only made things worse. Why would you be that way when you could choose quiet colours, keep things subdued? But sometimes, when he passed her in one of the wide, noisy school corridors, or at the tram stop or on the street near home, and he saw her ridiculous skirt, her shoes all tramped down at the backs, her gnawed nails, her untucked shirt and non-regulation bag, and, most of all, her fuck-off, fuck-you, fuck-everything face, he wanted to smile. He felt—not admiration, not really; it was simpler than that. It was almost a thrill, a rippling, airy feeling. It was a kind of delight.

There were only a few of them who still kicked the footy at lunch-time: Ryan, James Hanlon, Sam McKenna and Will Metcalfe. Everyone else now sat with the girls on the slope of grass behind the canteen. For this reason there was something reckless in the way they kicked. No pride was to be taken in it; quitting was imminent.

James stood, fingers fanned on the ball. 'Coming to Shareen's party, Macca?'

'Nah, we're going to Portsea.'

'How 'bout you, Metcalfe?'

'Yep.' Catching the footy and then booting it, blue eyes slightly crossed, stringy hair lifting from his forehead.

Ryan took the mark, reaching, his knee finding James's hip, boosting himself for a speccy, hands soft and ready, meeting the ball, bringing it down into the shelter of his torso, bringing his whole self into a curve and rolling, easy and slow, to the grass.

'Nice one, Mute, ya bastard,' groaned James from his sprawl.

Ryan lay with his eyes half-closed to the sun, the ball on his chest. Some year sevens pattered by, their voices reedy and insubstantial. Ryan could feel his own weight pressing him into the ground, the swathes of air required by his lungs, the roaring of his blood. For three years now he'd been taller than his mum, and hairy and deep-voiced since year eight. But it was only in the past few months that he'd found himself overcome by this private astonishment at his own body. He'd taken to admiring his arms after his shower in the mornings, although he could only fit them one at a time in the small, spotted mirror.

James's shadow fell over his face. The toe of James's shoe tapped the ball free. 'How 'bout you, Mute-o? Coming to Shareen's party?'

Ryan sat up. 'Maybe.'

The bell rang. Ryan followed the others. He watched them, their shoulders, their mugging sideways lunges, the grey shorts silly on their big man-legs. *My friends*, he told his mum when she asked who he was going out with on a Saturday night. But this year, year twelve, something had turned in Ryan's understanding of things, and a suspicion had crept in that these were not and had never been friendships, but place holders of some sort, an arrangement of convenience.

They'd reached the stage—despite not being ready for the sloping grass and the girls behind the canteen—of, at parties, getting drunk and saying things like, *Hard to believe this is almost it*, or, *I wonder if we'll stay in touch*, or, when more drunk, *You'd better stay in touch, ya bastard*, or, *I'm gunna miss you, ya cunt*. But it was Will and James and Sam who said these things. Ryan didn't say anything. And to him it sounded as if the others were following a script.

He had footy training after school and it was dark when he got home. His mum was still at work. He felt huge in the flat, crossing each room in three steps, his runners making sticky sounds on the lino. In the bathroom mirror his skin was shiny with grease and sweat. A new pimple was starting on his chin. Tenderly, delicately, he touched it.

'Fuck this,' he said, and went out.

He ran his usual loop, down the Avoca Street hill and through the park, around the cemetery, back up the hill. Then he did it again.

Anna and Junie Worth lived in a two-storey house partway down the hill. No other kids from school lived in this neighbourhood; most lived in the other direction, in quiet suburbs with big houses and flash cars and nice lawns.

On his second loop, passing Anna and Junie's house, he saw that the lights had been turned on in one of the upstairs windows. Their house was big for the area, but shabby. A tall tree grew in the front yard and the two upstairs windows could only be glimpsed through it from certain angles. Although he had no way of knowing, Ryan assumed that these were Anna's and Junie's bedrooms.

Girls' bedrooms—such mystery. He'd glanced in at Cassie Dean's once at a party and it had been like something from a movie—white wrought-iron bed, frilly pillows, teddy bears. He tried to use this setting sometimes for a fantasy about Melanie Geare—her legs against the frills, her school dress undone—but it didn't usually work. It was the teddy bears; he'd remove them, but they kept reappearing.

He didn't picture bedrooms like that inside Anna and Junie's house. If he tried to picture anything, all he got was the two girls standing there, one in each room, and the rooms empty.

On Saturday night he went to Shareen's party. He met Will and James at Brighton Station at nine-thirty—because early was not cool, Will said—and they walked through the hushed streets, past the big, tidy houses. Will had on a long-sleeved Quiksilver top and Quiksilver trackies, with Blundstones. James was all in Stüssy; his hair was wetted down and he smelled like Lynx.

'Don'tcha own any other shoes, Mute?'

'Sleep in them, do ya?'

No response was expected of Ryan—he knew this. There was nothing behind these jibes, no real malice or cruelty. It was just something they had to do, his so-called friends, another script, a way of staying at ease, of filling space.

Between the station and Shareen's they shared most of a small bottle of Southern Comfort. A heat came into Ryan's stomach, a hum to his fingertips.

Shareen's mother was at the open front door.

'Hello, boys,' she said. 'Come on in.'

She was one of the sporty mums, short hair and arms with slim muscles, a fine gold chain at the base of her tanned throat.

'How's your mum, Will? Tell her she needs to get that knee fixed so she can come back to tennis. We're missing her.'

'I think it's better,' said Will. The Southern Comfort bulged in his pocket. 'She's taken the strapping off, anyway.'

'Good to hear.' She ushered them through. 'Out you go. Everyone's out the back.'

There was a swimming pool, and a tennis court. A table with plates of snacks that nobody ate or even went near. Also, a rectangle of lawn that was being treated like the slope behind the canteen, except in darkness and with closer sitting, a bit of lying down, and even a couple of entanglements.

Some drama was taking place—girls hobbled urgently back and forth in their miniskirts and precarious shoes. Alicia Matthews emerged from behind a trellis flanked by Cassie Dean and Juliet Rodham, mascara tears black on her cheeks.

Ryan stood by the tennis court fence with Will and James and they finished the Southern Comfort. He looked for Melanie and saw her, eventually, sitting on a bench near the pool with Kristy Williams. James went off and came back with vodka and orange juice in a two-litre plastic bottle. It was strong, and after two swigs Ryan didn't want any more—the cyclone-wire fence was already wavering, the pool gently slipping sideways.

'Come on, Mute, ya wuss,' said Will. 'What's the matter with ya?'

'I'm going to the toilet.'

Ryan went into the house, into the back room, which was half a kitchen and half just a big space with two leather couches and a glass coffee table marooned in the middle of it. There was the smell of flowers, and hot pastry. Shareen's mum was behind the kitchen counter, doing something to the oven. She turned and smiled, but then didn't smile so much when she saw it was Ryan.

'You okay there?' she said.

None of the parents ever knew Ryan's name. Sometimes he got introduced, but they never remembered.

'I'm looking for the toilet, please,' he said.

'There's one out the back.' Shareen's mum opened a cup-board. 'In the cabana.'

Ryan went out again. Had he misheard? Wasn't a cabana a kind of sausage? There was a small building at one end of the pool—maybe that was what she'd meant.

He went the long way round, because this took him right past Melanie. There she was, laughing at something Kristy had said, her legs crossed, all bare and awesome. As he approached she got up. She didn't have stupid shoes like the other girls. She had sandshoes, except black, and her dress was drifty, red, with little white flowers on it.

'Toilet,' Melanie said to Kristy.

'Come straight back,' said Kristy.

Melanie laughed, and moved towards Ryan. 'Hi,' she said, brushing past.

'Wait,' said Ryan, and she stopped. He pointed past Kristy at the little building. 'Isn't the toilet in the, in the . . . um.' He didn't want to say the word, in case he had it wrong.

Melanie looked at him. 'The what?'

'Never mind.'

'O-kaaay.' She made a quizzical face, then shrugged.

'Thanks for taking such an interest, but I think Melanie can find the toilet by herself,' said Kristy from the bench.

Ryan's ears burned. He stumbled past and into the darkness of the entry to the shed, or cabana, or whatever it was. From there he watched Melanie skirt the pool and go into the house, and through the glass door saw Shareen's mum smile and nod and point to a room off the kitchen, which Melanie entered, closing the door behind her.

There were possible explanations. Maybe Shareen's mum was making all the boys use the outside bathroom, not just Ryan. Maybe there had been someone already using the inside bathroom when he'd asked. Maybe Shareen's mum had nothing against Ryan personally, but just didn't know him, whereas she knew Melanie well. But all of these were beyond Ryan's reach now.

'Fuck . . . you,' he whispered, very quietly, staring through the glass at Shareen's mum. Then, 'And fuck you,' super soft, directed at Kristy, who was slurping through a straw at something in a martini glass.

He entered the cabana, which had a television and sun lounges and a bar with nothing in it. Through a door in the far wall was the toilet. Fancy soap and a basket on the floor containing a pile of toilet rolls, the kind with little embossed flowers on them. He closed the door and locked it. Stood looking into the large, clean mirror. His pimple shone. He rolled his shoulders, made fists with his hands.

A vision entered his mind, uninvited, like the teddy bears with Melanie on Cassie Dean's bed. His mother doing the accounts, up late, her hair frizzing under the kitchen light, the worry in her shoulders, the dirty-white bathrobe. The way she read his report each term, frowning, long breaths going in and out of her nose, and the relief in her smile—*Well done, Ry!*—that didn't make the tightness in his gut go away. His mother serving dinner in her tracksuit and ugg boots, taking only one chop for herself. *You have the rest, love, you need it.* Her uniform on its hanger, her white shoes staying clean in their plastic bag. The Tiptop sandwiches she made for them both each morning, Vegemite and margarine.

He unzipped his fly, took out his cock and pissed at length, turning a full, slow circle, spraying the closed toilet lid, the walls, the door, and finishing with an extra good dousing of the toilet paper rolls.

Then he went out and past Kristy and across the tennis court. In a hidden corner he climbed the back fence and dropped down into the street.

He caught the train back to Windsor. The park lay, silent and dark and dangerous, the path winding into trees. He could have gone around it, but he didn't. His body felt agile and strong. No one was going to fuck with him. In he went, the air cool on his hot face. He didn't see anybody, but he kept an eye out—it was hard to know what might be going on in those shadows. Somewhere very far away there was the slow uncoiling of a siren, but inside the trees it was very quiet.

In the centre of the park was a cleared area with a children's playground and a toilet block, above which a harsh light burned, showing the sign that said MEN, and an entrance, black and still. He kept on, and was nearly through and into the next lot of trees when something moved, over to one side. He turned. It was Anna Worth, perched on one of the playground ladders, her hair pale, her face shadowy.

He stood like a dolt. What was the protocol here? Did they ignore one another? But this wasn't the tram stop—this was the park, in the middle of the night.

Anna made the decision for him. 'Hi,' she said. 'Did I scare you?'

'No.'

'You sure?' The playground equipment was made of dark timber, barely discernible from the trees behind. She almost appeared to be floating.

Clumsily, he crossed the tanbark. 'What're you doing here?'

She smiled, that same smile she gave when boys yelled stuff at her. 'What are *you* doing here?' she said.

'I'm . . . I'm going home. From a party.' He halted by the roundabout. 'Do your parents know where you are?'

'Jeez.' She jumped down off the ladder. 'What are you, the police? Do *your* parents know where *you* are?' She came over and got up onto the roundabout, reached down with a toe and gave a push. It began to turn and Ryan, on the opposite side, walked with it, slowly, a hand on one of the bars.

'My mum's asleep,' Anna said in a softer voice. 'Full of wine.' She sat down cross-legged, facing out, away from him. 'I get bored at night.' She made a flinging gesture towards the sky. 'Sometimes I like to sneak around.'

Ryan trod the tanbark. 'Well, I reckon you're crazy. You don't know what kind of freaks you might find out here. Bad things happen in parks at night, everyone knows that. You're asking for trouble.'

'What're you doing here then? Aren't you asking for trouble too?'

He didn't answer. There was no point. God, she was annoying. She was just determined to make life hard for herself. He sat on his edge of the roundabout and pulled his legs up. Around they went, back to back. A car gunned its engine, out on the road, and something shook the leaves at the top of one of the nearby trees.

'Why would you want to hang out here anyway, all by yourself?' he said, and was surprised by the anger in his voice.

'Why would you?'

'Oh, shut up! I wasn't hanging out, I was walking through. Do you always turn everything into an argument?'

'I just get sick of people telling me all the time what I shouldn't do.'

The trees slid past, then the toilet block light, then the trees. The anger left, as abruptly as it had arrived. The heat of the alcohol was gone, too. He was tired, he wanted home, his bed. But he'd begun to feel as if he was dreaming, the way he did sometimes at the end of a long training session, when he knew that if he stopped everything would hurt, and so he just kept going.

'I don't get you,' he said at last.

'You don't know me.'

'Yeah, but I see you around, I see what you do. Why do you dress like that? Why do you make yourself so ugly? Wouldn't it be easier to just, you know, be normal?'

No answer.

'Junie doesn't wear her skirt like that, she doesn't swagger around smoking at the tram stop and showing off. She's still— weird. Different. She's sort of cold. But she doesn't get too much of a hard time. Wouldn't it be better to be like that? Like her?'

'I'm not showing off.'

'Well, what are you doing then?'

'I don't know. But I can't help it.'

She put her foot down and started to push the roundabout faster. The toilet block light began to stretch into a long white snake against the dark.

'Don't,' said Ryan, swivelling to face her. 'I'll spew.'

She ignored him. She jumped down, keeping hold of the bar, and began to run around and around in the shallow trench of tanbark, leaning forward, pushing faster and faster.

Ryan felt himself being forced back against the bar. The trees shot past, then the toilet block snake, then the trees—dark, light, dark, light. Anna's footfalls pounded. She was laughing.

'Don't,' he heard himself call again, weakly. His head tipped back and he shut his eyes.

Then Anna's footsteps stopped, and there was a change in the movement of the roundabout—a shift in weight. In a furious silence they spun, and inside Ryan's head he saw the outward force, a hollow cone, cool and grey, its sides flowing through him. His stomach heaved and he opened his eyes and there, opposite, against the dark-light-dark-light, were Anna's knuckles, her hands on the bar, her white arms, the crown of her head. She was flying, face down, her body perpendicular to the ground, the spin sending her out, taut, like a flag.

It only lasted a couple more seconds, and then she descended, awkwardly, her legs dragging. Ryan unclenched and manoeuvred himself, lowered his feet. The roundabout slowed and stopped and he staggered on a diagonal to a tree and vomited, acid in his throat, at the back of his nose.

He stayed there for a while, spitting and wiping his mouth, and when he turned around Anna was sitting on one of the swings. He went over and perched on the lip of the slide. His edges felt blurred. The overcast sky was a very pale orange. None of this would exist in the morning, or at school on Monday.

'So who was at the party?' said Anna.

'Hanlon. McKenna. Metcalfe.'

'Right. Fuckheads.'

'Yep. I hate them.'

She moved back and forth, feet still on the ground. 'Really?'

'Yeah.' He was surprised—he hadn't known he was going to say it. He hadn't even known it was true. 'Yeah. They don't—they've got everything. Their parents are loaded, they never have to worry about . . . stuff.'

'Like you do?'

Something had shifted between them, something had been taken down.

'Yeah,' he said again, and the feeling was huge, like letting drop a heavy backpack he hadn't realised he'd been carrying. He thought for a horrible moment that he might cry, but it passed.

She swung, slowly, gently. 'Well, here we are,' she said. 'A lonely jock who hates his friends and a lonely weirdo who has none.'

He laughed. 'Here we are.'

'So,' she said, 'do you ever feel like you're not?' Her voice was languid, dreamy.

'Not what?'

'Not lonely.'

'Sometimes. When I'm running. Feels like I'm just, you know, a body. Feels good.' He glanced at her—her face was hidden. Her arms on the swing's chains were very thin and white. 'Do you?'

She skated her feet through the tanbark. 'At my nan's, at the beach, there are these huge rocks you can climb up, and there are all these sort of tunnels through the bushes where it's like it's your own world. That was kind of our special place. Me and Junie.'

'Don't you go there any more?'

'Junie does.'

'But not you?'

'Not any more.'

'Why not?'

'Well. Things are kind of divided, in our family. I'm with Mum, and Junie's with Dad. And Nan's on their side—well, she hates my mum, anyway. She doesn't say it, but you can tell. And Junie . . .' She swung higher; the chains creaked. 'It was our special place, from when we were close, and now we're not close, so I guess I'm kind of scared. That if I go there again with Junie and it's not special any more, then that would mean it's all lost.'

Ryan thought about those two lit windows in the house up on the hill, those imagined bedrooms. A sister, a sibling, a special place. This whole world that was Anna's, that she carried around inside herself, behind that skirt and hair and the scowling and spikiness. Something brilliant and warm and private—that he could never access—but something that she was now also outside of, a reflection, a memory, something she could hold and know, but not actually *be in* any more. He felt dizzy, with tiredness, with ideas.

'I think it's lost anyway,' came Anna's voice over the sound of the swing. 'Junie's changed. She hates Mum too.'

He'd only seen the mum a couple of times—a tall woman with dark hair, not like the other school mums, not trendy like them, or sporty. What was she? Stylish? Striking—that was the word. Junie had the same look to her, and maybe Anna would too, if she wasn't so floaty and pale. Something timeless in their features, old-fashioned. He thought of a picture he'd seen once of Ned Kelly's mother—a proud face, strong eyebrows and cheekbones.

He eased his legs out and folded his arms; it was getting chilly on the slide. 'Why do they all hate your mum so much?'

Anna was swinging high now, her hair streaking through the dark. 'Well, she did some stuff,' she said. 'She had an affair with this guy. Dad can't get over it.'

'An affair?'

'Yeah.' Her voice had changed again—now it was breezy and quick. She was swinging so high that the chains went slack each time she got to the top. 'An affair. And so what?'

139

The spell was breaking. Something—caution, a sense of risk—had returned to the air between them.

Back Anna flew, and then up again, and at the peak of the swing she left the seat and went curving out through the grainy air, arms spread, legs reaching, her neck long, and her landing was so light it seemed to happen in slow motion. She turned to him and put one hand on her hip.

'So what?' she said again. 'She fucked some guy. Get over it.' She had her chin stuck out, but she didn't look tough at all. And was her chin wobbling, were her eyes wet and blinking? Ryan looked away.

A breeze ruffled the leaves all around. Ryan got up. 'I'm going home.'

She didn't say anything, but when he started off towards the path she went with him.

They didn't speak again. Together they walked through to Avoca Street and up the hill, and when they reached Anna's house she turned into the driveway without looking back.

It was a long time later that Ryan heard about what had happened to Anna Worth. He was working as a lawyer, back in Melbourne after living in London for five years and Boston for three. He'd been at a dinner with old friends from university, in the city, and they'd gone on to have a drink at the Supper Club. He was leaving, and as he went towards the stairs that led down to the street someone got up out of an armchair and accosted him.

'Mute?' the person said. It was a man, lean, short-haired, with intense blue eyes.

'Sorry?' said Ryan.

The man grinned and clapped him on the shoulder. 'It is you! Mute, you old bastard, don'tcha remember me? Will Metcalfe!'

Of course he remembered. Those mad eyes. The hair, though, was different—it no longer hung in strings over his forehead, but was buzzed short, and patchy at the temples.

'Mute-o, I can't believe it!' Will exclaimed. 'What happened to you, mate? We missed you at the reunion. We tried to find you but it was like you'd disappeared. Gone without a trace. Like the fucken mystery man you always were.'

It wasn't really a conversation. They remained standing in the space between the back of the chair Will had been sitting in and the railing of the stairs, wait staff squeezing by, back and forth. More than once Will tried to make Ryan sit down with him and the other men he was with, and Ryan refused, each time saying that he needed to leave, although not actually doing so.

As he spoke, Will smoothed the front of his shirt, and into Ryan's mind sprang the image of him doing the same thing on the oval at school, Siamese eyes under that lank, pale brown hair.

Will said: 'Finance', and, 'consultancy', and, 'moved to Sydney', and, 'Macca, remember him?' and, 'coupla kids, lovely wife'.

Ryan said: 'Law', and, 'London', and, 'Boston', and, 'back now, new job'.

Then Will said: 'Few tough times', and then, 'engaged', and, 'lost her three and a half years ago', and, 'breast cancer', and, 'my depression'.

Ryan gazed at those eyes under their now slightly slackened lids—so incredibly familiar—the hand on the shirt, the way Will licked his lips before speaking. Pity ran in him like nausea.

'Shit,' he said, but then bit his lip. *I will not feel sorry for you*, he thought. There was a fuzziness in him though, a bafflement.

He had imagined the school reunion, when the invitation came—imagined it in two ways. In the first he stomped all over them, those fuckheads; wordlessly and brutally he took them by the collars of their pinstriped shirts and beat the shit out of them. This vision had come from nowhere, and shaken him with its explosive violence—he'd had to tuck it away as fast as possible. In the second imagining, which emerged later and with slow but forceful dread, he stood voiceless and meek amidst the preening and the designer suits, unable to respond to even the most superficial banter—a shame-filled sidekick, an underling, a toy. He put this vision away also, and tore up the invitation.

What he had failed to imagine was this—an offering on the part of one of the fuckheads, an opening. He did not know what to do with it.

Will drew himself up. He said: 'Better now', and, 'never forget her of course', and, 'wife', and, 'baby on the way', and, 'how lucky I am'.

Ryan was out of words. He seemed to be stuck in just looking, mesmerised by those eyes, that hair, that tongue as it performed its lip-moistenings.

Will did not appear to notice, and kept talking. It wasn't clear how he got to the subject of Anna Worth; perhaps it was to do with his being lucky, with ways in which things could have been worse. But suddenly her name was being spoken, and some dense screen within Ryan's memory collapsed and she appeared, completely intact, jumping up onto the tram, shuffling past the lockers in her ruined shoes, smiling her secret smile.

'Disappeared?' said Ryan.

'Yep. Vanished.'

'When?'

'Ninety-four. So our year twelve.'

'But how come I didn't—'

'No one knew about it, then. It must've been right at the end of the year, and it didn't get out, at school. You remember what Junie was like. She wouldn't've said anything to anyone. I only found out about it at the reunion.'

'From Junie?'

'No, she wasn't there. Just from some girls. Ladies, I guess they are now.'

'So Anna, she—what—ran away?'

Will shrugged.

'But she wasn't kidnapped or anything?'

'Nup. She just went off one day and didn't come home. Never been found. But she was, you know, troubled. She was into drugs. Well, that's what everyone said. Maybe she got mixed up with some bad people. Got in over her head, and . . .' Will's gaze had softened, slid down and to one side. Quietly he said, 'Never found. Terrible thing.'

Behind them one of his companions delivered a punchline and there was a round of hoots and roars.

'And you know,' said Will, looking up again, 'I feel bad. She got a hard time at school. Remember, we used to call her Worthless?'

'Not me,' said Ryan.

'Huh?' Will blinked. 'Yeah, 'course you did, mate. We all did.'

'No. I never called her that.'

Will put a hand on Ryan's shoulder. 'Come on, Mute-o. Don't try and tell me your shit doesn't stink.'

Ryan reached up and took Will's hand. It was warm and slightly damp. 'Don't try and tell me what I did and didn't do,' he said.

Will's eyes gave a startled flash. He tried to pull away but Ryan held on. They stood like awkward dance partners.

'You right?' said Will. 'Mute? You wanna let go of my hand?'

'My name's Ryan,' said Ryan. He let go.

Will laughed. He wiped his hand on his pants. Then he said, 'No it's not. Not to me—to me you'll always be Mute.' He swung out his arm as if to touch Ryan's shoulder again, but didn't quite make contact. 'Mute-o. Beaut Mute.'

There was an urge to do violence so vast and seething that the edges of Ryan's vision trembled. He breathed, slow and deep, focused on slowing his heart.

'Come and sit down, Mute,' said Will, in a new, gentle voice. 'Come and have a drink with me, for old times' sake.'

Ryan saw it then: Will was fond of him—or at least of the memory of him. Ryan stared into those blue eyes and saw in them a fondness that was easy, entitled and ignorant of its privilege, but also genuine and helpless.

'Mute-o?'

'Sorry,' said Ryan. 'I can't.' He tore his gaze away, looked down at the floor.

How close their bodies had come, so many times, out on the school oval—shoving and swinging and grabbing at each other, falling together onto the bruised grass, a sweaty, pimply mess of limbs. A brute closeness, but a closeness still. And perhaps it seemed sweet to Will now, untrammelled, but for Ryan it would always be heavy with compromise, with shame and envy and resentment—it was polluted, it was difficult, and the sweetness that lay somewhere in it was perhaps the most unbearable part.

Ryan lowered his head and pushed past Will. He went down the stairs and out into the February city night, into the noise, the streets filled with boozy crooked walkers, with taxis and arguments and barefoot women carrying their shoes.

Home in bed, Kim asleep beside him, his thoughts eventually loosened and circled back to Anna. He remembered her on the ladder at Avoca Park, flying from the bar of the roundabout, floating out from the swing. Her trembling chin, her brave, wet eyes. What difficulty, what compromise, had lain like dirt within the folds of her love, her lonely loyalty?

They went to have lunch with Ryan's mother. It was still strange, the new house, the old furniture shrunken and—if it was possible—shabbier. And Al, with his big, careful hands, his clean jeans. Taking the roast from the oven, apron tied.

'We're eating in here,' said Al. 'If that's all right. Margie's got a jigsaw going on the dining table she can't seem to finish.'

'That's fine,' said Ryan and Kim together.

There was a newness between the four of them. Something tender, almost painful. Each of them nursing the cautious joy of a person who had expected to be lonely, but now was not.

Ryan put the plates out on the scratched green laminex, thinking of his mother in the kitchen at the flat, up late with her ledger, her pencil. Her joke: *Come into my office.*

He left Kim with Al and found her in the dining room, taking napkins from the sideboard.

'Mum?'

'Yes, love?'

'Remember that photo from year twelve? The whole-school one?'

'Of course. You want to have a look at it? Show Kim?'

'Don't know about that. But have you still got it?'

She took him into the sunroom. Beige carpet, a built-in desk along one wall with her sewing machine on it, and a basket of clean laundry, a couple of her uniforms on top.

The photo hung next to the door, along with some of his individual school ones. He could barely stand to look at them.

'I was so proud of you,' said his mother. 'You were such a good kid.'

'You always say that.'

'But it's true. And I'm still proud of you. You were a good kid and now you're a good man.' She gave a nod. 'And now I'm going back to help Al, before I cry.'

He grabbed her hand for a moment, and she shot him a look, bashful, almost girlish, and he got a glimpse of the other person in her, the one that wasn't a mother, and which he could never know.

She went out and he moved closer to the whole-school photograph. He scanned the faces. There was Will, crazy stare not quite aligned, wetted lips grinning. There was Melanie, mouth bunched in a funny, transitory pout, eyes half-closed. There was Ryan, bad haircut, bruised-looking gaze. And there was Anna, head slightly back, unsmiling. One hand up—one fist punctuating the blue of her blazer, gripping the lapel.

Anna, Will, Sam, James, Ryan, Junie. Cassie, Juliet, Shareen, Kristy. All there, in the multitude of faces, each floating, separate in the blue. Some of them lonely, but none of them lost yet, or found.

PAINTINGS, 2008

ANNAS
by June Worth
All paintings oil on canvas.

Anna in the Garden at Avoca Street
A man stands in a suburban back garden, on a circle of lawn. Beside him are a wheelbarrow, a shovel and rake. Tears run from his eyes. He holds out his hands, in gardening gloves. The garden beds are crammed with flowers. A woman, naked, lies in one of them, among the flowers. She is smiling, her back to the man, reaching to something outside the frame. From the other side a tree leans in. On one of its branches stands a girl with blonde hair. She is high above the man and woman. She wears a blue school uniform, very short. There are red lines on her thighs. Her arms are over her head. She is poised, as if about to take off into the sky.

Anna at Dad's Flat
Inside a kitchen. A girl with dark hair lies on her back on a round table, staring at the ceiling. Balanced on her stomach

is a plate with a roast chicken on it. The man from the first painting sits at the table, eating a chicken drumstick. Against one wall, low down, is a red stain, with broken glass under it. The blonde girl is under the table, lying on her front in a one-piece swimming costume. She is reading a book and eating a round fruit: a plum, or a peach.

Anna at Mum's Boyfriend's House

A bedroom. The bed is covered in flowers, and on it the naked woman lies on top of a naked man, a second man, not the one from the other paintings. Their faces are pressed together, their arms around each other. Outside, through the window, is a yard, concrete, corrugated-iron fence, completely bare. The dark-haired girl stands outside looking in the window. Behind her is the man from the other paintings, his hands on her shoulders, his eyes closed. Behind both of them the blonde girl, in the swimming costume, rises into the air, arms out, toes pointed, as if floating away.

Three Annas in the Garden with Mum

A garden bed, overflowing with flowers. In the flowers lie the woman and the blonde girl. The woman is on her back, her arms around the girl, who rests her head on the woman's chest. Both the woman and the girl wear peaceful expressions, their eyes closed. A long white cloth is wound around the girl, binding her arms and legs. One end of it trails onto the grass, and has the word PERMISSION printed on it. The other end passes under the woman and up to the fence top, where a second girl with blonde hair sits, unwinding the cloth from her limbs. She wears a school uniform and her legs have red marks. Overhead, in a tree, a body lies along a branch, completely wrapped in white.

Anna at Esther's Birth

A hospital room. A woman, recognisably the dark-haired girl from the other paintings, sits in the bed, holding a newborn baby. The baby is wrapped in a long white cloth, the end of which trails off the bed. The woman gazes down at her child, smiling but also crying. The trailing cloth runs along the floor and up to the open window, then out. The part of the cloth that goes up the wall and over the windowsill is torn in places, and stained yellow and brown, and also with what looks like blood. Outside the window is a city in darkness, a streetlight showing falling rain.

Anna in Her Other Life

A young woman with blonde hair stands on a city street, hands on hips. She wears jeans and a t-shirt, and sandals. On her t-shirt is the word MAYBE. Nearby is a rubbish bin, and beside that a suitcase, opened, on the ground. The suitcase is empty. Out of the top of the bin pokes a blue school dress and some wilted flowers with broken stems.

Annas in the Garden at Our House

A garden, not the same as the one in the other paintings. Vegetables planted in rows, a shed. No flowers. The young mother from *Anna at Esther's Birth* and a young man sit on the grass. The man holds the arms of a toddler, who is trying to walk. Both the man and the woman gaze happily at the child. The woman is kneeling on a suitcase, as if holding it closed. Flowers and their broken stems stick out through the opening of the suitcase. Above, in the sky, float a blue school dress, a girl's swimming costume, a long white cloth with bloodstains, a paperback book, a plum or peach with a bite out of it, a lit cigarette with smoke. Standing behind the toddler is a teenaged girl, the same blonde girl as in the other paintings. She wears black, long sleeves and long pants. She is calm, smiling, healthy-looking. Standing behind the toddler's mother is another blonde girl, like a twin, also in black. This girl is gaunt, with dark-shadowed eyes and bruises on her face. Her posture is stooped and crooked. She is reaching towards the mother's head and has taken hold of a lock of the mother's hair. She is also smiling.

JOHN

It was Kathy's idea that I come here.

Oh, Kathy's my new . . . my new . . . a new person in my life.

I suppose I should give you some background. And also, I've never done this before, even when my marriage was, and when my—my daughter . . .

I'm sorry.

Thanks, it's okay, I've got a handkerchief somewhere.
  All right, sorry about that, I'm sure you see this a lot, ha ha.

Okay then. Bit of background. So I was married; Helen and I got married when we were in our early twenties. We met at university, at college, we were both from the country, and we got married, well, because in those days you had to, if you wanted to—you know.

Well, sleep together is what I mean. So we got married and, God, now that I think about it we were so young. Anyway, we finished our studies and I've had a very steady career, I'm an accountant, I'm from a long line of accountants, and Helen works for these pharmaceutical companies. She's done very well, actually—better than I have, if you're talking about pay. So we had a normal life, and we were quite happy; well, at least I was happy.

Two children. June, she's twenty now. And Anna . . . Anna. Sorry.

Sorry. Okay, so Anna. Well that's what I'm here to talk about, what happened with Anna.

We never thought there was anything really wrong. She was a funny kid—funny peculiar, I mean. She had a very active imagination, so, you know, she'd read a book that was a bit scary and she'd have nightmares for weeks. And say she was going to a birthday party, she'd be waiting by the door all ready two hours before it was time to go, and all the way there she'd be talking about what was going to happen, what the kid was going to say to her when she gave them the present, and what games they would play and what was going to be inside the pass-the-parcel and how she would win it this time because she hadn't won at the last three parties, and so on. And she would've been talking like this for days, you know . . . And then when I picked her up afterwards she'd get in the car and burst into tears because none of it had worked out the way she, well, not just wanted—I mean she had convinced herself that this was how it was going to be.

It probably started pretty young. Three or four, but it was still happening at nine or ten, past the age where you'd expect a kid to do that kind of thing.

Fantasies, yes, that's a good word. And when they were, I suppose, revealed to be fantasies, she just couldn't cope. I mean, she'd be upset for ages, and you couldn't do anything. We'd just send her off to her room, you know, send her off to cool down. It sounds terrible, but it got to the point of, here we go, another one of Anna's tantrums. We got . . . desensitised, perhaps you'd say. But you just couldn't, I mean, if every time she went like that you sat with her and cuddled her and . . . Sorry.

What am I thinking about? Well, I'm thinking that maybe that's what we did wrong, that we didn't comfort her more, back then. Or even just that we let her be like that, and we acted like that was normal life. To have this kid who . . . She did other things too, she had these tics, and she sort of picked at her hair, pulled bits out. I think she also had trouble sleeping; I'd go in to check on her before I went to bed and half the time she'd still be awake.

Oh, you know, just lying there.

The tics? It's hard to remember. They changed, too. Blinking. Tapping on things. One was a cough, she did that for a while . . .

Look, I have to be honest and tell you that I didn't give any of this much thought at the time. It was just, that's Anna, that's what she's like. These things she did, well, I suppose they seem significant now because of what happened. But we weren't to know what was going to happen. And all kids have their strange little habits and things. And almost all of them turn out okay.

No, her teachers never said anything about the tics. She did well at school, when she was younger. Primary school, I mean.

Okay, so Helen and I broke up. Junie would've been about twelve, so Anna was about ten. It was Helen who ended things, and I, look, I didn't cope very well. I was pretty much destroyed, to be honest. I mean, I just couldn't believe she'd throw it all away, everything we had. At first that was all I could think about. I felt like I still loved her. I did still love her, I wasn't even angry about the affair, I just thought, look, what we have, we're so lucky, come back, don't—

Yes, she had an affair. Didn't last. Well, it lasted for a while, but, you know, long term it didn't last, and now she seems to have a different bloke every month. From what I hear. Anyway, for a while there I would've forgiven her, I reckon. I would've given it another go, anyway. But she didn't want to.

No, I wasn't angry. Not then. I've been angry with her since, but not then, not for that. Funny, isn't it? I was just very sad and, well, depressed, I suppose. It sounds hard to believe, I know, but I always felt really lucky with Helen, like she was too good for me. I just couldn't believe my luck, to be honest. And when she left me, well, it was terrible, just terrible, but at the same time there was this feeling of, yeah, that I was lucky to have got what I did. Of her.

Well, I think it was probably really hard for the kids. Confusing. Especially because Helen, well, she moved that bloke straight in. And when that failed, then she had another one. I mean she had a lot of blokes, as far as I can tell, and I don't know how much she hid it from the girls.

I didn't think it was great. But I didn't want to fight with her. To be honest, I think deep down I still had that hope that she might want to get back together, especially since it hadn't worked out with that first bloke. And also maybe I'd just got into the habit of not saying anything. I mean it was her business, I couldn't ask her to stop.

Look, maybe when I say a lot of blokes I'm exaggerating. All my information's based on what the girls said. A bit from what Helen might mention to me, but we weren't that friendly, we only talked about the girls really. I mean, maybe they weren't all boyfriends, but from what I could tell she became very socially active after we broke up. So some of these blokes I'd hear about, maybe they were just friends. Some were definitely boyfriends though.

No, none of them lived with her—not after the first one, anyway. But I don't think she'd keep them quiet; I think they all met the girls pretty much as soon as they were on the scene.

Yeah, so anyway, Anna seemed just the same to me, but over the next couple of years she started getting into trouble at school. Helen and I, we always communicated about the kids, we made an effort to do that. So we talked about Anna, what was going on. She was getting in trouble. Smoking, wagging school, that kind of thing. We didn't like it, but we just thought she was going through a phase. Funny, the tics had stopped.

Yeah, by secondary school they'd stopped. It was like they were replaced by this other stuff, this bad behaviour.

So I'd get these calls, from the teachers, from the principal. And, look, this was a private school. I mean it cost a bomb. I wasn't all that impressed actually. It's their job, you know, to discipline her while she's at school, that's what we were paying them for. So I'd tell them that. You know: Do your job.

Well, to Anna I'd just say, Behave yourself. Stop being a smart-arse.

Yes, I saw it as being inside her control.

No, not like the tics. She was older now, she was choosing what she did. So yeah, I just told her to stop it. Pull up her socks.

Well, Helen thought differently. And this became a problem. As things got worse with Anna, Helen and I started to fight about how to deal with it. Helen, well, she just gave Anna whatever she wanted. If Anna didn't want to go to school, Anna didn't have to go to school. If Anna wanted to stay up all hours of the night watching TV and then sleep all day, that was fine with Helen. But I thought she needed discipline. I would've been dragging her to school in her bloody pyjamas. I would've been switching off the TV at nine pm and saying, Bedtime.

Well, the thing is, I had no chance to do things my way, because she stopped coming to my place. Junie still came. In fact, when she was in year twelve Junie asked if she could come and live with me. I think things at home were just too disruptive for her to focus on her studies.

Yes, she did, she lived with me that whole year. And Anna didn't even visit, not once. And that was the year it really went bad. I mean, I haven't told you how bad this got. Anna was a law unto herself. I found all this out later, but apparently she just came and went as she pleased, and she'd stay out overnight. Helen didn't know where she was. This was a young girl, you know, fourteen, fifteen, and she looked younger, she was small, and she didn't mature physically till quite late. This was a child, sleeping God knows where. She wouldn't tell Helen where she went, or who she was with.

And the school said they were concerned about drugs. That she was using drugs. But obviously they didn't have any evidence.

Shit, I don't know. I have no idea. How can you tell? She wasn't, you know, shooting up in front of us or anything. She was always skinny and pale, and all that sleeping all day and watching TV all night, well, she didn't look great. But I hardly saw her, for that whole time. I only saw her if I went round there, to the house. Which I did, as much as I could, but that didn't end up being very often.

It just seemed like every time I went over there was some sort of drama. Anna would throw a tantrum about something. And it was also Helen. She'd be quite welcoming at times, but at other times I think she got worried that I'd scare Anna off. It was ridiculous—I mean, this girl was holding us to ransom.

Well I'm not. Not with Anna, anyway. I have been angry with Helen. Very angry. I think she stuffed it up. I think the situation was worse than she let on, and she should have . . . we should have got help.

I mean, I was completely on the outer. Helen had all the power. You know, because Anna still had some connection with her. Helen was the one Anna would come home to, when she did come home.

And what happened . . . I'm sorry, I'm going to get emotional. What happened was that one time Anna went off and days passed, and then weeks passed, and she just didn't come back.

No, nothing. No contact whatsoever. She's just gone.

It's been three years.

There was a police investigation. And they found nothing, they were fucking useless, pardon me. And they just seemed to give up really fast. They were saying things like, If someone doesn't want to be found there's not a lot we can do.

This is a child we're talking about!

She was fifteen. I said that; didn't you scribble it down there in your secret little notes?

Okay, maybe I didn't say it. Sorry.

Sorry about that. I just get fired up when I think about the cops.

Phew, okay, sorry.

Useless, yes. Well, that's the truth—I'm sorry, but it is. In a matter of weeks they were saying, We've done all we can. And I'm not even sure what they did.

I'm being sarcastic. I know what they did. I know this stuff backwards. They ticked all the boxes. Not that there were many to tick in Anna's case. They check the hospitals, of course. They usually check with DEET and Medicare and places like that, but Anna wasn't old enough to have her own dealings with any of them. She did have a bank account, I opened the girls one each so they could put their savings in, when Anna would've been twelve or so. But she'd hardly made any deposits over the years, and it hadn't had anything in it since before she disappeared.

Look, I'm not saying they didn't tick all the boxes. I know we're not the only family in the world to have had something like this happen. I know all the statistics; I've had them quoted at me several thousand times.

Well, the cops reckon they get an average of fourteen people reported missing per day, in Victoria. But ninety per cent of these people are found within twenty-four hours. Generally speaking, if someone doesn't turn up in the first few days, well, they're unlikely to ever turn up at all.

So, you know, when Anna didn't show up straight away they more or less stopped looking for her. They'd ring up once a week and give me these bullshit reports, which were always just them basically saying they had no news.

Yeah, they rang me, because I was the one who'd reported her missing. That was once Helen finally told me. Anna had been gone for three days by then.

No, she hadn't done anything about it. She said this had happened before, but then Anna had come back, so she'd just assumed this time would be the same.

I mean, this is just unthinkable to me, that you'd let a fifteen-year-old girl go out like that without saying where she was going or for how long, or who she was with. In my day, you asked your parents' permission to do things.

Anyway. That was Helen.

Oh, right, okay. That was quick.

I'm okay. Sorry for losing my cool.

Yes, right. I'll see you then. Do you take Mastercard?

American Express then?

Oh, okay, I'll have to send you a cheque.

🙠

G'day. Ah, do we just continue from last time? From where we were up to?

Right, the police. Yes, you could put it that way: I was unsatisfied with their investigation. What they did, well, that wasn't enough for me. I kept thinking there'd be some sort of next stage, you know. But it was like they'd given up. It was just these stupid phone calls. Sorry, Mr Worth. No activity on her bank account. No sightings reported.

Then, after maybe six months, Helen said she had to move out. Of Avoca Street, the family home. She said she couldn't stay there, it made her too upset. But one of us had to be there, you know, for if Anna came back. So she moved out and I moved in again.

And then. Well, I went a bit . . .

Okay, so what happened was that I decided to do my own investigation. I started at the school. I spoke with all the teachers, the school counsellor. I tried to talk with some of the kids but the school didn't like that, said I had to go via the parents. So I did that, got some phone numbers, visited some families. It was awful, I have to say. You can see that when it comes to this stuff I'm an emotional person, well, I tend to cry, and, you know, I'd turn up at someone's house to talk with their kid and usually it'd be the mum who'd let me in, and often she'd get upset, you know, commiserating with me. I mean it's every parent's worst nightmare. But I'd have to hold it together because I couldn't be this blubbering mess in front of the kids.

That did lead somewhere. To this kid—Grimmo, they called him. He wasn't at the same school, but some kids knew him, said he'd been hanging around with Anna. I got hold of him. He was a real shit, pardon my language. Rude, wouldn't look at me, answered every question with a grunt. Anyway, all he'd say was that he and Anna had caught the train a couple of times to Belgrave. When I asked why, he just shrugged. When I got right in his face and asked why, he said, To look at the forest.

Don't know. To get drunk? Or take drugs, out in the forest? I don't think they were practising their boy scout skills, let's put it that way. But he had an alibi. Completely solid. He was on a school camp the whole week that Anna went missing.

Anyway, yeah, so I went through the school. And I didn't get much. But a few kids said they'd seen her in the city, hanging around with, you know, undesirables. So that was the next stop, the city. And at first I thought I might be getting somewhere. I mean, ninety-nine per cent of people would just look at the photo and say, Nup, don't know her, never seen her. But then there were a few leads. They never went anywhere, though. It was always this second-hand information, you know, someone would say, Yes, I know her, I saw her last year and she was hanging around with this guy. So then I'd try to find that guy. But then, when I did, he'd say it wasn't Anna, it was a different girl. Or someone would say they heard she caught a train to Sydney, but then someone else would say they heard it was Geelong.

Yeah, I went to Sydney, I went to Geelong. I went to Ballarat and bloody Broken Hill and Moe and every place anyone mentioned. I'd do it on the weekends, take the Friday off work, or the Monday. Hang around scungy train stations and bus depots, talking to these people who are . . . well, I used to think they were another species, most of them. Not like us. I mean, these people, they're rough as bags, out of it on drugs or booze or bloody soda bombs or whatever, anything they can get basically, and they've got missing teeth and they're filthy, and half of them can't even use the English language properly; they'll say things like, I done this and I done that, instead of I did, you know?

So, to be honest, I had very little regard for these people, my whole attitude was, well, I was horrified at the thought of my kid having anything to do with them. But one time I was in at the police station and I asked to have a look at the missing persons register. That was a miserable experience, I can tell you. I mean, the sheer quantity, bloody hell. The number of unsolved cases, and on half of them it says that the family has grave fears for the person, they think they were murdered. I mean, all these people, all these faces, you're just looking at face after face. And these people are somewhere, out in the world, and nobody knows what happened to them, and half of them are probably dead, you know, dead bodies, buried somewhere, or burned, or at the bottom of the bloody Yarra. And all the rest of us are going about our business. Maybe we're even walking right past them, or over them.

But anyway, back to my point: some of these faces are young. Some are even kids. And they look so innocent and small, you know, like—like Anna . . .

Sorry. Ahem. So you look at these people I was meeting, on the streets, at the train stations, and you think how could anyone become like this, how could you have so little dignity? But then you think, well, they were all kids once. They were all, well, like Anna, once.

Okay. So. So I went on with this investigation, every day after work, and every weekend. Showing people the photo, asking if they'd seen her, writing it all down, taking their photos if they'd let me, so I had a record of who I'd spoken with. But also, you know, I was actually looking for her. Anna. Always. I tried to be realistic—I mean, she'd been going off and coming back, that had been a bit of a pattern, and then something had happened, you know, to put a stop to the pattern; she'd gone to another city perhaps, or, or . . .

But still, I couldn't help thinking maybe it was just that, who knows why, but she'd decided not to contact us, and she was in fact still right here in Melbourne somewhere. Probably living rough, probably in bad shape. I tried to prepare myself for seeing her, you know, a bag of bones sitting in a doorway somewhere.

I'd be . . . Shit, sorry.

Ahem. I'd be catching the tram into the city and I'd picture myself finding her. I'd see myself going up to her and kneeling down, and her looking at me. I'd think about what to say. I'm not angry, you're not in trouble. You need help. We're going to help you. Come on.

Phew. Sorry. Ah.

Pardon?

Well, I think she probably needed to go into some kind of clinic. That kind of help. You know, if it was drugs, and I'm not going to fool myself and say for sure it wasn't drugs.

So, yeah, my investigation. Maybe it was being in that house all on my own—not that I spent much time there—and maybe it was this other thing that happened . . . But anyway, it got a bit out of control. I mean, I didn't see it at the time, but I was very much, I was consumed, I suppose. Junie started saying that she was worried. About me, my behaviour. A few times she showed up when I was in the city, you know, doing my rounds, she'd come and find me, and try to make me stop. She'd say, Go home, you need a break, you can't keep on doing this.

Well, Helen tried too, but I wouldn't talk to her. I'd hang up the phone if she called. A couple of times she came to the house but I wouldn't answer the door, I shouted out that I didn't want to see her and she went away.

They had a right to be worried. Looking back now, I reckon the police had contacted Helen, asked her to have a word with me.

Well, because I was making a nuisance of myself. With them. You know, turning up at the station all the time and asking to talk with the bloke who was in charge of Anna's case, telling them what I'd found out. Bringing them my own reports, I suppose, ha! And I'd do things like go and check in some out-of-the-way cop shop to see if Anna's poster was displayed, and then if it wasn't I'd kick up a stink.

The other thing?

Oh, right, yes. I actually think now that this might've been a big factor in me getting so, well, obsessed.

Okay. So this is going back a bit, this was maybe ten months after Anna went. And, you know, there'd been nothing. The cops hadn't come up with anything, and I hadn't either, and actually I think at that stage I did have this idea of putting some kind of a limit on it, you know. Like at the end of the year I'd stop. This was towards the end of winter. Actually it was spring, September. But then I got a call, from the cops, and they'd found—they'd found a girl.

It was a body. And it matched Anna's description, and I had to go and see if it was her.

I mean, fucking hell.

And it wasn't Anna, I saw that the moment they showed me her face. It was just, you know, a completely different girl. And Anna had this scar on her shin, here, she cut it badly when she was about seven, on these steps at my mum's place. So she'd had stitches and everything, it was quite a big scar. And this girl had a scar too, that was one of the things that made the cops think it was Anna, but this girl's scar was different, and it was in a different place.

So anyway, it wasn't Anna. And I went off, my legs were shaking so much I could hardly walk.

No, I didn't tell Helen. I didn't see the point.

No, I didn't tell anyone. Who would I tell?

Oh, actually, I might've told Junie.

So I went off and I got in my car and then I just sat there. I was trying to say to myself, it's not her, it's not her, that's a good thing, she's still out there, that's what this means. But I had this terrible feeling and I just couldn't get rid of it. And I didn't know what it was.

I didn't know what it was, I just said that.

Oh, okay. What it felt like . . . Ah, sort of sick, in my stomach, a lot of the time. Dizzy, too, like something had happened to my balance. Sort of like I was floating around without anything to hang on to. And it didn't go away. I'm not talking hours here, I'm talking days, weeks. And the only thing I could do, to feel like I had my feet on the ground, was to keep on with this investigation. It became a routine. I had my different places where I went after work, the train stations in the city, and these spots along the river, and then another time I'd go to St Kilda, or the bus terminal, and it was like a track I ran along, on auto-pilot in a way. I mean, looking back on it now it ended up not really being about finding Anna. Well, that's not what I mean, of course it was about finding her, but in a funny way it ended up being about more than that.

Yes, I think you're right. It did sort of hold it off. Because when I stopped being busy, when I wasn't at work or doing my rounds with the photo, that was when it came back.

Yes, a definite connection. I mean, it started the moment I saw her, when they pulled back the sheet.

Yeah, of course it did. Yeah, it made me think exactly that. I mean, that wasn't the main thing on my mind, I have to say, because the main thing was the absolute horror of seeing a dead person, a young girl, dead. That was, it was, you know, very affecting. But yeah, somewhere else there in my mind was the idea that, okay, this could be Anna, what if it was Anna, how would I feel?

Well, this is the thing. And maybe this does explain the awful feeling, where it came from. Okay, so, people talk about resolution, about how the worst thing is not knowing, and that finding someone dead is better than not knowing. But seeing that girl, it just made me think, right, this would not actually be an end point. There would still be so many things you wouldn't know. I mean, they can probably tell you how someone died, if they drowned, or if it was a drug overdose or, or, God, homicide . . . But nobody can tell you why. Why she went off, why she put herself in these dangerous situations, why she wanted to take drugs, if that's what she was doing. And you're never going to find out, if she's dead.

I have absolutely no idea. She was loved, you know, she was a smart kid, she had a good brain. She had every advantage in the world. I mean, when I look at the opportunities my kids've had that I never got . . . There was the break-up, and of course that's going to affect the children, but break-ups happen all the time without kids going off the rails.

I really just don't know. Do you think that might've been what the awful feeling was, the idea that I might never find out? That the chances are there will never be a resolution to this, an end point?

Yeah. Yes, I think so.

Well, I said before that I reckon I'm over it. And I've certainly put a stop to the, you know, the obsessive behaviour. Meeting Kathy's what's done it. But I do still get the feeling sometimes. It makes me sort of restless, like I want to get up and do something, go for a run, or jump in the ocean, to, you know, distract myself, escape.

Or do my rounds with the photo of Anna, okay, yes. But I don't. The way I see it now, I'm like an addict, and that behaviour, my investigation, you know, that's my drug. And I've gone cold turkey. And that doesn't mean I don't care about Anna any more, or that I don't think about her all the time, every time the phone rings . . . It doesn't mean any of that.

Support? Well, Kathy. She's the big one. She's the one that got me to stop.

Well, she didn't come along and say, Now look, you sad loser, this is very unhealthy behaviour you've got going on here, you just stop it right now, ha. No, it was just, you know, meeting her. Meeting her and her showing an interest in me, well, that made me look at myself from the outside. And it made me see that I'd, well, you know—I'd gone a bit mad, and I needed to stop.

Yeah, so Kathy's my main support. And I've moved out of the house. Helen and I have agreed to rent it out for a year. And then we might sell it.

Well, of course there's this feeling of, shit, what if Anna did come back, and neither of us was there, or what if she rang and the phone was answered by a stranger. But it's been three years. If she was to come back, if she wanted to contact us, then we have to trust that she'd work out how to. You know, go to the cops. She was a smart kid. And she'd be . . . she'd be eighteen now.

Which is hard to imagine.

Look, I can't—I can't tether myself to this thing any more. I mean, that could've been the rest of my life, that searching, that endless . . .

Or some other thing, some other way of, I don't know, hiding. Booze, or gambling. So the way I see it, I have to make a new start. Kathy's from Canada, and—I mean, she wants to give it some time, a year or so, to make sure we really are suited. But she'd always planned on going back, and I think that when she does I should go with her, go and live there. Junie's grown up now, and I don't have any other reason to stay here. And it just feels, it does feel a bit risky.

Yeah, that I might get like that again. Obsessed.

Time's up? Okay. Well, thanks.

Next time? Oh. I thought . . .

No, look, really. Well, of course there's more. We could go on forever, couldn't we? I haven't even told you about my mother, ha! But I've said what I needed to say. Thank you, it's been good. It's—I've—it's—been dealt with.

ANNAS

1995, in the city. A Friday night, very late, so in fact Saturday morning. Junie leaves The Lounge with two other people. Sweaty, ears ringing. Five or six vodka sodas, no dinner. She trips at the bottom step and only just keeps her footing, hurtles past the bouncer, grabs at the wall.

Junie is eighteen. It's spring but it's cold. She's with Laura, her housemate of one month, and Matt, a boy from her anthropology tutorial. None of them know each other, really.

'Walk home, or taxi?' says Laura. 'Where are you going, Davie-boy?'

'Fitzroy,' says Matt. 'And it's Matt.'

'Okay, Davie-boy,' says Laura. 'We're Carlton, so shall we all share a taxi? I have . . .' She feels in her bag, then her pockets. 'Five bucks.'

Laura is lazy, Junie knows that much. Laura is partial to hungover Sundays on the couch under her doona, hogging the TV, with cheese on toast and what she calls equalisers—joints of very weak leaf mixed with dried oregano. Laura wears op-shop dresses and laddered tights, and Doc Martens. Her large thighs press together.

'Fuck,' says Matt, 'it's freezing.'

'I've got ten dollars,' says Junie.

'Fabulosity,' says Laura, and starts waving at taxis.

'Come to my place?' says Matt to Junie, in a whisper.

Junie doesn't answer, but she'll go. Does she like Matt? Not really, not from what she knows of him. He takes himself too seriously and talks too close.

When they have sex Junie will be dry, and she will apologise, and say it must be all the vodka. And she'll try to avoid kissing.

But first, no taxis stop, and then no more taxis come, and they begin to walk up Swanston Street towards Carlton, something, some part of Laura or her clothing, creaking quietly.

They cross Lonsdale Street, and then as they're crossing Little Lonsdale Junie turns her head and sees someone who looks like Anna. The person who looks like Anna is wearing dark clothes and so her hair shows pale down her back. She is thin, in sneakers and baggy jeans, and she is walking away, fast. Very quickly, before Junie can even stop walking herself, the person has gone, around a corner.

'Hang on,' says Junie to Laura and Matt, and runs. But when she gets to the laneway she thought she saw the girl go into there's nothing. It's a dead end. Junie runs all the way down it, past big black shapes—bins, piles of boxes—but there's no one there.

'Sorry,' she says, back with Matt and Laura. 'I thought I saw someone I knew.'

'Oh,' says Laura. 'I assumed you were rushing off to have a little vom.' She leans her head on Junie's shoulder. 'I'm tired,' she says. 'Will you carry me?'

It had been night, and Junie was drunk enough for the headlights of cars to leave luminous trails as they passed. And could

Anna's hair have grown that long in only, what, nine months? Had it even been hair—could it have been a scarf, or a light-coloured bag hanging from a shoulder, and for a blurry moment it had looked like . . . ? Was the person in fact a girl? What had made Junie think it was a girl, and not a small woman, or even a boy?

It is possible she hadn't seen anyone at all, but still, for days, months and, with less frequency, years, in the dark of her mind the frail figure flashes up and turns the corner, again, again, again.

⋘

1998, on a tram, a Wednesday evening. Junie is going home from an art opening she has left early because if she stays she'll drink too much. She rents her own flat now, but as a consequence is always broke.

A large group gets onto the tram and clogs the front half of it, where Junie is sitting. It's a sports team of some sort—all men, muscled, clean-cut. They bawl unintelligible in-jokes.

'Oi, Damo. Whatchya keep-ums?'

'Geddout, ya moong.'

She considers moving, but she's hemmed in. She turns to the window. It's summer, the light heavy and golden. Late office-leavers in their muted colours walk along the footpath outside the Fitzroy Gardens; beyond them, on the grass, sprawls a small mob of rough-looking men. One lies on his back, knees up, in wide shorts from one leg of which lolls something pink and puckered. There is a roar of appreciation from the sports team.

Junie shifts her gaze again, and through the scrum of meaty legs and eye-level crotches catches sight, across the aisle, of another seated passenger. A shoulder, a wan arm, bent at the elbow. Restless fingers. Black singlet, small breasts, no bra.

Junie's breath catches. Her heart thrums.

One of the sportsmen shifts and a chin comes into view, some hair, black, but that means nothing, hair can be dyed. Lips, very thin. Too thin. But still . . . Teeth appear. Wrong, wrong, wrong. A lump in Junie's throat. Sweat behind her knees. But those fingers, that arm . . . She cranes through the tangle of men. *Lift your arm*, she silently begs the woman who isn't Anna. *Hold your hand like that again. Please.*

***

2011, the island, an afternoon. January, school holidays, any day of the week, time is not being closely monitored. Paul and the younger two children are at the beach. June has stayed behind with the oldest, Esther, who has been sick—a virus, a fever, a wakeful night. June hopes that they both can sleep while the house is quiet. They lie on the big bed in Paul and June's room, under a sheet. The curtain in this room is missing some of its rings and sags near the top, letting in the light, which is hard, and somehow projects the green of the lawn in a watery oblong against the ceiling.

June's throat is sore, her joints ache, as she pulled the curtain closed the glare outside sent a black shimmer of pain through her eyes, but she doesn't recognise what's happening to her. It might be that she refuses to. Her youngest child is a toddler but she still feels as if she is recovering from something, and has felt that way since his birth. There is nothing wrong with her, and she takes an iron supplement. She just didn't know how hard three kids was going to be, and illness on top of this general exhaustion is not a welcome prospect.

Sleep crashes down, and June fights her way through a series of hot, dank nightmares from which she comes close to waking a number of times, feeling the room and her daughter there, but unable to open her eyes. It's because she fell asleep first, before Esther, that she is so filled with dread in these half-awake moments—this, and the fever. There is a terrible sense of some unspecified failure, a lapse of responsibility.

At last she gets herself awake, hauling up her eyelids with a mighty effort. The sun must have lowered in the sky because the green projection is gone, and the room is filled with a deep orange light. June is lying with the sheet clutched to her neck and her knees drawn up. Her skin is slippery with sweat, her mouth dry, her head pounding. She is looking at the curtain, the shape of the window behind it, the knobs of the wooden rings on their rail, the cobwebs in the corner. Behind her she can hear breathing, deep and even. She is sick—now she admits it.

Everything's okay, she tells herself. *It's just the fever.*

But the dread will not pass. She knows what she has to do: turn around and look at Esther. But she can't. Because there is an idea there, in her mind, from one of the dreams, perhaps, which float overhead and drift below, crowding her, clinging like seaweed, that the child behind her is not Esther, but Anna.

Anna, sleeping, a girl again, hair orange in the orange light, bitten fingers slack against the sheets, face calm and babyish. The silky skin of her eyelids. The tip of her tongue showing between her lips as if it, the tongue, can remember and mourns thumb-sucking.

June's eyes must be closed again because everything is warm and dark. Anna is out of the bed, she has woken up and is sitting near June's feet. *Junie*, she says. *I am so sick of all my books, I am just so bored of them. Imagine if I went outside and I was looking on the ground for a new book, and one just appeared.* She starts to bounce on the bed, pushing off from the floor and then thumping down beside June's feet. *Imagine. If. Every. One. Of. Those. Spiky. Weeds. Turned. Into. A. Book.* Her bouncing gets faster and lighter. Her voice ruptures, unwinds. *Erv. Ook. Weeb.* Her fingers bat at June's leg.

June jerks upright, gasping, throwing off the sheet. Esther is there, her dark hair, her striped t-shirt. Sleeping. From the laundry comes a muffled banging. The washing machine: sweat-soaked sheets from last night have unbalanced its spin.

The front gate gives its opening squawk, and there is Maggie's voice, and Paul's. June flops down again. Her heart thumps. There isn't time. She wants more time. She wants to go back to something.

✈

2012, the island again. Easter, the chill gathering in the evenings, the days closing down rapidly. June has gone by herself to the supermarket in Cowes to buy chocolate eggs. They will have to hide them inside this time—last year something got to them in the backyard, rats, or possums. There is a photo of the children holding their mangled tinfoil prizes, three forlorn faces, the littlest with actual tears, the other two hamming it up, knowing such tragedy will not be allowed by their parents, that replacement chocolate will be provided.

The town is jammed with SUVs. Lines of cars inch up and down the main street; at the roundabouts, where signs painted on the ground warn pedestrians to give way to vehicles, groups of people venture forth, hesitate, fall back again. June parks in a back street and walks, avoiding the roundabouts. She passes the CWA, which is closed, a lowered blind covering most of its window display in what could be seen as a demonstration of withholding, of disapproval. As if the tourists, thronging to Bakers Delight, to Coles or to the surf shops, would care. She passes a cafe that was once called—mystifyingly, because it appeared to sell the same 'cappachinos' and toasted sandwiches as the other island cafes—Café Praha. June has no special connection to Café Praha, in fact never visited it, but for some reason it's stored in her mind, along with other, perhaps more obvious landmarks, as an emblem of the old island.

The Shell House. The old penguin parade, sans concrete stadium, where you just sat on the beach behind a line of staked rope. The old supermarket with its rectangles of speckled linoleum, green, pale yellow, salmon pink. The CWA, smelling of wool and lemons, where children of all ages were—and are still—frowned upon, despite most of the items for sale—jumpers, bootees, baby blankets, knitted toys—being for them. The Anchorage general store, which sold jelly rats and Fags before they became Fads. And Café Praha, not at all Czech.

June crosses at the traffic lights, new, to the Woolworths, also new. She is almost at the entrance when she sees the woman. Sitting on a bench. Leaning forward, elbows propped on knees. Cigarette, skinny legs. Long hair, dull blonde, dry-looking, kinked at the back from a ponytail elastic. Her face is hidden.

Why would she be here, now, this place, if she'd avoided them all this time, if she'd made herself disappear? But there's no reason to this, no logic. June knows what can't be; what she wants is to be mistaken, she clutches at error with both hands, she stands without moving, almost not looking, barely breathing.

It's a mist, a detergent bubble with sliding rainbows, an egg-shell perished in the sun. To examine it is to break it; all she can do is exist, with it, for as long as it allows. It sits right in her chest, and each careful inhalation finds its edges, but also crumbles them.

The woman's fingers rise to her hair. June lets go of caution, takes one deep, full breath. What if, what if, what if?

⁂

And now back again, right back to 1995. January. Anna has been missing for one month. Approximately—there is no specific start time for the missing-ness, because Helen at first didn't think she was missing. When John went to the police it was a Monday, late morning. Monday, December the twelfth. But the last time Helen saw Anna was on the Friday morning; Friday, December the ninth. Before she left for work Helen had gone to Anna's bedroom and seen Anna there in bed, still asleep.

They have gone over this many times, and they go over it again now. It's a Saturday evening at Avoca Street. John has that day been helping Junie move her things from her room in his flat into a room in a group house in North Carlton. She starts her arts degree in a couple of weeks. Orientation. A process she will hate, with its enforced socialising, its jollity, its undertones of initiation. The only thing about it she will embrace is the drinking.

The idea of getting to know something, of orienting yourself, of a framework of references, an ordering of time and place, will seem ridiculous. Because everything, the whole world, has been collapsed and then reopened in a new way. There is no framework, there is no certainty, there is, above all, no predicting.

Junie can look back on the past, when Anna was there. She can see, behind her, that world, where things were aligned. And then there is a signpost, a marker, which is Anna being gone. And after that the void opens, and the plank appears, the plank reaching over the void, the plank that you have to walk on, even though right in front of you it ends, and there is only empty space. But as you walk, as you wake each day in the world of No Anna, you step and a bit more of the plank appears below your foot. Only enough, though, for that one step. No Anna, today. This is all you know.

But none of it has happened yet, the laughable and miserable Orientation, the bands playing in the Union Square, the plastic cups of beer, the evenings at pubs, the booze-clouded, regrettable sex with someone called Chris and, another time, with someone called Nathan. Now Junie sits at the table, tired in her body, and looks past John at the bottom of the stairs, visible through the doorway that leads from the kitchen to the front of the house.

'So you went to work,' says John, 'and when you got home there were signs that she'd eaten something, and . . .'

'Weet-Bix,' says Helen. 'She'd had a bowl of Weet-Bix, and left it here, at the table.'

'What, so you're her maid now, are you? Why didn't she put it in the dishwasher?'

'I'm not her maid. I don't clean up after her. She usually puts her dishes in the dishwasher. Perhaps she just forgot that time.'

Helen's mouth is rimmed with worn-off lipstick. She turns and turns her glass on the table. They are all drinking wine.

John sighs. 'Sorry,' he says. 'Okay, so she took a bag with her.'

'Her usual bag, her backpack.'

'And it didn't have anything extra in it.'

'As far as I could tell, no.'

'And she locked the back door and put the key in the hiding spot.'

'And I don't know what time that was, but I think before two pm because that's when I called and she didn't answer.'

'Although she might've been in the shower.'

'Or even asleep, still.'

'So it could've been any time up until five or five-thirty.'

They go on and on, combing out these facts. Junie rubs at a splinter embedded in her thumb. She glances towards the back of the house. Then again at the stairs.

'And there were no messages,' says John. 'No missed calls at my work. From her.'

'And none at mine either.'

'And she seemed normal? Well, as normal as—'

'John! She *was* normal! Things were just, she'd been struggling a bit, at school and—'

'Right, the school business. So on the Wednesday you took her for a tour at the whatsit, the special—'

'It's a community school.'

'Right, for dropouts.'

Now their voices snap down fiercely.

'John! I was just looking at options. To keep her engaged with her education. For God's sake, it wasn't working where she was, even you would have to admit that.'

'Well, to be engaged with your education it does help if you actually go to school.'

'She's not a baby. They get beyond the age of telling them "because I said so".'

Junie gets up. She goes to the toilet in the upstairs bathroom, which has become, since Junie has gone to live with John, Anna's bathroom. The things in the shower are the same as they always were: the soap, the shampoo, the face washer hung over the edge of the screen. Through specks of dried toothpaste Junie in the mirror looks the same as always. On the vanity top is a toothbrush and tube of paste. A hairbrush, with a floss of Anna's hair in it. In the top drawer, old make-up, inherited from Helen. A stump of lipstick, dry mascara. They've always been there. From dress-ups, very long ago, or a school play. Anna doesn't wear make-up, or at least Junie has never seen her wear it. Hair elastics, sunscreen, Impulse deodorant. Nothing new.

The second drawer down had been Junie's, and still has some things she left in it; Body Shop perfume oil, chapsticks, more hair elastics. Nothing changed.

The third and last drawer contains, as always, pads and tampons.

Anna's room is the next one along from the bathroom. The door is half-open, and the blind must be up, because it's not dark in there. From the hallway Junie can see the bookshelf, the foot of the bed, the rumpled covers. She turns back, goes partway down the stairs and stops.

Here was where she sat one night and heard Helen and John arguing, when she was twelve, when they were still together. When John said, *Is there someone else?* Something had gathered in the house then, a presence, invisible. The air had bulged with it. And a similar presence is here now, and has been since these evenings began, since the day she got home from school and John, waiting for her, said, *Something's happened. We've got to go over to Helen's.* It's at the edges of the rooms, and it's behind the doors, around the corners. It's an impossibility. It's Anna, but she's not there.

CHRISTMASES

1994, Avoca Street. Anna missing two weeks. Presents for her will remain under Christmas tree, unopened, until packed away along with tree (synthetic, reusable, purchased circa 1980) by Helen in late January. When Helen moves out of Avoca Street in August 1995 presents will be transferred to her new house, and will remain in storage until she moves again in 2001, when they will be donated to the Salvation Army, still wrapped but with cards removed.

For Anna from Helen: a necklace, silver, eye-shaped pendant, Egyptian style, commented on by Anna herself at St Kilda markets, Helen returning later to purchase. Wrapped in paper saved from last year. For Anna from John: copy of *Huckleberry Finn*, hardcover, gold-edged pages, marbled endpapers. Bought Christmas Eve at bookshop near John's flat. Gift-wrapped by bookshop staff. For Anna from Junie: nothing.

For Junie from Helen: maroon long-sleeved top from Sportsgirl, velvet trim at neckline and cuffs. Wrapped in paper saved from last year. For Junie from John: same as Anna's, above, except *Tom Sawyer*. For Junie from Anna: earrings, silver-plated (cheap), small studs in shapes of palm trees.

For Helen from Junie: Vanilla Nourish Body Lotion. For Helen from Anna: earrings, silver-plated (cheap), large hoops with hammered texture.

For John from Junie: box of handkerchiefs. For John from Anna: nothing.

No gifts exchanged by John and Helen.

Cold ham, chutney, green salad, egg salad, cheese, biscuits. Olives, chocolates, cherries. White wine, red wine, sparkling wine, expensive. All purchased at Coles and Liquorland on Christmas Eve by Helen. Tinned apricots and custard, purchased by John at 7-Eleven on Christmas morning.

Helen: I thought you were getting the pudding, John.

John: . . .

Junie: He forgot.

Helen: Oh, well. I love tinned apricots!

Junie: . . .

John: . . .

Helen: That ham was all right, wasn't it—for Coles.

John: It was nice.

Helen: How sweet of Anna to get you those earrings, Junie.

Junie: I can't wear them. I have a reaction to the cheap metal.

Helen: Well, I'm sure Anna didn't know about that when she bought them.

Junie: . . .

Helen: Well, I think it's lovely that she got you something.

Junie: As opposed to how not lovely it is that I got her nothing.

Helen: Junie! Come back! I didn't mean . . .

John: Let her go.

(Helen pours more wine.)

John: No more for me, thanks.

When Helen finishes her own glass of wine she will reach across and take John's and drink that. She will drink the best part of two bottles of wine.

In Anna's room, upstairs: unmade bed, Sheridan sheets from outlet (gift from Helen a year earlier); half-drawn curtains, dust motes, tumbleweeds of carpet fluff; musty smell, tobacco, vanilla; top of desk entirely covered, top layer including *Essential Mathematics 10*, A4 school notebook marked *Anna W, 10 C, Humanities*, two empty cassette cases labelled in pen, Anna's writing—*The Breeders* and *Smashing Pumpkins*—hair tie with small orb of matted hairs attached like a bead, hardcover notebook, A5, unlabelled, paperback copies of *The Chocolate War, On the Road* and *The Great Gatsby*, small wooden box with carved flower on top, containing cigarette papers and a few crumbles of marijuana leaf, two cigarette lighters, small round jasmine-scented candle, three-quarters burned, various pens and pencils. Blu-tacked to wall above desk, posters of The Breeders, Sonic Youth, Nirvana, photograph of Anna and Junie swimming at Red Rocks Beach, aged approximately eight and ten years respectively, project poster from primary school: *Phillip Island and it's* [sic] *Chicory Kilns. (On Victoria's Phillip Island you will find many cute little buildings with pointy roofs, but did you know what they were once used for?)* On floor, pair of jeans, inside out, pair of underpants, also inside out, being 'worn' by jeans, grey windcheater, inside out, various socks, t-bar school shoes with backs trodden down, school jumper, inside out, school dress, inside out. Bookshelf with books including *Snugglepot and Cuddlepie, The Magic Pudding, Seven Little Australians*, as well as, filling two shelves, *Choose Your Own Adventure* paperbacks, arranged in series order.

Hardcover notebook on desk contains drawings of trees, faces, Egyptian symbols, and one page of Anna's writing. *I live with my mother, things are sad but we laugh a lot, the laughing and the sadness are actually almost the same thing. They are connected, anyway. It gets to be like a power, it gets so big I feel like a giant, like I could take the whole world inside my heart. Doesn't anybody else see how beutiful* [sic] *this world is? Tonight I got up on the roof and watched the sun going down and it's like the most massive high you could possibly get, and I was straight sober. It comes from sadness, isn't that funny.*

In Helen's room, downstairs: bed semi-made, Sheridan sheets from outlet, bought same time as Anna's, curtains open, window open, carpet vacuumed. Faint scent of cosmetics—synthetic apple. On one bedside table, tube of hand cream, paperback copy of *The Bonfire of the Vanities*, box of tissues. Inside drawer of bedside table, condoms, lubricant. On other bedside table, nothing. Inside other drawer, nothing. Chair with pair of tan stockings draped over it, also dark green skirt and ivory camisole; on floor under chair, black shoes, mid heels; on top of chest of drawers, framed school photographs of Anna and Junie, aged around six and eight respectively, framed wedding photograph of Helen's parents (black-and-white), framed university graduation photograph of Helen (black-and-white). Inside left top drawer of chest of drawers, lingerie, red, black, pink, lace. Inside right top drawer, cotton underpants, white, pale blue, yellow, two bone-coloured bras, elastic puckered, another bra, greyish, formerly white, pilling on straps.

When Junie comes back into the kitchen and she and John prepare to leave Helen is in the back garden unsteadily pulling up weeds.

John (by the gate, whispering): Do you think you should stay, Junes?

Junie (not whispering): Why?

John (whispering): You know, to give Mum a bit of . . . I mean, she looks like she needs someone to . . .

Junie: . . .

Helen (calling): You off then, you two? Hold on—take some parsley. There's so much, it's seeded itself all over the garden . . . Here. Actually, hang on, let me get a plastic bag.

(Helen goes inside, colliding gently with the doorframe as she does so.)

Junie: I'll wait at the car.

John: Wait a minute. Junie . . .

Helen: There you go. Where's Junie?

John: She's gone out to the car. She said to say goodbye.

Helen: Oh, okay. I'll come out and wave you off.

John: That's all right. You just take it easy, Hel. Why don't you have a bit of a lie-down.

Helen: I'm fine. I'm fine! Tired from work, that's all.

John: . . .

Helen: Oh, Johnny, where is she? I keep expecting her to walk in. It's silly, but I woke up this morning and I was sure she was there upstairs, in her bed.

John: . . .

Helen: Whoops, sorry!

John: You right? Here, come and sit down.

(John helps Helen into the kitchen and into a chair.)

Helen: I'm fine! I'm fine!

John: Here, drink some water.

Helen: That chardonnay was good, wasn't it. Where is it, I might just have one more—

John: Come on, Helen, no more wine. Drink some water and go to bed for a while.

Helen: I'm sorry.

John: It's all right. Just lay off the booze, okay? Things are hard enough, without you—

Helen: No, I mean I'm sorry for everything. I think I made a mistake.

John: What are you talking about? Are you talking about Anna?

Helen: I'm talking about us. You and me.

John: Oh God. Please don't.

Helen: But Anna too! If I hadn't fucked it up, the marriage, then maybe Anna might not have—

John: Just stop. There's no point.

Helen: I've failed you all! Everything's my fault!

John: Helen, I have to go. You're being ridiculous. You've had too much to drink.

(Helen cries into one hand, clutching at John's arm with the other. John pulls away from her and walks out.)

John (getting into the car): Look, Junes, I really think you should stay.

Junie: No.

John: Mum's quite upset. I don't think she should be by herself.

Junie: She should be upset. It's all her fault.

John: Can't you just go in there and be nice to her? She's your mother.

Junie (under her breath): Cannot wait to move out and get away from this family.

John: What did you say?

Junie: Nothing.

John: For Christ's sake! Are you not at all worried about what's going on, or do you only think about yourself? Anna is missing. It's been more than two weeks. We don't know what's happened to her, if she's even alive. What if she's been—taken, by someone? What if someone is doing terrible things to her?

Junie: . . .

John: Have you thought about any of that?

Junie: . . .

John (starting the engine): Yeah, well, you just think about it.

⁂

1996, Avoca Street. Anna missing two years and two weeks. No presents for her under tree. No tree.

For Junie from John: forty dollars cash in envelope, no card.

For John from Junie: copy of *Gabriel Gaté's Television Recipes*, purchased from second-hand bookshop in Carlton. Wrapped in paper torn from cheap A3 sketch pad.

Ham, soft white rolls from a packet, lettuce, purchased at Safeway by John on Christmas Eve. Praise French dressing from fridge. Peanuts from pantry. Panettone, cream, purchased by Junie on Christmas Eve in boutique Carlton deli. Beer, Melbourne Bitter, from fridge. Wine, red, inexpensive, from pantry.

John: I thought you could use it to get some art supplies. I didn't want to get them myself in case I got the wrong thing.

Junie: Thanks, Dad.

John: Gabriel Gaté, how sophisticated. Let's see, Classic Duck a l'Orange, ooh la la. Crème Caramel. I could host a dinner party.

Junie: Are you going to see Nan?

John: Well, I thought I might drive down and visit, but I don't have much time off work and I want to go to Geelong, actually—I'm trying to get a hold of this bloke who reckons he saw Anna in October, about a month before she went missing. I had a chat with him a few weeks ago and I thought he might have some useful information, but I haven't been able to find him again and the other day someone told me he'd moved to Geelong. Hang on, where's my notebook . . .

Junie: It's all right, Dad, you don't need to—

John: No, no, here we are: Murray, aged mid-twenties, question mark—it's hard to tell with these people, they can look a lot older than they are, drugs are very ageing evidently . . . Anyway, yes, blue eyes, short hair, tattoo on neck, spider or scorpion, met with me at Spencer Street Station on Friday, December the sixth, six-twenty pm. Fairly certain he saw Anna back in October '94.

Junie: Can we please talk about something else?

John: Murray living at the time in squat in East Melbourne, dealing drugs to kids from various private schools, reckons he did a roaring trade, didn't actually sell anything to Anna but claims she was with a group he met with a few times, which included that Grimmo character.

Junie: Dad, can we please talk about something else?

John: That Grimmo, what a nasty piece of work.

Junie: Dad, are you looking after yourself?

John: Never met a kid so damn rude.

Junie: Dad? Are you eating good food? Vegies?

John: I mean, you'd think he'd lift his game out of respect, or sympathy, or something, jeez. But every question I asked, it was just, *Dunno. Yep. Nup. I dunno.* This is an educated kid, good family, every advantage. Those dropkicks at the train stations, Murray and his lot, you can excuse them, they don't know any better. But Grimmo, shit, if I was his dad I'd give him a good clip round the ears, tell him to smarten up his act. What on earth was Anna doing, hanging around with someone like that? I'm going to have another beer, how about you?

(John opens two stubbies of beer, puts one down in front of Junie and drinks from the other.)

John: Anyway, this Murray bloke, when I first met him what he said was . . .

Upstairs, in Anna's room: curtains drawn, dark, stuffy, smell of dust with very faint trace of vanilla. Bed made, sheets clean. Floor clear, carpet vacuumed. Desk bare. Posters and photograph still on wall.

Downstairs, in John's bedroom: dark, curtains drawn, human smell, bed unmade, chair with John's clothes on it. Nothing on top of chest of drawers. On one bedside table, glass of water. In drawer, one pen. On other bedside table and inside drawer, nothing.

꜠

1996, later same day, Helen's townhouse. Tree, with present for Junie, and three or four bottle-shaped presents for Helen's friends.

For Junie from Helen: pack of Van Gogh notecards from the National Gallery; forty-five-dollar gift voucher for Eckersley's Art and Craft.

For Helen from Junie: Rose and Lavender Bath Soak.

For Shanti from Helen: bottle of sparkling wine, mid-range.

For Helen from Shanti: voucher for massage.

Sliced turkey, cold, sliced ham, cold, cranberry sauce in a jar, potato salad, green salad, various cheeses, muscatel grapes, cherries, chocolates, crusty white bread, dips, sparkling wine, all purchased by Helen from shops on Acland Street, Christmas Eve. Supermarket plum pudding, custard, cream, brandy butter, courtesy of Shanti.

Helen: Oh. Bath soak. Thanks. I'll hang on to it, I suppose, for if I move again one day.

Junie: Don't you have a bath?

Helen (laughs, cheerily): No! No bath.

Junie: Oh. Sorry.

Helen (laughs again, not as cheerily): Never mind. I know, why don't I give it to Shanti? You've got a bath, haven't you, Shanti?

Shanti: Oh no, you keep it, Hel.

Junie: Here, give it back, I'll get you something else.

Helen: No, no, it's fine, really.

Junie: No, really, it's all right, I can get you something else. I forgot you don't have a bath.

Helen: Did you keep the receipt?

Junie: No.

Helen: Well, don't worry about it then.

Junie: . . .

Helen: Open yours, Junie. It isn't anything flash, sorry. But useful!

Junie: Thanks, Mum.

Helen: Pleasure! More champagne? Shanti? How was Dad, Junie?

Junie: You sure you don't want me to get you another present?

Helen: Is he looking after himself?

Junie: I'm sure they'd let me return the bath stuff without the receipt, if I exchange it for something else.

Helen: I hope he hasn't been making a nuisance of himself with the police again.

Junie: What about soap? They have nice soap.

Helen: What did you have for lunch? Did he cook?

Junie: Can I turn this music down a bit, please? It's giving me a headache.

Helen: Of course. I'm sorry, I didn't realise it was so loud.

Junie: That's okay, it's just giving me a headache.

Helen: It's Maria Callas.

Junie: It's still giving me a headache.

Helen (laughs): Oh, Junie, you're such a card. She's always been such a card, hasn't she, Shanti? Have some more turkey, you two. It's not bad, for Safeway. Have some cranberry sauce, that's the best part. I can't wait for the pudding! Brandy butter, my favourite!

Shanti: Mine too. Which genius thought to combine those particular ingredients?

Helen: I love Christmas!

Shanti: Well, I don't. Christmas as a single woman with family on the other side of the world is often quite depressing. So thank you for inviting me, Hel. Cheers.

Helen: Cheers. This champagne's good, isn't it?

Helen's room, seen from doorway: bed with white linen, neatly made, linocuts on wall, female nudes, green and pink, built-in cupboards, cane chair with cushion. On one bedside table, tube of hand cream, glass of water, copy of *Cloudstreet*. On other bedside table, glass of water, folded newspaper.

In bathroom, two toothbrushes in holder. Shaving soap, man's razor.

In kitchen, in draining rack, two bowls, two coffee cups, coffee plunger. On kitchen wall, blu-tacked, sketch of Helen, nude, lying against pillows.

Helen: Do you know what I've been doing?
Junie: . . .
Shanti: What?
Helen: I've been playing squash!
Shanti: Good on you!
Helen: You probably don't remember, Junie, but I used to play, when you and Anna were little. Shanti and I played twice a week, during our lunchbreaks, didn't we? It's great fun, and it keeps you so fit!
Shanti: You are amazing, Hel. I don't know where you get the energy.
Helen: You should give it a go, Junie—it'd do you good to get some exercise.
Junie: . . .
Helen: Well, look at that, we've managed to polish off two bottles. Would anyone like a glass of riesling? I think that's all I've got—hang on, let me have a look.
Junie: I'd better get going.
Shanti: So soon? We haven't had the pudding.
Helen: Here we go, have a bit of this, it's not bad. I had lunch with Pauline the other day. She said she saw you, Junie, at the cinema.
Junie: . . .
Helen: She said you were with someone. A nice-looking young man!
Junie: . . .

Helen: Oooh, I remember those uni days! The world was your oyster! Although, of course, I managed to get myself involved with Dad pretty early on, so—

Junie: Thanks for dinner, Mum.

Helen: I don't know about you, Shanti, but I had such low self-esteem then. I had no idea how gorgeous I was. I just wish I could go back. The things I'd wear! The things I'd do!

Junie (muttering): Don't want to picture it, actually.

Helen: But you know what else? It's all about your state of mind. Some days I feel just terrible, I look at myself in the mirror and I think, Who's going to want you, you old crone?

Shanti: Oh, Hel, what are you talking about? So many men want you.

Junie (standing up): I'd better get going.

Helen: It's like Anna.

Junie: What?

Helen: It's like thinking about Anna. There are times when the most awful thoughts come into my mind, about what might have happened to her. That she might have suffered. Or be suffering now. But then all I have to do is, I force myself to picture her floating through life, loving life and being free, and having a wonderful time. I can just see it, this gorgeous girl, this young woman, the world is hers. Radiant! That's the word. She's radiant, and—don't worry, these are happy tears.

Shanti: Oh, darling.

Helen: It might have all ended so terribly, but when she was here we had some lovely times, some beautiful moments; she was so full of love, that girl, and that's what we need to remember, to focus on, her *spirit*, that gorgeous spirit she had, and, you know, it's still here! It's here even if she's not! We can keep it alive, by remembering those beautiful moments.

(Shanti embraces Helen. Helen laughs, sobs and kisses Shanti's cheek, then opens one arm to invite Junie into a three-way hug. Junie picks up her bag and walks towards the door.)

Junie: I really have to go.

THE BAD CAFE

Junie caught the tram into the city. She was going to meet John for a farewell lunch, because in a week John was moving to Canada with Kathy, his soon-to-be second wife. Kathy was thin and short, with mousy hair she raked back into faux-tortoiseshell combs. She dressed as if from the Rivers catalogue, daggy jeans and chequered shirts and sleeveless parkas, and was prone to announcements about what she could and couldn't eat, and why. *I can't eat eggs, they clog me up. Beer gives me thrush. Grapes make me toot.*

It was a Wednesday lunchtime and the tram was half-empty. Junie had a book she should have been reading, *Primitivism in Modern and Naive Art*; she held it open on her lap while looking out the window.

Junie had not had much to do with Kathy. Every now and then John invited her to their house for a barbecue, but she'd only gone to three of them in two years. They were awkward. John seemed to have nothing new to say, instead retelling worn anecdotes about travelling with Helen in Europe in the early seventies, or about Junie and Anna as children. The Sheep's Eye Soup in the Istanbul Cafe story, or the Argument Over the Map in the Black Forest story, or the Junie Hiding Under the Table at Her Own Birthday Party story, or the Anna Cutting Her Leg on the Steps at Nan's story.

When the stories concerned Anna, John's chin might soften, his eyes become bright and moist, but there was nothing of the fixed expression that belonged to his time of being obsessed with finding her. This was a relief to Junie, although she still felt nervous every time the subject of Anna came up.

The other thing about John telling these stories was that he didn't leave Helen out of them. Helen in fact played a starring role in several, such as the Black Forest one, in which she threw the map to the ground and jumped on it. This also made Junie nervous, or at least very uncomfortable. Kathy didn't appear to mind at all, but went on sitting in her plastic chair, nodding and smiling, holding her plate of whatever it was she was okay to eat.

It was hot in the tram, and Junie took off her coat. She yawned. The swaying, the dinging of the bell—not a real bell now, a recording of one, but with the same brisk, officious tone— the stop-and-start rhythm, the sleepy overheated air, all made her feel like a kid again, riding home from school on a dull, wintry afternoon. She slipped into a half-dream of Avoca Street, from the time before Anna went, before the house took on the feeling of a stage with actors who squinted under their spotlights and paced along the curtains, clawing madly, seeking entry to wings that could not be entered, and in which certain players may or may not be waiting. The old Avoca Street, before all of that. Its after-school hush, its kitchen bench still littered with breakfast things. The strange pleasure of being the first one home, the only person in the whole house. A feeling of secrecy, something almost sexual—and also a shyness, as if the house itself was watching.

Avoca Street had been sold. To a couple who were both doctors, Helen said. *Very nice people. Very interesting. The house will be perfect for them—they'll be very happy there.* When she said this, Junie had prickled all over with annoyance. Why did Helen have to use the word 'very' so much? And how could she know the doctors would be happy? She couldn't, it was impossible. Yet Junie felt jealous of this impossible happiness, and angry with Helen for bestowing it upon the doctors. Why did Helen always have to do this, always jolly things along? And in the process give away things that weren't hers to give?

Junie lived now in her own flat, above a shop, on the other side of town. She was depressed, really, but things were better than they had been a year ago, when she was still with Lee. Poor Lee. Lee had come at her like someone taking a test they have studied very hard for, and because Junie had believed that love was supposed to be effortless, and somehow complete—there, or not, cleanly, devoid of any messy mediating factors such as expression or communication—this, Lee's *trying*, had eventually become intolerable.

It had ended, untidily, during a week Junie spent at Nan's house on the island, only a few months after Nan's death. Late autumn, the chill rising from the ground. She had taken work for her university course but didn't do much of it. She walked on the cold beach. She spoke on the phone with Lee, their voices fitting together like two heavy stones, their grinding pattern set.

Running baths and lying in them until the water went cool. Dressing in the same musty clothes. To ease the ache in her throat, drinking what was left of Nan's whisky, and then her sherry, and then her brandy, waking in the black night dry-mouthed and sick, the hollow knock of her elbow against the wall wrenching her back to childhood.

She'd met a woman on the beach and they'd somehow come together for one reckless, drunken evening, an episode that flutters in Junie's memory, tissue-thin, with Swiss cheese holes and a vague red pulse of embarrassment, not something she'd voluntarily revisit. She'd been an artist, the woman, and good—one of the wisps of memory holds a dim shore, a sketchpad, pastels, grey- and green-tipped fingers bringing forth waves that sprang and flicked with not only life but *wetness*—Junie has forgotten her name though.

Now Junie was beginning to see that love probably had a lot more to it than she had thought. Also, and this was an uncomfortable thing to admit, that Lee's diligence had not been completely voluntary, but inseparable from her own slackness, her refusal to contribute—that her reluctance had only drawn him, helplessly, into further effort.

She still saw him sometimes, at uni, in the distance, and his sweet, round face and nervous, bouncing walk made her feel guilty, and relieved, and lost.

John had chosen the lunch venue. It was an inner-city office workers' cafe, the kind of place Junie would privately call a bad cafe. John favoured such places—greasy tables, bain-maries, misspelled whiteboard menus. He seemed to take pleasure in their basic, oversalted and generally un-nutritious food, and would always order the least healthy thing. Chips and gravy; roast pork with extra crackling.

John was not fat—or not too fat, anyway. His small paunch had remained the same size for as long as Junie could remember, apart from the temporary shrinkage that took place during his search for Anna. He clearly didn't eat like this all the time. Junie could remember the meals from when he and Helen were together—sensible, family food, lots of vegetables, dessert only occasionally. And she'd been to those barbecues with Kathy, where it was much the same, except without eggs, or beer, or grapes.

There was something furtive, something illicit in John's enjoyment of the crackling, the gravy, the giant chocolate-chip biscuit with his coffee. This, the childishness of it, brought on in Junie a surge of tenderness, and an unbearable irritation.

They were the same feelings that had plagued her when he was doing his searching, that year he lived alone at Avoca Street, when the paunch went away and his hair became noticeably thinner and greyer. When she would ask, *Dad, are you eating enough? Are you looking after yourself?* And he wouldn't even answer, just say something like, *So I found this bloke who reckons Anna was camping with him and some other people in a tunnel near Spencer Street Station, in January. He reckons she caught the train to Sydney with someone called Luke.*

Junie saw John through the window of the bad cafe, already seated. The cafe was busy, and some dirty cups and plates were being removed from John's table by a waitress. John said something to the waitress and they both laughed.

An evening at Avoca Street, long ago. Helen and John in their work clothes, in the kitchen, cooking dinner. John had been out to a long lunch, a business thing, at a restaurant that was at the time very fashionable, and Helen had wanted to know what he'd eaten. It was a light-hearted conversation; there was a tone of festivity in the house, perhaps because of the lunch, because of John's afternoon of fun, his brief escape from everyday life.

Oysters? Helen following John across the kitchen. *Did you have oysters?*

John, grinning, opening the fridge: *I'm not saying!*
Champagne?

Maybe.

Was it good? Was it French?

More grinning, eyebrow waggling.

Let me smell your breath!

And then Helen was grabbing his arm and they were scuffling, their grown-up bodies ridiculous and slightly frightening as they shoved and pushed and laughed.

Junie remembers listening from the table, looking up from her spelling book, a strong sense of a loss of bearings, of upset. Why was this? Were there already undercurrents in the marriage? Was Helen already having her affair? Junie is hazy on the timeline, having only the information given to her by John during his oppressively sad post-break-up monologues, to which she had tried not to actually listen. So it was possible that this high-spirited interaction had been laced with genuine tension. Or perhaps it was simpler, just a normal childhood revelation— that parents had their own, separate connection, and also their own, individual needs; that parents could want things from one another, and that these things could be withheld.

'You going to eat those?' John pointed with his fork at the soggy pieces of roasted capsicum and eggplant that had fallen out of the bottom of Junie's toasted sandwich.

'No. Go for it.' Junie watched as he speared the rubbery morsels and put them in his mouth. 'I don't know how you've got room though.' John had just eaten a huge chicken parmigiana.

'I don't.' John groaned, wiped his hands, patted his stomach. 'I'm so full. What a pig I am.'

Over lunch, he had told Junie about Toronto, where Kathy was from, the snow and cold in winter. *I'll get all my cold-weather gear over there, it's cheaper and they have the proper stuff.* The house Kathy owned, which had been rented out, but which was now empty and waiting for them. *On a hill; Kathy says if you climb up on the back fence you can just see Lake Ontario!* The job he had already got over there. *The internet, tell you what, makes it all so bloody easy.*

He had asked about Junie's master's, about her painting. Whenever this happened, she always tried to keep her answers practical, telling him how large or small the canvases were, what kinds of paints she was using, what her rented studio was like. But often he still insisted on asking what the paintings were of. This was difficult territory—John had never tried to hide his bewilderment at both Junie's art and her desire to be an artist. *I just don't get it,* he would say, screwing up his face.

Junie told herself that this didn't matter—that she didn't do it for him. Still, she couldn't help but sense a stubbornness in his 'not getting' of her work, a refusal, as if what he was doing was in fact dismissing it. Also, she thought he might be embarrassed by it, and by her doing it. This was not helped by the fact that her art and her need for it were things Junie was herself embarrassed by.

But your work is about shame, she had been told by one of her teachers—her favourite teacher, a life-changing teacher. *It costs you, but that's why it's good, why you must keep doing it.* She held this close, this instruction.

She had occasionally been able to see that John's behaviour might come out of protectiveness, of a fear of seeing her fail financially, or suffer humiliation; that he wished for her a safe career.

'They're figurative,' said Junie now, mumbling.

'What does that mean?' said John. 'They've got numbers in them?'

'No, figures. You know, people, and things. As in, they're not abstract.'

'Oh. Right.'

There was a pause. John looked around the cafe. He cleared his throat, worked his lips. These were signs that he was about to say something he found tricky.

'I'm going to miss you!' said Junie brightly, getting in first.

'Oh. Yes. Me too. I'm going to miss you too, I mean.'

Junie felt herself flush. She'd got it wrong; it was something else he'd been preparing to say, a different tricky thing.

Again, the throat-clearing, again the lips. Here it came.

'Junie, do you think about Anna, still?'

Junie swallowed. She hadn't expected this. 'Of course.'

John gave a short laugh. 'Don't worry.' He put his hand, briefly, over hers. 'I'm not going back into all that. This is different. I've had—a kind of breakthrough.'

'Okay.' Her heart sank.

John smiled, his eyes crinkling. 'You should see your face. Not that kind of breakthrough. Don't worry! I'm over all that, I promise.' His eyes became soft again, and sad. 'No, it's a, you know, a personal breakthrough, in how I think about the whole thing.' He took a deep breath. 'I think she's dead. Don't look at me like that, Junie. I do. There's no other explanation. She had no reason to leave us, to run away. To never be in touch—not in five years—just to let us know she's all right. So, yeah. And who knows how it happened.'

Junie's chest felt tight. Under the table she worked at a hangnail.

'I know,' said John. 'It just doesn't bear thinking about, does it? You could drive yourself crazy. Like I did! But here's the thing. She'd gone out to the Dandenongs, on the train, right, with Grimmo or whatever he was called. On the Belgrave line. And she was always climbing things, remember? Even as a little kid, always jumping and climbing and falling off things. So I reckon she went out there again, another time, without Grimmo—he was on a camp, remember, the week she went missing—and she was trying some stunt, off the track, up on a cliff or something, and she fell. And she was on her own, or whoever she was with got scared and ran, and hasn't ever reported it. And she's never been found. The chances of someone coming across her up there, if she was deep in the bush, away from the tracks, well, they're pretty much non-existent. I've done my research.' He drank some water. 'All I hope is that she didn't suffer. That it was quick.'

There was a brief silence. Junie, feeling an expectation of agreement or even of approval and being unable to give either, also drank some water.

'So,' said John eventually. 'That's what I think. I've decided on it. She's dead. It was an accident. If there was pain, it's over now.' He sat back and folded his arms.

She was walking away from the bad cafe, towards Bourke Street, when she heard him call her name. She stopped and turned and he caught her up, half-running.

'I forgot to give you this.' John held out a plastic shopping bag, from Myer. 'For June the fifteenth, since we won't be here.'

Junie took it and glanced inside. Department store wrapping, weighty, anonymous. A card with his slanting writing on it: *Happy Birthday Junie, with lots of love from Dad and Kathy.*

'I hope you like it,' said John, making an apologetic grimace. 'I had to ask for help, from the girl in the shop.'

She caught the tram back to her flat. She felt immensely heavy. When the tram got to her stop she could barely drag herself out of her seat.

The next week, the night before John was due to leave, she rang him, and was relieved to get the answering machine. She said that she couldn't make it to the airport to see them off— something had come up, a meeting with her supervisor at uni, she couldn't change it, she was sorry. She wished them a good flight, said she was looking forward to visiting. She switched off her own answering machine, and when her phone rang an hour later, and then three more times over the next hour, she didn't answer it.

She was lying on the couch, having drunk almost a whole bottle of wine, watching a film on SBS about a girl in Turkey who had been sent to jail for a reason that either wasn't clear or that Junie had missed, when she heard the clang of the gate from the laneway behind the shops and footsteps on the metal stairs that led up to her flat. Junie snatched the remote and turned off the TV. Then she scrambled over the back of the couch and lay on the floor behind it.

The flat was very small; there was a tiny bedroom and a tiny bathroom, and then there was a third room about the size of the other two put together, which was the kitchen and living room, where Junie was. This was the room the door opened into, the only door in or out. The door had a pane of glass in it, near the top. A dusty lace curtain hung over this pane, so that during the day the view of rooftops and the laneway below was mostly obscured. At night, if the lights were on inside, it was possible to see in through the lace. There was a lamp on in the room. If you were to look in the window you would see, to one side, the kitchen part, the bench and stove and the bar fridge, and to the other side, Junie's wonky op-shop work bench against the far wall, and the couch, facing you. You wouldn't see Junie, though, because she was lying on the floor behind the couch.

'Junie?' It was John. He banged on the glass. 'Junes? You there?'

He knocked again, and called again, and then at last there were the sounds of him going back down the stairs and the gate clanging closed.

Junie lay on the floor for another minute or so and then she got up and sat on the couch again and poured out the last of the wine. It was cheap chianti, from the bottle shop two doors along. She drank that and then opened another bottle.

The gift, when she unwrapped it, was a scarf—a shawl really; large and square—of fine wool, deep grey with a paisley pattern around the edges in orangey-pink and soft blue and green. Junie didn't like it. She put it away.

She forgot she had it, and when she came across it again ten years had passed. She was in her mid-thirties, and called herself June. By this time, she had visited John and Kathy in Toronto twice. She had seen Lake Ontario from the top of the fence and up close, and walked through Wychwood Park in the snow.

She had met John at Melbourne airport when he visited in 2007, a week before her thirtieth birthday, with Esther holding on to the hem of her coat and baby Maggie in her arms. And when John cried at seeing the children for the first time she had fought her tenderness for him—because she always did; because she couldn't unharness tenderness from pity when it came to John—but something had ripped its way out and she'd cried too. The two of them crying, there in the loud and busy airport, with people passing close by, and Esther climbing on the trolley that held John's bags. And then John's quiet tears stopped, but June's didn't—they became uglier and more abundant, no longer tender, no longer pitying, but furious and grieving. And John gave her his hanky, and put his arms around her, and said, 'Junie. Sweetheart.'

When she found the scarf after all this time she put it on and looked in the mirror. She thought of John in Myer, in ladies' accessories, waiting for the attention of the salesgirl, awkward amidst all the sparkling femininity, the bright lights. She imagined the salesgirl holding up two scarves for John to choose between. It was up to June how she imagined John doing this, and so she made him do it with care.

She wore that scarf all through the rest of her thirties. It suited her.

GRIMAUX

He sits by the dam. He doesn't fish, although there are fish in there—it's full of trout, stocked with trout, like a shelf, a larder, a bar fridge. He has a folding chair. There are tadpoles in the shallows, sperming about. He thinks of nets and jars. He thinks of his son, whom he's not allowed to see.

He is landed gentry, but only in so much as he has the land. He works, when the local council needs another set of hands in blue Hard Yakka and a hi-vis vest—he labours on roadsides, he sprays weeds, he replaces fox baits. He is thankful for it, for the occupation; the money doesn't matter much, his living costs have become astonishingly modest. And the work is casual, and tends to happen in blocks of two or three days, leaving plenty of time for sitting by the dam. For reckoning.

He wonders sometimes what the other guys would think, if they knew about this undeserved inheritance of his, this picturesque and unloved investment, site of not one pastoral family scene, nor even, later, once true acrimony set in, refuge for either of its purchasers. Its rows of untended grapevines, its dam of gleefully breeding, uninterrupted trout. Its whimsical gate sign, GRIMAUX. A fairy-tale name, as people have insisted on telling him his whole life. Was there ever a less apt association? The 'grim' part, he supposes, has proved fitting.

(Someone was French, back on his father's side—memories of his father's study with its poor choice of deep pink paint, so you felt as if you were inside a cut-open body; the plasticky smell of photo albums, a family tree with confusing vowels. This was early on, when his father would show him such things, consider him worthy. Before he proved his unworthiness, and proved it again, and went on banging down hard on the nail of proof with a million deceitful hammers.)

What would Omran think? Of this dam, these vines, this unearned landed-ness? Omran in his hi-vis, with his bored dark eyes, who lost it once as the two of them tried to unclog a public toilet that some genius had wedged a shoe into, and cried out, his teeth flashing white: 'Before I come here, I am *engineer*, I am greatly valued, my parents are proud, and women desire me!'

He sits by the dam, not diminishing its stock of trout, and not catching its tadpoles in jars with his son, who in any case is probably too old now for such things. He sits and knows that he is fortunate, and cursed with ingratitude.

He was smart, at school. And his parents were wealthy, and busy, and seemed to have simply lost interest in the whole idea of a family. He turned fourteen with two sisters already grown and gone, and understood his home to be a place in which time was somewhat bitterly being marked. He grew quiet, and began to get quietly into trouble.

He has it roughly divided into sections, for ease of riffling. Home, parents, early life. That's pretty boring—and generally leads to unadulterated sadness, which he's not a fan of. He prefers blends, such as shame and regret, or horror and remorse. These are more broadly abrasive, but less intense. So, there's

Early Life: Lonely Bowls of Froot Loops and Hello Dad's Liquor Cabinet. And then there's Secondary School: Booze, Pot, Rubbish Speed and Rubbish Acid. Then Early Twenties: Better Speed, Better Acid, Further Adventures in Psychedelics, and Introducing Heroin. This is followed by Mid-Twenties: Heroin, a Love Story; Late Twenties: Heroin, O Heroin!; then Early-to-Mid-Thirties: Still here, Heroin?

Sometimes he uses a colour-coded system. It's more direct, and also expansive—impressionistic. Green for psychedelics, fun times: Belgrave, looking down on furry hills, green shade, green moss, green fans of ferns opening; Dee, with her hair dyed green, her nose-ring, her springy flesh, her round child's face, unsullied. (Okay, there's a bit of mild tragedy in green too.)

White for smack, the good times: white sugar in the bowl, coffee in the mornings before the first hit, the teaspoon of many uses, the early, needful wakening, white dawns in the sleeping city, holding off just a moment longer, the white buzz of possibility, *Perhaps I won't today*; a fat white moon over a backyard, Dee's white limbs on a blanket, dry grass, the white surge in his veins; a road trip, white dust, white clouds over a river, Dee white and naked in the water, white bark of trees, a white eternity of stoned-ness under a white sky.

Black for smack, the bad times: black bruises, black scabs, black under Dee's eyes when she cries, their ugly black dance of begging and blame; black streets, black doorways, black waiting; a quick search of the glove box for his father's black wallet; rotten black finger of a dealer on the edge of going under.

Yellow for getting clean: shaking yellow afternoons, yellow sweat, yellow eyes in the mirror, yellow light globe on all night, yellow of his son's hair, imagined.

Red for damage (rarely used, too awful to go straight into): red spray of blood on tiles; red ambulance lights; red ribbon on flowers at the funeral; red scratch marks on his face, red under Dee's mother's fingernails, her face red raw.

Pink is for hope (often visited): the pink face of his newborn child; the pink tulips beside the bed; pink curtains framing Chloe as she gave her pink nipple into the tiny pink mouth.

He believes this to be his work, his real work, these reckonings by the dam. He understands that to someone like Omran this would seem an inconceivable, disgraceful luxury. But he has, for no apparent reason—all right, for the kid, for that sweet pink hope—resolved to stay clean. And, in order to do so, to as best he can untangle the vast and rigid mess of his motives, reveal and dismantle the tripwires that are his misdirected hankerings. To tough it out, to stare himself down.

Nobody cares if he does this or not. No one will believe it, if he does pull it off. (He tries not to dwell too often on this fact. It is, in any case, impossible to accept—hope, for all its gentle pinkness, is unkillable.) In detox they talk about rock bottom. Perhaps for him, this is it: he is alone, and he has been given up on.

Thinking like this, after decades—a whole lifetime, really—of pressing anything remotely like insight into a harmless paste with the heel of his habit, is difficult. He is having to locate muscles like someone recovering from a spinal injury, straining into the unknown, pushing with all his might for the slightest stirring, the merest wiggle.

He fucked it up, the chance with Chloe, with the kid. He slipped. Chloe had known he would; they'd both known. *I'm sorry*, he said. The battered old appeal, but emptied, this time, of expectation. He was quite simply sorry, moved to a frank and general sorrow—by the dreariness of failure, the ordinary greyness with which even this precious opportunity was brought undone, by his own indefatigable and banal destructiveness, by Chloe's necessary, enviable strength, by the whole damn situation. *I'm sorry*, he said. *Me too*, said Chloe.

He fucked it up with Chloe and the son and heir, and that sealed things with his father. That particular door has at last been slammed, and barricaded. From his mother a more resigned closure, but, he thinks, one as sincere. This was how he got the property—a farewell gift from her, a last provision, thrust at him with the heartsick finality of the terminally disappointed. *This is all you get, understand. Do what you like with it. Liquidise it and put it up your arm for all I care, but you will get nothing else, nothing more, from me.*

The tadpoles spurt, the trout send up silver bubbles. He rummages. Of late he has found himself returning to matters filed under Green. This is probably his easiest material, his time of baby steps, light on despair, rich with what were still relatively simple pleasures—its angsts almost laughably naive. Even remembering Dee the way she was then is not always painful; more often it's like thinking of a different person from the one she ended up being, and ended as, full stop. Interestingly—is any of this interesting? Is his whole life a bore? Probably, but who cares, he is free to wade; surely this is the chief pleasure in finding oneself not being given a shit about by any other human being on this earth? Interestingly, other than Dee, he is hazy on who else he hung around with in those days. But he works to draw them out. He's not sure there's any reason for this, other than the general benefits of flexing his poor, wasted mental muscles. But random dipping does usually end up getting him somewhere worthwhile—meaning somewhere that hurts.

He struggles with his dipper, his imprecise and atrophied probe. Johnno? Thommo? Boofhead type, acne. He's got the name wrong, but the boy is coming into focus now: meaty shoulders, rugby tops; an unsuccessful mushroom-seeking venture in a borrowed car, culminating in a visit to a small-town hardware shop, and chroming in a cemetery.

Megan? Stoner girl, into death metal, skin-tight jeans after (and before) they were in fashion. Showed him how to roll amps, although he always preferred his joints sans speed; stimulants were never his thing. What he sought was not sharpening, or bolstering, or delusions of grandeur; what he sought was obliteration. Thank God—imagine how much more insufferable he might have been had he gone in that other direction. He wouldn't have made it—he would have wiped himself out in a toxic streak on a road somewhere, or fallen under a train, or got himself shot by the cops, thrown himself, demented, railing, stringy fists and champing jaws, into the hail of bullets.

Ah, here comes something, from the Green days: Anna. He has opened this particular treasure box a few times. There was a reason to remember Anna. Anna vanished, apparently, and her father came to him, asking questions. A man bristling with need. He descended onto the white leather Grimaux couch and cushions shot out in all directions. His clothes were scruffy, his hair in want of a trim. He had a little notebook, and wrote in it pedantically, pursing his lips. *And which station is it? And how many times did you go?* He would not be sold short; he pressed, he insisted, he got down on his knees and stuck his face right up close—close enough to see blackheads. There was no defence against this desperation other than to withdraw—not that there was far to go; any further would have meant imploding.

Regret: that he couldn't find it in himself to say, *I am so sorry about your daughter. I am so sorry I can't help you.* Shame: for his selfishness, his lack of compassion. No excuses.

He sits with it, for a while. Then goes on, to Anna. This is ripe, this territory. He has circled it on other visits, touching only with fingertips. There is work to be done, if he is able.

Here is what he remembers of her. Pale skin, on the surface of which freckles seemed to float. Beautiful, gold-red hair she roughed with her hands to make it stick up at the back and let hang into her eyes. A body too young for her age, that made you feel afraid when you saw how credulously, how boldly, she sent it into the world. A smile to make you cry, so pasted-on was its mystery.

She was hungry for a certain kind of wastedness. Not for oblivion, and not for escape either. He, having only a blind and one-dimensional intimacy with his own need, felt wary when faced with hers—there was nuance there, there was, dare he call it, sophistication. Heightening, that's what she was after.

He thought at first that she was desperately sad, and romantic with it. That she was—and weren't they all—in love with the full range of minor-key emotions, from the intensely glorious to the lumbering: melancholy, woe, anguish, downheartedness. At her school they learned French, and once, peaking, her eyes all ravenous pupil, she whispered to him, *Tristesse, isn't that the most beautiful word?* But what he realised, eventually, was that for her it wasn't only about sadness—she was just plain romantic. On the train back from Belgrave she showed him a poem, in a book. She spoke the final line of it: *Childe Roland to the dark tower came.* It thrilled him—how could it not? But he hid the thrill. He stayed safe. He would not—could not—come out of himself to where she was.

All this he knew when her father arrived, drilling with his questions and taking his notes, and trying to make eye contact. And none of it could he give over—which would have been a better gift than nothing. Which would have been an act of kindness. (Shame. Regret.)

The sun is nearly down. Mosquitos are rising from the dam's moist reeds. What a waste his life has been. If regrets were silk handkerchiefs he could sew himself the world's biggest parachute, find a cliff and float gently down, to—what? To a place of no regrets? To a mattress of forgiveness? Not deserved. To a field of spikes fashioned from every act of forgiveness he ever betrayed? To an ocean of tears, filled with sharks fed only on betrayed forgiveness? Oh, shut up. Get your hand off it. Here is the downside to so much musing, to lengthy, unfettered rompings of the mind.

He forces one more moment of honesty, a small punishment. They are necessary. The truth is, he couldn't do it even now— look her in the face, Anna, were she to be magically un-vanished and here before him. He would quail still at her passion, the absoluteness with which she gave herself over to feeling, the challenge it threw out: *Live!* He would turn away from it, as he did the first time, terrified and ashamed of his fear, his stumpy little claws dug in.

She wouldn't have become a junkie, that girl. She would have made the most of life, of living. He hopes that she did. And now he sees what must come next, in this series of arduous and miniscule advances. Kindness is still possible. Anna's father is, most likely, still out there. He is, most likely, reachable.

He goes into the house. He looks up the school, and he sends an email.

And then he plays a record, on his parents' state-of-the-art seventies turntable. Mulatu Astatke: 'Tezeta'. The rolling piano, the warm guitar, the hovering, feathery sax. So much space between every sound. It's like a sigh; it's like tender evening light in which a drink might be poured, in which forgiveness might be offered. There is no one here to forgive him, and forgiving himself is something on which he is yet to establish a position. But he can have a drink. Soda water and lime, his sober treat. He pours it, and the fizz is pleasant, calm, suitably comforting. He raises his glass. He will drink alone. He will drink, a father, who does not know his child.

PART THREE

HELEN

Helen grew up in a country town. Her father was the doctor, and their house was at the back of the surgery; their laundry stood side by side with the supply room, where there were shelves filled with kidney basins and rolls of bandage, and brown-paper packages of suture thread and needles, and sinister coils of rubber hose, and large white squeezable bulbs, also rubber, the purpose of which Helen never discovered, and, upright in a corner, the spare cylinder of laughing gas.

The smells of the surgery and the smells of the house bled into one another: disinfectant, the pine-y sweetness of tongue depressors, carpet powder, beeswax polish, roast dinners, Bon Ami.

Helen's father was a tall man, with a face that was mostly eyebrows and nose. His eyes were small, and hid behind black-framed glasses. He wore his dark, thick, wavy hair combed down with Vaseline tonic from the cabinet in the bathroom. Helen knew this only from the smell, of the tonic and of her father—in their house nobody entered the bathroom while another person was in it. Alongside the tonic lay her father's shaver, which had a heavy stem with an embossed, criss-crossing pattern that was strangely soft to the touch and made Helen think of reptiles.

Helen's mother had been a nurse but now she ran the surgery, sitting behind the waiting room desk in her brown wool skirt and yellow blouse with the buttons that looked like pearls but weren't. Her face was round, with very fair, almost invisible, eyebrows and lashes. She wore no make-up, but her lips were naturally a pronounced pinkish-red; the bottom lip was plumper than the top one, and she had a habit of pulling it in with her teeth and then letting it slide back out, so it was often wet and shining. Her hair was fine and mousy, unfashionably long, pulled into a low bun. At night she put it in a plait, which went right down the back of her nightdress, as far as the soft and rounded shape that was her bottom released from its daytime strictures.

Helen saw this—the plait and the nightdress—very rarely, only when she was sick and her mother needed to come into her room in the middle of the night. Usually, Helen got ready for bed and went down to say goodnight to her parents in the sitting room—where they would be fully clothed, her father reading the newspaper, her mother sewing—and then when she saw them again in the morning they would both already be up and dressed. In her mind, they existed only as daytime people, their bodies sheathed in their clothes, their hair arranged, their feet shod. So this vision of her mother in her nightdress, with the curves of her body loose under the cotton and her long wispy plait hanging down, pale at its tip, lurked like a kind of spectre, something that might have been imagined.

In all her life, Helen never saw her father undressed, or in anything less formal than slacks and a short-sleeved shirt. When she was twenty-eight years old she saw his bare feet for the first time. He was dying, in hospital, and she was visiting, and a sheet came untucked. The feet were large and had yellow, brittle-looking toenails, and Helen looked away, struck by a terrible sense of shame and transgression.

As a young child she knew that her parents must have done something to make her be born. She knew that the thing they must have done involved nudity, and private parts—she knew this from what other children said at school. This idea was absolutely impossible. And yet there was that spectre, of her mother in her nightdress, with her girlish hair and her softened body. And sometimes, late at night, inexplicable sounds could be heard coming from her parents' bedroom—an odd, silly giggling, in what was recognisably her mother's voice, although her mother never giggled like that in the daytime, nor laughed in any way. When this happened, Helen put the pillow over her head.

Helen's parents were old. This understanding did not come to Helen until she was almost an adult herself—while she was a young child they, like all adults, seemed ageless, outside of time. Much later, when it was too late to find out, Helen did wonder why they had taken so long to have her, their only child. Had they believed children were not possible, for them—had she been one of those unexpected, last-minute, miracle babies? Or had they not meant to have her? Had she been an unexpected, last-minute mistake?

The heavy black telephone in the downstairs hallway rang sometimes in the night, calling Helen's father to emergencies. Occasionally, if things were too desperate for the drive to be made to the city hospital, these emergencies were brought in to the surgery, and from her bed Helen might hear shrieks and wails, doors banging, cars coming and going—but never the voice of her father. Her father never raised his voice, which was deep and precise and dry. It was a voice that hadn't ever needed to be raised, that was certain of being attended to, of being, as Helen's mother would put it, minded.

Every weekday at noon Helen's mother left the desk in the waiting room and went back to the kitchen, and made lunch, and set the table for Helen's father. At a quarter past twelve her mother ate, standing up, at the bench. At just before half past twelve, her mother put her father's lunch on the table and filled his glass with lemon cordial, and dropped in four ice cubes.

For lunch Helen's father had cheese-and-tomato sandwiches with salt and pepper, and butter Helen's mother softened by putting a pat of it on a saucer and holding the saucer over the steaming kettle. Or he had leftover meat from the night before, reheated: grey, greasy slices of lamb; a chop with its curving bone so like a handle, although nobody in that household would ever eat with their hands; sausages that made popping sounds in the frypan and sent up a dancing haze of fat. With the meat there was often potato salad with tiny green jewels of gherkin, and mayonnaise Helen's mother whipped by hand, staring in a mistrustful way down into the bowl, her whole body tensed and rocking with the beat of her wrist, in a way that Helen would be reminded of for the rest of her life by the action of a washing machine on spin, and—a much less welcome association—by certain urgent frictions of a sexual nature.

Helen's mother, and Helen, when she was home during school holidays, did not have the same things for lunch as Helen's father. They had the crusts of the loaf of bread with only a scrape of butter, and the end bits of tomato; they had half each of the smallest sausage, which was burnt; they had the cold scraps of lamb and the driest potatoes. They did not have mayonnaise. They did not have cordial with ice. They ate side by side at the bench, quickly, bent forward so that no crumbs would drop onto the floor.

When the clock showed half past twelve on a weekday the kitchen was ready for Helen's father, his lunch on the table, his napkin folded, the ice cubes shifting gently in his glass of cordial; the frypan, the wooden spoon and mixing bowl, the cutting board and knife washed and dried and put away; the bench wiped. Helen's mother was back at the surgery desk. Helen, when she was home, was outside—or, if it was raining, in her room.

Once—only once—Helen crept down the stairs and to the door of the kitchen while her father was in there eating his lunch. She saw his jacket hung over the back of one of the empty chairs; she saw his large hand resting by his place; she saw his white shirt and his tie and his black glasses and the brisk munching of his jaw. She saw the ripple of his throat as he swallowed. He reached for and lifted up and drank from his glass of cordial, and the ice cubes in it made a silvery sound. Then he turned his head and looked at Helen. His eyes, distant behind his glasses, moved slowly over her as if she was a part of the doorway, or of the bannister of the stairs behind. Then her father turned his head back and put down his cordial and took up his sandwich, and resumed his biting and chewing and swallowing. He did not look at Helen again, and she withdrew and ran upstairs and hid behind her bedroom door. She used her fingernail to flick up the edges of a scab on her elbow and then peeled the soft middle bit from the sticky, pink skin underneath. Then she put the scab in her mouth and ate it.

Dinners were not the same as lunches. At dinnertime they all sat together, and they all had the same food, more or less, although Helen's father got the best and biggest of everything. They ate in the dining room, and special plates were used, and special cutlery. Helen's father disposed of his dinner quickly, efficiently, and then he put his knife and fork together, set his forearms down on each side of his plate and interlaced his fingers, so that his knife and fork and plate were encircled by his arms and hands. Then, his gaze fixed somewhere to the left of the mantelpiece, he began to talk.

His talk was musing and leisurely, and it was always about his work. He spoke in long sentences that were filled with medical and anatomical terms, making no concession to his listeners. He expected no response, and in fact did not appear to be conscious of any audience. This was not storytelling; there was no art to this talking, nothing in it glittered or flashed, despite the potential of the material. Years later Helen would tell friends that her father was the only man in the world who could put you to sleep with a story about draining a boil that yielded half a pint of pus.

Every now and then Helen's stultified brain would, despite itself, catch at promising words—*hernia, psoriasis, ocular rosacea*—but these never went anywhere other than back under the surface of the colourless and unrelenting tide. *Now take this morning,* her father might begin, *a fascinating case*—but it wasn't, ever.

Helen always tried to make her dinner last so that she would have something to do while her father talked. This was clearly her mother's trick—as the soporific mist of Helen's father's voice filled the room, Helen's mother's small, rather puffy hands busied themselves with a minute and pedantic dissection of whatever was left on her plate. One string bean could get her through two cases of diabetes and a heart murmur. Helen tried, but her plate was always empty even before her father had laid down his cutlery, hitched in his chair, and established the arm-and-hand fence around his own. Her stomach gurgling—because she was never completely full, completely satisfied—she ran the edge of her fork as quietly as possible over any left-behind smears and down both sides of her knife, then sucked it, the tines pinching her tongue. Then she sat holding in yawns and trying to inconspicuously lick all around her lips and into the corners of her mouth, in case she had missed any traces of food.

When at long last Helen's father had finished talking, he undid his hands and lifted his forearms from the table. Immediately, released, Helen and her mother got up and began to clear. While they did this, and while they packed any leftovers into the refrigerator—which was still new, and which Helen's mother took care to open only when absolutely necessary and to close as quickly as possible so as to save electricity and the seal around its door from wear—and washed and dried the dishes and put them away, and gathered up the tablecloth and took it out into the yard to shake, and wiped the bench and table, and swept the floors, Helen's father stayed in the dining room, leaning, hands in pockets, against the mantel. He wore an expression of removed interest, like that of an anthropologist observing an exotic tribe. When Helen came with the broom to sweep under and around the dining table he stuck out his foot and interrupted her sweeping, twitching his eyebrows and bending his thin lips in a roguish smirk. He never touched Helen, but if it was her mother with the broom he would reach out suddenly and scuttle his fingers up the side of her torso and into her armpit. *Look out*, he'd say, *there's a big white spider that lives in the chimney. Have you seen it?* When this happened Helen's mother shrugged him off and went on with her work, but she would also smile, just a little bit, and her lower lip seemed wetter and redder than usual.

Helen, watching this, felt a distinct and pressing revulsion. Her father's 'white spider', his quirking eyebrows—these were somehow connected with the sight of her mother in her night-dress, and the giggling sounds in the night. Helen would go back into the kitchen, where if she was lucky there was a potato in the refrigerator small enough not to be missed. She ate it so fast she got a burning feeling in her chest as it went down.

The two worst things a person could do, in the time of Helen's childhood, were to be wasteful, and to have tickets on one's self. This was, Helen would later recognise, because of the Second World War, which lay like a thick layer of soot over the recent memories of her parents and every other adult she had anything to do with. It was because of the war that money was tight, and nothing was to be taken for granted, and comforts must be hard-earned and modest.

In the house of Helen's childhood, though, there was something more being acted upon than frugality and a general sense of caution. Helen's parents, it would seem, subscribed to a fundamental belief that life was not to be enjoyed.

But what about Helen's father's cordial? His mayonnaise, his generous helpings of butter? What about his post-dinner talks and the satisfaction with which he concluded them, removing his arms so Helen's mother could take his plate? What about his foot poking out, his smirk, his 'white spider'? And what about Helen's mother's little smile, her moist lip, her giggle in the night? Rationed, contained though it might be, enjoyment was allowed for in this household. Enjoyment was had. Just not by Helen.

Sometimes the Dysons came to dinner, sometimes the Parkers. Neither couple had any children, and when they visited it was as if Helen's parents didn't have any either. Helen was fed early, in the kitchen, a boiled egg and one piece of toast, watching as her mother made a dessert, measuring sugar, melting butter, pouring boiling water around a pudding basin set in a baking tray, and then carefully sliding the tray into the oven. Helen's mother's cheeks were pink, her lip shone, a small frown appeared between her eyebrows. Helen didn't like the white of the egg, but she ate it all, spooning up the flabby pieces, scraping the shell clean. Her toast would already be gone. At the bench, her mother ran her finger around a bowl in which delicious things had been mixed together—butter and sugar, or cream and sugar, or egg white and sugar. Helen's mother licked her finger and made a little sound of pleasure. Helen watched. Then her mother took the bowl to the sink and washed it.

Helen was sent up to bed before the guests arrived. Sometimes she went to the top of the stairs and listened, and heard her father's voice droning. Much later, when she had left home, she would think that her father's talking was probably the reason people didn't come for dinner very often.

She tried to say something about this to her mother once, when she was in her twenties, living in Melbourne, married to John. This was in 1974, before the children. Her mother came to stay for a night, because she had to see a specialist about a mole on her arm—she wouldn't come to the city otherwise. She had not visited Helen while Helen was at boarding school, nor while Helen was in college, and until now she had not visited this rented flat either.

In the time since Helen had last seen her, Helen's mother had become smaller, and afraid-seeming. She sat on the edge of the lumpy green couch with her coat still on, the heels of her small black shoes catching on the threadbare rug. She didn't want to try the wine John offered her—she didn't usually drink wine, and wasn't sure she'd like it. She regarded the chicken casserole Helen served with suspicion, and ate only a few mouthfuls.

Over dinner John made some gentle and diplomatic enquiries regarding the mole and the specialist, which Helen's mother answered with a minimum of detail. Helen's mother did not ask Helen or John anything about themselves.

Helen ate two large helpings of casserole and had to stop herself from licking her plate, a habit she had fallen into since living with John. She cleared the table, sweeping the leftovers wastefully into the bin and imagining she could feel her mother watching in horror. Then she poured out the last of the wine for John and herself and arranged a plate of cheese and biscuits.

The three of them sat in silence for a while, and then John excused himself and began to wash the dishes. Helen waited for a reaction to this—she suspected that her mother had never seen a man wash dishes. Helen had a little speech ready, about gender roles and equity. But her mother didn't even seem to notice; she just sat there with her hands in her lap. Her hair, which had faded rather than turned grey, was pinned back in the same old style, but there must have been less of it now because it was more a knot than a bun. Every so often she moved her lips as if about to say something, but no words came out. She seemed utterly lost, and Helen was gripped—perhaps out of empathy or perhaps out of a need to end her own discomfort at having to be in the same room as this ghost—by a big, warm, physical urge to have her returned to her own kitchen in the house behind the surgery. More than anything, Helen wanted to be able to magically transplant her, to lift her up with a huge, invisible hand and deliver her, and then to have the relief of seeing her there, restored to herself.

Full of casserole and wine and cheese, and taking this eruption of sympathy for some kind of breakthrough, Helen sailed on into a poorly judged and unplanned attempt at forging a new connection. It was the seventies, after all. She reached across as if to take her mother's hand, but found no hand there to take. Undeterred, she placed her palm flat on the tabletop.

Remember, she said, gamely, *the dinners? At home?*

Her mother blinked and bit her lip.

Remember, said Helen, *how we sat there, while he talked and talked? Like we were these—receptacles, for every single detail, for whatever might happen to drift through his mind?*

Helen's mother's head trembled, the way a very old person's might.

It was too late, but Helen tried a laugh, as if what she'd just said might be changed into a joke.

Her mother drew in her lip and cast her eyes down and Helen, with a flattening, cold and lonely shame, saw—not for the first time, because it had been so much a part of her childhood as to in fact be her childhood, but in the broader light of an adult understanding—that her mother's loyalty to her father was absolute. It had and would and must come before all else.

On the desk in Helen's father's consulting room there were jellybeans in a jar, which were for children who had been brave. It's not clear how Helen knew about this as she never went into the consulting room while her father was working, but somehow in her mind she had an image of her father opening the jar and holding it out over the desk for a child to reach in and help themselves.

When she was about five years old Helen, climbing on the timber seesaw at school, slipped, and an inch-long splinter embedded itself in her leg, just above the anklebone, a dark mean spike that showed through the skin, only the very tip of its tail end poking out. She limped through the rest of the day with it hidden under her sock, and by bedtime the flesh around the splinter's tail was hot and red, and had risen up like puff pastry around the fork holes in a pie.

The next morning her mother noticed, and she was taken into the consulting room by her father, who lay her on the high examination table and mopped at the splinter with a cotton cloth soaked in a brownish-yellow liquid that stung like fire. Then he put one big hand right around the calf of her leg, and with his whole heavy forearm pushed down on her thigh and hip and the best part of her upper body while he used a scalpel to open the skin and then a pair of tweezers to dig and grasp and draw the splinter out. He was holding her that way to stop her from struggling, but Helen did not struggle. She lay with her head to the side, her eyes on the jellybean jar. As the disinfectant burned, as the scalpel cut, as the tweezers probed, she stared at the jar. Red, she thought, I want a red one. If not red, then white. If not white, then purple.

When the splinter was out her father held it up for a moment, turning it this way and that and examining it. He looked pleased. Then he dropped it into the wastebasket, swabbed again at Helen's skin with the mustardy disinfectant, and wrapped a bandage around her ankle. He glanced at his watch, lifted her down from the table, and set her on her feet in the doorway. *Off you go, or you'll be late for school*, he said, and then he shut the door.

Helen wasn't quite through the threshold, so when the door closed completely she was pushed by it and had to take a couple of small, hobbling steps to regain her balance. The waiting room was empty. Helen turned around and looked at the big closed door, and then she looked at the place behind the desk, where her mother would soon come to sit, and then she looked at the two lines of chairs that would soon be filled with people waiting to see her father. Her ankle throbbed. She drew in a breath and let it out with a small, experimental whimper: *Ow*. Nothing changed. The clock on the wall went on with its smooth ticking. A tremor ran through Helen, low down, between her hips, and a fart fluffed out. She bent at the waist, took the gingham cotton of her school dress in handfuls and used the fabric to waft the smell, warm, bold and familiar, up and into her nostrils.

After the splinter, every Sunday afternoon when her parents were both safely outside gardening and Helen was supposed to be resting in her room, she went downstairs and into the empty surgery and took one, just one, jellybean. Her heart hammered and her mouth ran with saliva. She returned the big glass stopper to the neck of the jar, and then she squatted and backed herself into the space beneath her father's desk. She sat on her bottom with her knees pulled up. Breathing loudly through her nose, she sucked the bean into a tiny, translucent slip of gelatine, its chemical sweetness transferring to her spit, her tongue, the insides of her cheeks.

At boarding school the food was soft and leached of colour— stews, mashed potato, soggy vegetables, gravy, puddings. The serves were not generous, but you could go back for seconds, and Helen did. There was white bread and margarine, salty and doughy, and you could have four slices if you wanted to. The girls were allowed to take a piece of fruit for later and Helen took an apple, but also hid a banana in the sleeve of her jumper. She ate it after lights-out, under the covers, the sweet lumps sliding down, the smell sulphurous and furtive.

> Dear Mum and Dad, I hope you are well, I am still not going very well in spelling but I am second top of the class in maths. On the week ends we are allowd to spend our pockit munny at the shop, they have choo choo bars that make your teeth black, or choclit frogs. You can have two servs of dinner. There is desert evry singul night, last night it was jelly, red or green.

She wrote letters like this, and then she tore them up and rewrote them without all the food, which made them very short.

Then, in third form, she realised that she was fat and changed to brown bread, no margarine, and only one helping of dinner. The fat went away. Helen saw herself: her legs were long, her face was pleasing, she didn't have pimples, and her breasts were nice, not too small or too big. Her hair had thickened and was dark and shiny, and took well to the backcombed styles the girls did for dances, and for when they went to the shops on a Saturday afternoon in the hopes of seeing some of the boy boarders from the brother school in the same suburb.

Boys noticed Helen. Boys approached her at the dances, and on Saturdays at the shops, where the advances were sideways and idiotic, but advances nonetheless. Helen was ready for them—it wasn't hard, you just had to smile, and not say much—and she found that she liked what came next. Every glance and every stare, and later every kiss and every compliment, and every eager and fumbling touch, and then every heated brush of skin on skin, and every bit of softness and hardness and wetness, every taste of saltiness and sweetness—Helen opened up, and down they slipped, one after the other.

She was not distracted from her studies though. She was bright, and she didn't want just to be a wife, a prospect a lot of the other girls seemed happy with—looked forward to, even, talking after lights-out about engagement parties and how many babies they were going to have. The boys, the clandestine meetings, the whispers, the touching—these were Helen's rewards, the secret treats she would give herself when her essays were finished, her French verbs learned, the diagrams in her physics book neatly ruled off.

She sat her matric exams with a tender, exquisite feeling between her legs—she would do well, she knew, and then she would take her pleasure.

After boarding school came university, and then John, and marriage, the early years, their first flat, where the ill-fated dinner with her mother took place. She would come to look back on this time—the years in the flat, and the trip they took to Europe—as the happiest of her life. Gloriously, untenably happy.

They spent four months driving a campervan through Italy, France and Spain, unwashed and flat broke and thinking only of the next meal, the next campsite. Looking back, Helen does not remember reading, or meeting other travellers, or even visiting many tourist destinations. She remembers the food they ate, sausages cooked on the camp stove, bread and cheese, round purple grapes from a roadside stall, watery red wine drunk from enamel cups; she remembers the pallor of their tangled limbs in the light that came pink through the campervan's curtained windows.

Back at the flat, she more or less did as she wanted, stayed as long as she liked at work, cooked and ate and drank whatever took her fancy, and washed the dishes only when they ran out of clean ones. They spent whole weekends naked, eating nothing but toast and bacon and eggs, the bed full of crumbs, the news-papers sliding to the floor as they rolled and grappled and yelped and laughed.

From the first day of boarding school there had been a sense of release—from her parents, from the dim and hushed and repetitious and disapproving house of her childhood—but there had still, at school and then later at college, been confinement too, some restraints and rules. It wasn't until she was with John that she felt at last delivered into true freedom.

It was Helen who wanted the baby. Her body wanted it, with a blunt, impatient hunger, and John, though he was happy to wait, to continue enjoying what they had, conceded readily enough.

And so Helen was pregnant, and rushed through the preg-nancy, working as hard as ever despite mild disapproval from older men at her office, and outright frowns from older women on trams—women who still wore hats when they went out in public. *Take it easy*, John said. *Slow down*. But Helen did not. All her appetites seemed to double—on a Saturday morning she would eat two plates of bacon and eggs and then pull John down into the bed with her, heaving herself onto him. *Should we be doing this?* said John, from the far side of her enormous belly. *I mean, with the baby?* But Helen did not answer, and did not stop. It seemed that Helen pregnant was not a woman with a baby inside her, but simply a bigger, hungrier Helen.

There was a baby, though, and she was born, eight pounds and dark and difficult. Day and night June wailed like a thing possessed, falling into only brief periods of sleep before waking to cry again. She cried while being rocked, while being pushed in the pram, while being sung to or patted or left alone in her cot. Helen's world was suddenly reduced to the flat. She went out only to do the grocery shopping, as fast as she could, since June would cry through the whole excursion, prompting pitying looks and unsolicited advice from strangers. None of this was what Helen had expected—but then again she had not expected anything. She had not thought about what it would be like to *have* a baby—she'd only felt the burning desire to *make* one.

Helen was forced to wait—for John to come home at the end of each day and take the baby, and also for the six-week mark, when June would be able to go to crèche. Waiting did not suit Helen. She spent that six weeks rearranging furniture, washing curtains, cleaning and sorting the kitchen cupboards, putting all the photos in albums, filling in the pages of June's baby book. Much of this work she did to the sound of crying. Insistent, sturdy crying from the bassinette on the floor of the kitchen. Muffled, exhausted crying from behind the closed bedroom door. Quavering, kittenish, just-woken-up crying from the pram. Furious, lusty, clamorous, mournful—whatever tone June's crying took, or seemed to take, the message was the same: *I am here*, her crying said. *Tend to me.* And Helen did—of course she did. And there were moments of sweetness: the smiles, the cooing, the closeness of feeding, June's tiny lips working, her fingers curled, warm and milky, against Helen's skin. But these were small islands in the sea of demands. And whenever the crying started there was something sharp in Helen that twisted away, that said, *Not now. Not yet. Not me.*

John was very happy. June's smiles, her wobbly head-lifts, her triumphant rollings-over; the tidy house, the repertoire of boring recipes Helen had grudgingly mastered; Helen herself, returned to her usual size, her appetites no longer colossal, waiting for him when he came home—his joy at these things was so simple, so childlike, so straightforward as to be enviable.

If she had been the kind of person who looked for such things, perhaps Helen might have seen it then, the fatal mismatch, which was not in temperament, not really, but more a matter of pace. John was a stayer, but Helen, who had escaped something—her childhood—now seemed compelled to move through life on a forward tilt, her mouth always watering for more.

Things eased, in time. June settled and by three months was sleeping through the night, as most babies did in that era of closed bedroom doors and ignored crying. Helen returned to work four days a week, and felt less desperate. She began to fill her weekends with activities—pottery classes, life drawing, yoga—during which John was happy to stay home with June. A balance was struck, between John's contentment and Helen's restlessness, and like two acrobats they gripped one another and leaned and reached and resisted in all the right places, and together held the pose.

Then came Anna. Not a mistake, but not planned either—because there was no plan, nothing was being mapped out, things were just happening—a fact that John accommodated readily, unquestioningly, happily, and Helen was unable to accommodate at all, and so tried to disregard. Beneath Helen's eternal busyness, her headlong onward rushing, there now lay, faint but definite, the queasiness of someone who has bitten off more than she can chew.

Anna was easier than June. She was not freakishly easy—she was just a regular baby, who cried at times but was generally able to be settled, and more or less relied upon to sleep—but in comparison to June she was easy. And Helen fell in love with her. Perhaps it was because of her unexpected easiness, because she was so responsive, where June had bawled and fought and so often held herself stiffly against any embrace. Perhaps there was something deep and primal and psychological going on, to do with Helen not identifying with this second-born child in the same way she might have done with June, and therefore being free to simply love her. Whatever the reason, Helen delighted in Anna, in her sandy-pink wisps of hair, in her creamy skin, in her creases and folds and her snuffles and cross-eyed gazes, in the warm and miraculous weight of her, the cushioned feel of her bones through her flesh.

It was not that Helen hadn't felt wonder and delight at newborn June, and it wasn't that Helen didn't feel wonder and delight at June the toddler, with her sturdy legs and her conscientious frown and her pointer finger fatly extended as she stood over a tower of blocks, commanding: *Ookit my done, Mama*. Helen loved June as much as any mother loves a child—but it was, as some loves are, at times painful and murky and hampered. And Helen's love for Anna—even as Anna grew into a twitchy, contrary, worrisome child—was not ever anything but huge and clear and swooning. It was like the pleasure Helen took in food and sex, and Helen would, from Anna's birth until Anna's disappearance—and even beyond, into Anna's absence—turn to it in the same way she turned to these other pleasures, compulsively, blindly, heedlessly.

Helen's father died first, in that hospital in which his large and rough-skinned feet were so mercilessly exposed. He had gone in because something was wrong with his heart, but when they anaesthetised him for exploratory surgery he, as if in reaction to the undignified nature of the whole business, did not regain consciousness. There were no goodbyes. Helen was told by a nurse, over the phone—her mother not able to speak—and then left the children with John to go and help, by which time her father's body had been put in a coffin and the lid put on. She did not ask to see him.

There was a funeral attended by many, and a wake attended by very few. The wake was at the house behind the surgery, which was smaller and shabbier and darker than ever. Helen's mother insisted on catering, assembling sandwiches at the kitchen bench and baking a cake. The pitiful turnout resulted in an atmosphere of awkward intimacy. There were the Parkers—the Dysons had moved to America long ago—and there was the driver of the local ambulance. There was the priest, who was young and new, and had given an apologetically vague eulogy at the church. Then there was Mrs McPherson, who suffered a great many maladies and had been a regular visitor to the surgery since Helen was young. Mrs McPherson had not changed—her legs were still vast and bumpy, and she wore the same navy sack-like dress, and the same hat that was a not-quite-matching navy, topped with a spray of semi-disintegrated yellow felt flowers. She was supposed to have trouble with her blood sugar and therefore watch out for sweet things, but two slices of cake vanished while she was standing alone at that end of the table, nodding and sighing and glancing around.

These five were the only guests. A bunch of flowers and a typed card had arrived from the company that supplied the surgery with medical equipment. There were no speeches.

Helen went alone into the kitchen and found a plate of shortbread biscuits on the bench—brought, presumably, by the Parkers—and crammed two in her mouth before bringing the rest out to the dining room.

I really shouldn't, said Mrs McPherson, but out went her dimpled hand and a number of biscuits appeared to fly up into it.

I hope you have been well, said Helen. She was not sure if Mrs McPherson even knew who she was. Mrs McPherson, who had icing sugar on her nose, didn't answer, but turned to retrieve her handbag and then went lumbering off.

There was a whiff of something sweet and fumy, and Helen realised it was alcohol, and at the same time thought she heard a sloshing sound coming from some part of Mrs McPherson or her bag as both exited the room.

Helen's mother would not sit down. She poured tea and cut the cake and passed out cups and plates and cake forks and napkins, and offered sandwiches, and, once some had gone, rearranged the remaining sandwiches on the serving platters, and refilled the teapot and the milk jug, and swept up into her hand and threw into the fire a little pile of sugar that the priest had accidentally spilled, and poked the fire, and put more wood on it, and gathered up empty plates, and brought out more whipped cream, and put the kettle on to boil one more time, and again emptied the teapot and filled it with fresh leaves.

Mrs Parker hovered like a mosquito. *Now let me*, she said, and, *I'll do that*, but Helen's mother ignored her and went on with her work, frowning faintly, as if listening out for something or someone.

The ambulance man ate a sandwich and drank a cup of tea and then slipped away. Mr Parker made conversation with the priest, eyeing the young man's modern, dark suit and understated collar. *Can't tell 'em from us normal fellers these days*, he whispered to Helen, reaching for the milk.

And I believe you're married, Helen! said Mrs Parker. *And have children!* Her teeth were crooked—Helen had never noticed, never been close enough to see.

Yes, said Helen, who had biscuit stuck in a paste against her gums.

Then Mrs Parker did an extraordinary thing. She leaned nearer and tapped Helen on the wrist. *Your mother is very proud of you*, she said. *Of your career. She's always telling me—*

But there was a sound, a call, and Mrs Parker broke off, and threw back her head like a dog scenting the breeze, and the call came again and suddenly everyone was rushing from the room.

Helen went last, out into the hallway, which had become very crowded. They all had their backs to her, and were clustered around the entrance to the downstairs toilet, and Helen caught sight of a pair of large, pale legs stretched out on the floor. It was Mrs McPherson—she had fallen, and was now making strange, airy noises that sounded more joyful than despairing.

She's hit her head, said someone.

Hit the bottle, said Mr Parker, out of the corner of his mouth.

Oooh, oooh, called Mrs McPherson.

They got her up, and onto the sofa in the sitting room, and asked her questions such as, *Do you remember what happened?* and, *What's the date today?* and, *Can you tell me who the prime minister is?* Mrs McPherson lay with a half-smile on her face, nodding and sighing and looking off into the distance.

It occurred to Helen that Mrs McPherson might not be capable of answering these questions at the best of times—and it seemed that everyone else had the same notion, because nobody pressed the issue.

Perhaps a cup of strong black coffee? said Mrs Parker, but there was no coffee in the house—Helen's father had not approved of it.

Mrs McPherson was brought a cup of tea, and she drank it, and eventually rose quite gracefully from the couch and walked in a skating sort of way to the front door, and left.

The priest went soon afterwards, and then it was just the Parkers. Mrs Parker took Helen's mother by the shoulders and said, *Now, you are going to go upstairs and lie down. Helen and I will do the dishes.*

Helen's mother, surprisingly, allowed this. Mrs Parker went up with her, and Helen had a vision of her mother being helped into her white nightdress and having her knot of hair undone and plaited for her. She pictured her mother lying in bed like a child, being tucked in.

Mr Parker went out to his car and returned with a newspaper, and settled on the couch. Mrs Parker reappeared, and she and Helen went into the kitchen, where Mrs Parker washed and Helen dried and put away.

You wouldn't remember, said Mrs Parker, *but Mrs McPherson wasn't always like that. She had a husband, a builder, he fell from a roof. Your father was called out. His back was broken, Mr McPherson. Lay in bed, couldn't do anything, couldn't move his arms or legs. There's a word for it.*

Quadriplegic, said Helen.

Yes, said Mrs Parker. *Well, he died, eventually—there were more things wrong than the broken back.* She shook her head. *A terrible mess.* She looked at Helen. She was a small woman, with large breasts so firmly strapped in that they looked as if you could rap your knuckles on them. *We can't know what it's like*, she said, *you and I, to be without someone you have come to depend on.* She puffed out her cheeks and made a weaving motion with her head. *What am I trying to get at here? What am I trying to say to you? Ah!* She nodded, and narrowed her eyes. *I don't think your mother is going to go to pieces, Helen. But I think she will seem different, from now on, to us. She will in fact become a different person. Do you understand?*

Helen nodded, but she didn't understand.

Helen's mother, as far as Helen could tell, did not become a different person. Not at first, anyway. She appeared to go on being the same person, living her life in service to Helen's father, as if he had not died but gone away for a while, and would return. The surgery was shut down, but Helen's mother continued to live in the house. It was not clear what she did in there all day.

Mrs Parker somehow acquired Helen's phone number and began to ring her up, not often, as long-distance calls were expensive, but perhaps every few weeks.

She's cut herself off, said Mrs Parker. *I keep inviting her to things but she doesn't want to come.*

Oh, said Helen.

It's a worry, said Mrs Parker. *I think she should be getting out more, seeing people.*

Yes, said Helen.

In another call Mrs Parker said, *I think I'm beginning to be a nuisance to her. Yesterday she didn't answer the door, but I knew she was there—I think she was hiding from me!*

Oh, said Helen.

Do you think you should come? There's only so much I can do.

Really? said Helen.

Well, you are her daughter, said Mrs Parker.

Helen sighed. *I'm not sure I'd be welcome,* she said.

Helen was certain that the sense of relief she'd felt when she finally left home for boarding school had been shared by her parents. The house behind the surgery had, she was sure, only ever been meant for two—she had been an appendage which they'd tolerated, and it had seemed right that she should, when the time came, remove herself and leave them alone.

When Helen called, her mother sounded the same as she always had, which was quiet and unforthcoming, and uninterested in Helen and John and their children. There was even the same very subtle tone of irritation, as if Helen was interrupting something.

How are you? said Helen.

Well, thank you, said her mother.

At this point, when Helen's father had been alive, Helen's mother would say something like, *Your father has been very busy*, or, *Your father has had a cold*, or, *Your father's had to cut the lemon tree down because it was full of borer*. But now she didn't say anything more, she just stopped.

What have you been doing? said Helen.

Washing the shelves in the supply room, her mother might say, or, *Making marmalade*, or, *Tying up the runner beans*.

Nothing seemed to have altered, other than that Helen's father was no longer there. During these exchanges Helen felt the way she always had during phone calls with her mother, which was claustrophobic and agitated. Afterwards she would go to the fridge and drink milk straight from the bottle, or get a knife and cut a small chunk of butter and put it, salty and slippery, on her tongue, or open the jar of muesli and pick out fat, sticky raisins, or find John and slide her hands up under his shirt, or if she came across one of the girls, ply her round cheek with smacking kisses, take her compact little body onto her lap and squeeze it.

Nothing had changed, and Helen was still rushing headlong through her life—her adult life, which was never supposed to have had her parents in it—but there was a tiny little thing that sometimes came flitting in at her from far off to one side of her consciousness. It was to do with what Mrs Parker had said at the wake, about her mother being proud of her.

It was Mrs Parker who rang to tell Helen that her mother had 'taken a turn', and was in the hospital. This was three and a half years after Helen's father's death.

Helen had not done as Mrs Parker suggested and gone to visit her mother—since the funeral she had not visited at all, and Helen's mother had not visited her. They spoke on the phone every few weeks, and the phone calls always took that same course, with Helen making unrequited enquiries and receiving brief and reluctant-seeming domestic reports. At Christmas Helen's mother always claimed that she had 'people' coming, and would be terse when Helen rang, excusing herself as quickly as possible, saying she must get back to the pudding, or the mince pies, or the 'bird' that was in the oven.

Mrs Parker must have given up on Helen, because her phone calls had petered out within a year of Helen's father's death. Helen didn't know if Mrs Parker had also given up on Helen's mother.

She's taken a turn, said Mrs Parker now, over the phone.

Oh, said Helen. *Is it her heart, or . . . ?*

It's a turn, *Helen*, said Mrs Parker meaningfully.

A turn, repeated Helen, failing to understand. *So do you think I need to . . . Should I . . . ?*

You will need to come, yes.

When Helen arrived at the hospital Mrs Parker was there. Helen's mother and Mrs Parker were sitting side by side on two chairs in a private room. The bed lay empty, its sheet tucked smoothly in.

Why aren't you in the bed? said Helen to her mother.

Helen's mother did not respond, and did not look up.

She won't get into the bed, said Mrs Parker. *Will you, you silly thing?* As she said this Mrs Parker put her hand over Helen's mother's, and gave it a couple of light, almost playful pats.

Then Helen's mother said, in a strange, girlish voice, *We're going to learn three dances,* and Helen understood at once what had happened. A number of things that she had been holding at bay came slopping down onto her—things that her mother had said, over the phone, during the preceding six months: that she was bottling peaches from the tree; that she needed to go and wash her red crepe dress; that Eileen Mackie had come to stay. But there wasn't a peach tree in the garden of the house behind the surgery, and Helen had never seen any sign of a red crepe dress, and Eileen Mackie—Helen remembered now, although she hadn't at the time of the phone call—was not even a friend of Helen's mother's, but a moderately famous singer who had occasionally given recitals in the town, long ago, when Helen was a small child.

We're going to learn the waltz, said her mother, in her new, strange, lisping voice, *and the foxtrot. And there's another one . . .*

Helen thought that she might be about to have diarrhoea. She sat on the end of the bed, clenching against the loose, watery feeling.

What is the other one? What is it? said Helen's mother, her voice craven, whining, her head still lowered.

Never mind, murmured Mrs Parker.

Helen organised for her mother to go into a home. She and Mrs Parker cleared out the house behind the surgery, finding shoes in the oven and biscuits under the mattresses, and, on the desk that still stood in Helen's father's old consulting room, a plate holding a mouldering fried egg, and a cup of tea that had grown a floating disc of rank-smelling green curd.

The house and surgery were sold, and the money was enough to pay for the home, for at least as long as it would take—which, as it turned out, wasn't very long.

Helen did visit, now. Once a month she drove the three and a half hours, sat with her mother for forty minutes, and then drove back again. It would have been more practical to have chosen a nursing home in Melbourne, or at least somewhat closer to Melbourne. But Helen had not done this, and her justification was vague. It was so that her mother could be in familiar surroundings, she told John—but this didn't make sense, since the inside of the nursing home was not familiar to Helen's mother, and since once she was in it she did not leave, so never again encountered any of the parts of the town that had been known to her. When John questioned her further Helen said, at last, that she simply felt that her mother belonged in the country, in the town she'd lived in for more than fifty years, that it 'felt right' that she stay there. John pointed out that if you didn't know where you were then you probably didn't mind where you were, and said that it would be easier on everybody to have Helen's mother closer. Helen would not be swayed. *She belongs there*, she said. What she really meant—and she did admit this, but only to herself—was that her mother belonged away from her. That the two of them must be kept, cleanly, apart.

Sometimes, during these visits, Helen's mother recognised her, sometimes not. Sometimes her mother thought she was somebody else—once she thought Helen was Eileen Mackie, and cried, saying how beautiful her voice was. The nurses said this sort of thing was normal—and also that it was normal for dementia cases to hold on to the practice of making small

talk even when all understanding of themselves and their surroundings had gone. *Hello*, said Helen's mother, and, *Very well,
thank you, and yourself?* and these phrases did indeed seem to
be automatic.

Helen's mother, the nurses said, was 'a lovely patient'. Helen
took this to mean that she didn't cause any trouble, like some
of the others—the old man who came shuffling down the corridor, bare-legged and gleeful and surprisingly fast, his pyjama
top flipping up at the back to show his flat, sagging bottom; the
woman who shouted out from her room, hoarsely, incessantly,
Fuck! Fuck! Fu-uck!; another woman who Helen saw sitting up
in bed, using both hands to scoop stew from a tray into her
own lap.

Helen's mother mostly sat in silence, her eyes cast down, her
lower lip jutting. Her body inside her dressing gown was very
small and—unlike her old night-time body, plush and curving
within its nightdress—looked dried out, insubstantial. Helen
sat with her, every now and then looking at her watch. She
made herself stay the full forty minutes, and it was excruciating. She was often plagued by the diarrhoea feeling that had
overtaken her in the hospital that day with Mrs Parker, and the
hush of her mother's room would be broken by rude internal
burbles and groans.

Helen didn't speak to her mother beyond saying hello and
goodbye, and if her mother came out, as she occasionally did in
the early months, with a nonsensical statement such as, *Shall
we go to choir?* or, *Nobody told me the Barkers were coming*—and
then, later, as her words went awry, *It's just a tish*, or, *They're my
smerts*—Helen did not respond.

Once, when they had been sitting in silence for some time,
Helen's mother, who had not replied to Helen's greeting nor

acknowledged her presence, suddenly shifted around in her chair and fixed Helen with her gaze. Her face softened and she smiled. Her expression was melting, rapturous—it was, undoubtedly, a look of love.

Helen moved in her chair.

Helen's mother's eyes followed her.

Mum? said Helen. *Mum? It's me, Helen.*

But the look had gone, slid away.

In the end she just lay in bed, her eyes closed. She was not even very old—she was in her early seventies—but she looked old and small and papery, her hair and skin pale, her soft fingers moving against the blankets as if seeking a comfort that was always just out of reach.

The nurse who rang to tell Helen her mother was dead sobbed over the phone. *She was my favourite*, said the nurse.

Helen, standing by the telephone table in the new house at Avoca Street, felt upstaged. Wasn't she the one who should be crying? But if she started now it would seem competitive. How nice it would be to cry—to collapse into it, to release the tight, cold feeling at the back of her throat, to sob herself into a quiet emptiness. But Helen crying and Helen's parents, it would seem, were mutually exclusive.

There was something about her, said the nurse. *You know?* She had a rough, smoker's voice. *Still waters run deep, I s'pose.*

Helen had to work hard not to slam the phone down. *I'll come tomorrow morning*, she said.

Helen found Mrs Parker's number. Mrs Parker didn't cry— she tutted, and sighed. Helen's mother had clearly disappointed Mrs Parker. Helen wondered if it was because she hadn't become the different person Mrs Parker had spoken of that time in the kitchen—if it was because she hadn't become the right sort of different person.

There was a service, of sorts. Nothing churchy. Helen, Mrs Parker and the nurse from the nursing home watched as two men in cheap suits lowered Helen's mother's coffin into the grave in which Helen's father already lay. The gravel-voiced nurse cried. Mrs Parker sighed. Helen's bowels sloshed and cramped.

Driving home, Helen was visited again by that gnat of a memory—Mrs Parker in the dining room of the house behind the surgery, her fingers tapping Helen's wrist. *Your mother is very proud of you.* Perhaps she should have asked Mrs Parker to tell her more about this, more about her mother—the person she was when she was with Mrs Parker, the person who was proud of Helen. But she couldn't. The idea of her mother harbouring this secret regard for her was as unbearable as the memory of her mother's giggle in the night all those years ago, or of her father's 'white spider'. She would not barge in now to where she had never been welcome. And anyway, what would be the use? What might she find? Love, perhaps, love like a dirty secret, twisted up and shoved into a dark corner—and what would she do with that?

Helen reached to the passenger seat, to her bag. She rustled through it, one-handed, but found only an empty liquorice allsorts packet. With her finger she wormed into it, and then sucked, dug sugar from under her nail with her teeth.

She would leave love out of it. But this pride her mother felt—assuming it had existed; assuming it wasn't a figment of the imagination of Mrs Parker, with her strong and whimsical and unsatisfiable expectations regarding Helen's mother—why was this kept hidden from her, Helen? Was it the old fear of spoiling a child—as if an entire upbringing of rigorous denial could be undone with one word of praise? Helen gave a weak laugh. Was it because of Helen's father—the exclusive devotion he had required, which had set the shape of their family and held it so firmly bound? Perhaps. Helen felt a moment's envy for Mrs Parker, her mother's confidante, an outsider.

The road was borne up, along a crest. Knobbly sun-bleached hills fanned out, strewn with boulders and small whippy-looking trees. Helen put down the window for a moment to let the hot wind into her hair.

Another memory arrived, quick and sharp and unannounced: her mother coming in from the surgery with a white apron on over her usual yellow blouse and brown skirt. Her mother going to the supply room, her steps brisk. Her mother's practised hands tearing open rolls of bandage, shaking a vial, dropping a fat syringe into a kidney basin. Her mother being a nurse— helping her father, on a busy day? She couldn't remember now, the context was not there. Only the expression on her mother's face as she worked—attentive and absorbed, and, yes, proud.

It was Helen's career that her mother had been proud of, according to Mrs Parker. It was not Helen's marriage or her children but her career that her mother had paid attention to, been interested in. Had it been envy, then—stemming from her mother's frustrated pride, her neglected intelligence, her unsatisfied ambition—which had stood between the two of them?

Just for a moment, Helen felt it, an untainted sympathy. Only a snatch, like the grey-green toss of leaves at the corner of her eye as the fence lines flew past, the dams, the clumps of trees. And then it was gone, once again beyond her.

She drove along the freeway. It was summer, and the pad-docks under the high sky were silvery and ragged. There were no clouds. The world seemed very big, and possibly uncaring, but she was moving through it, she was wide open, and whatever it offered she would gather up in great armloads and devour.

PART FOUR

OTHER BEACHES

SHELLY BEACH

Shelly Beach was off the island, back over the bridge and around towards Kilcunda, away from Melbourne.

Shelly Beach was no more shelly than any other beach. In fact, less. The sand was coarse, and sand is made of shells, in part, ground-up shells, tiny pieces of them, but there weren't any whole shells, none at all. There were big brown-grey rocks at each end, and flat darker rocks across the middle, going out into the shallow water, and pockets of sand and rock pools, and huge crashing waves beyond.

It was at Shelly Beach that nine-year-old Anna climbed onto the biggest rock and disappeared over the other side, to where monstrous, invisible explosions took place, from where jets of spray shot into sight, high in the air, then seemed to pause before breaking apart and slapping back down.

Nan running, slow in the grainy sand, slow on her thick brown legs.

Junie standing by the towels, bite of apple in her mouth, eyes locked on the empty place, the fountains of spray.

Nan running, Junie standing, and, in a rainbow mist, wet hair pressed pink to her scalp, limbs froglike on the shining dark rock, a grin of determined triumph only slightly slipped— Anna, reappearing.

It was at Shelly Beach that twenty-one-year-old Junie, squinting into a sunset, shivering in a jacket that had been Nan's, having drunk before driving perhaps one more glass of whisky than she should have, magicked Anna back again. Just for a moment. Junie's eyelids lowered, the light stretched and shimmered, the sea jostled, gunmetal, glittering—and Anna, grinning, watery, came crawling over the rock.

But there was nothing beautiful in this. No relief. No marvellous falling away or splitting open of the Junie she was, the Junie she'd become. No return to anything unreachable or longed for or forgotten. Instead, fury, narrow, violent, unstoppable. *How dare you? How could you? Why? Why? Why?*

She drove back to the island, to the empty house, too fast, skidding at the Anderson roundabout, revving up the hill.

And it was at Shelly Beach that forty-year-old Paul told thirty-seven-year-old June that he was having doubts about their marriage. This was in the summer, Esther and Maggie and Cal busy in the rock pools, four or five other groups of people set up along the sand—umbrellas, drink bottles, bags of food— someone's small tan dog trotting in important loops from camp to camp.

They were seated on the same, sideways-spread, towel.

'It's not working,' Paul said in a quiet voice. 'I keep thinking it'll change, but it hasn't.'

Panic. Salt on her lips, dripping from her hair. She seized another towel, stood, wrapped herself, sat back down. 'What're you doing?' she hissed. 'We can't talk like this here.'

'I'm sorry.' His lips were shaking. 'I've been trying to say it, but I keep losing my nerve.'

Cal ran up with a clump of wiry purple seaweed. 'Look!'

'Nice one, Callie!' June reached for her sunglasses. 'Can you find another one like that?' Watching him run back down the sand, aching at his eager legs, the dimples over his elbows. Turning to Paul, whispering: 'How long have you felt like this?'

'A while. I don't know. It's happened before, and then I thought everything was okay . . .'

'When before?'

'When you were so angry all the time, when Cal was a baby.'

'But I haven't—I'm over that. Aren't I?'

'I don't know.'

'Well, I thought I was.'

He was shielding his eyes with one hand, elbow on knee. 'I'm not so sure,' he said.

'But since when . . . ?'

'A year. Eighteen months maybe.'

Her mind leaped, frantic. It was the three kids, so much harder than she'd thought it would be. It was her painting; she hadn't had a show for years, it was so difficult to get anything started, or finished. There were parts of herself that she was waiting to get to—this wasn't quite it yet, the life she meant to have. Had she neglected to let Paul in on this, the incompleteness of things?

'But why didn't you *tell* me?' She spoke too loudly—a woman looked over.

They both waited until she looked away again. Then Paul said quietly, 'I should've. I fucked up. I'm sorry.'

His hand was on the towel between them, the hairs on the backs of his fingers beaded with water.

'What can we do?' she said.

A shadow moved in. Drips fell and pocked the sand. June looked up at the children, all three, standing there.

'We're hungry,' said Esther.

And, at the same time, Maggie: 'What's the matter with you two?'

It was the next week, at Shelly Beach, that June, standing on one of the high flat rocks, looking down on Paul and the children playing in the shallows, began to laugh.

She was thinking of her possessiveness, its hugeness, how it had seeped into every corner, surrounded them both. It had been vile, and she at its mercy. Yet they survived it. What had brought them down, the two of them—what she now believed had brought them down—was something so much smaller. A hairline crack. It was this. Once, perhaps two years ago, in the deepest of red-wine nights, Paul had said that he was afraid that she, June, would one day betray him. Have an affair. Do a Helen. That it was somehow in her blood.

She laughed, up on her rock.

And of course this was snatched up by the terrible part of her that was always searching for confirmation, for judgment. She had not been able to see where in Paul this statement came from—his frailty, his need. She had only been able to take it personally. Always she had held herself so rigidly away from Helen, away from the parts of herself that might have Helen in them.

This was what it meant to be her, June—to not be Helen, to not do what Helen did.

She could see now what she should have done, when Paul had said that. Just loved him, like he was a child, heaped her love and attention on him, allowed him his moment of insecurity, been big enough to allow it. Instead she had reacted, hardened, turned away.

She laughed into the wind, tears sliding from the corners of her eyes. For all her efforts not to be Helen, not to be selfish, not to betray Paul—because of these efforts!—she had betrayed him. Herself, too. She had betrayed them both, thrown them both over for an obsession with, a devotion to, the shadow of the thing she was most afraid of being.

PAUL

Paul, as a young man, had two very near misses in cars. When he says young man, he means eighteen, nineteen, having only just got his driver's licence. In the darkness over the bed where Paul and June lie a young man appears, climbing into a car, light and slender, very serious. Thinking himself grown but so young—a child, really.

He was driving home after being out, seeing bands. He'd had a fight with his girlfriend. Was he drunk? He doesn't think so, actually; more just angry. But he shouldn't have been driving. And it was late, it was wet, he was going too fast around a corner—you know Brunton Avenue, where it curves around beside the MCG? Yeah, there. And the car just spun out, did a complete three-sixty. Nobody saw. It was so weird. No other cars around, him just sitting there, his heart going a hundred miles an hour. He yelled, to nobody, *Did you see that?* Threw out his arms. *Fucking hell, did you see that?* And then a car was coming, and he had to start the engine and get out of the way. Drive off home like it never happened.

And then the other time, very similar scenario, but it was in Sydney. Maybe a year later. Crown Street, Surry Hills. In fact, almost exactly the same situation—a fight, and driving when he shouldn't've been, and doing stupid stuff, going too fast.

This one a few people saw—he remembers there was a couple walking along the street and when he came out of the spin he was right there, beside them, and they jumped back and grabbed on to each other. That was the worst part, seeing how close he'd come to actual damage, to hurting someone.

The cars spin circles over the bed. June—or is she still Junie?—listens. Their bare skins touch, under the sheet. This is before the children, when they sleep naked, when there is no one they might need to not be naked for in the middle of the night. They are at Airey's Inlet, in a borrowed house. They have been at the wedding of some friends, on the beach.

Once Paul was hitchhiking, in New South Wales, and it was late, he'd mistimed things and ended up in a car in the dark with this guy, somewhere between Mullumbimby and Byron. He was even younger then—seventeen, maybe even sixteen—still at school, this was during the holidays. And the guy, the driver, who'd seemed okay at first, started to ask a few weird questions. *How many girls have you slept with? Do you like blowjobs?* And then Paul saw that the guy had his penis out. And Paul said, *Stop here please.* And the guy said, *No, no, I'm not stopping.* And Paul said, *Please stop, I want to get out.* And the guy said, *Just show me yours, then I'll stop.* And Paul said, *No thanks, just stop, I'm not interested in this.* And the guy stopped and let him out, and drove off, and left him, skinny kid on the roadside in the dark, middle of nowhere, full of relief.

He climbed a fence and slept in a paddock. He had his sleeping bag, and anyway it was summer, he hardly needed it. Woke up to a circle of staring cows.

Another time he was walking home from a party, very late. He was maybe fifteen. Eastern suburbs, off the main road, just houses, quiet area. And someone was standing under a tree. And Paul got a bad feeling. And then a second person stepped out of the shadows. He never got to see them properly. They were men, that's all he knew, and they meant him harm.

He ran, jumped a fence, cut through someone's yard, climbed another fence. Hid, for a long time, behind a shed.

And one time—so stupid!—Paul went swimming by himself, at Anglesea, off season, no surf patrol, nobody there, not one person on the beach or in the water. He was fourteen. He had a wetsuit his cousin had given him and he wanted to try it out. He got caught in a rip, did all the wrong things. He panicked, tried to fight his way back in, got really tired. Luckily the waves weren't too big, that was probably what made the difference. He fought and fought, thinking, Shit, I'm going to die. And then he turned over on his back and floated for a few seconds, trying to catch his breath, and that was when he remembered what you're supposed to do. And he let it take him out—so far out, it was scary. He thought about sharks.

And the thing is, nobody tells you that once you've swum across until you're out of the rip, the swim in might still be hard. He was so exhausted, and he was out so far. It took a long time to get back in. He didn't think he was going to make it.

The beach wedding had been beautiful, but at the reception afterwards Junie drank too much and when Paul tried to get her to leave she wouldn't go. At first she laughed and tried to make him dance with her. *Five more minutes*, she said. *Come on, Paulie.* And when he said, *No, really, let's go*, she said, *You're no fun.* And then, when he said, *We need to leave*, she said, in a loud voice, *Why? Am I embarrassing you?* And then she realised she was going to be sick, and ran off behind some trees.

He found her and they left, and back at the house he helped her have a shower and get into bed, where she cried and said, *I don't know how to be happy, I don't think I can be.*

And now it's the next morning, early, and they're awake and Paul is talking in the dark.

Do you see what I'm saying? says Paul. *Something happened to her, but it was just bad luck. Something might have happened to you, or to me—something nearly did, more than once.*

But what about the cutting? says Junie. *What about the drugs?*

People do that stuff, says Paul, *and get over it. People do all kinds of dark things and end up okay. Maybe you don't know how strong she was, underneath.*

At this time, the time of the beach wedding, the time before children, the time of sleeping naked, Paul speaks like this often. Sensibly, lovingly, he clears a place and sets down in it the possibility of an Anna—and so also a Junie—who is sturdy and whole, as sturdy and whole as he is.

It's a lovely thing to do for someone. And there is a sense, at this time, that things can be squared away, that Junie's hangups are not only approachable, but solvable. And perhaps they were, then. Perhaps they would have been, if Junie and Paul had stopped there. If they hadn't had the children. If they'd both let Junie go on being the child. But it's unlikely.

And anyway, life got busy, and they had the kids, and Junie became June, and because June didn't get drunk at parties and cry and say that she didn't know how to be happy, they both thought she'd grown up and got over things, and that there was no longer anything to be fixed. And when it became clear that all was not well in the marriage, what also became clear was that Paul being logical, Paul being kind, Paul being the grown-up, wasn't going to help this time. And, in any case, he'd gone on being those things all along.

The fact was that June couldn't go back to being the child, to having him look after her. Which was sad, because it had been a beautiful thing, his looking-after, and it had, at the time, worked. Their beginners' idealism, the simplicity and sweetness of their good intentions—June would have to mourn these. And she would have to find other ways through the mess.

NOOSA

A missed call every now and then, perhaps once a month, is quite usual. They are not, technically speaking, always missed calls—most often they are in fact ignored calls, when she switches the ringer to silent and puts the phone, still haplessly vibrating, back in her bag, or face down on a bench. This is done with a kind of hasty, squeamish efficiency, the way one might shoo a fly out through a window. If messages are left, she deletes them without listening.

So she ignores the first call. But then when she sees, at five-thirty pm, that there have been another three—genuinely missed, during school pick-up and swimming lessons and grocery shopping—she thinks, *Shit.*

She goes to Paul, who is sitting on the edge of the bed, putting on his running shoes.

'Uh-oh,' he says, when he sees the screen with its trail of red caller IDs. He bends once more to his laces. 'You'd better ring her back.'

She looks at his thighs, their long muscles, his fingers tying their precise knots. 'Of course I will,' she says. 'What kind of a person do you think I am?'

He stands.

'Actually, don't answer that,' she says.

They laugh.

'Do you want me to wait?' he says, indicating the phone. 'In case it's something—bad?'

'No. Thanks. It's all right.'

He goes, and from the window she watches him half-walk, half-jog down the path and onto the street.

Some sort of equilibrium has been recovered. Paul has agreed to give it another six months, and they are on a waiting list for counselling. There is a general sense of reprieve, a lightness almost; there has been more laughter, and also more sex. Mostly June feels grateful, and pleased by him, his body, his mind— like a death row prisoner with a last meal, she's savouring every moment. And she is being more honest with him—almost reck- lessly so—and it's not as terrifying as she might have imagined. He receives her attempts at honesty square on, with delicacy, and with just enough humour. They are both *trying*. But there are times, too, when she feels as if she is on probation.

A male voice answers Helen's phone. 'Hello, June?'

'Oh. Dev. Hi.' She is flustered, and then suddenly fearful— adrenaline saws at her, her knees give, and she plonks onto the bed. 'Is—is everything okay? With Mum?' How easily the word slips out, a bleat, a blunt nub of a cry.

'Yes. Everything is okay, no worries. She just has a little problem with her health.' Dev's musical, European voice—*war- eeze, lee-dle*—is very calm. But she's not sure what it would take to make Dev not calm. Inappropriate jokes skim her panic: *A lee-dle problem. She's had both legs amputated, no war-eeze. She's on life support, she's in a coma. No war-eeze.*

She shakes her head, pinches herself above the knee. 'What sort of problem?'

'Well, she had just a little virus, nothing too bad, but she has lost her hearing now. This can happen, apparently.' *A lee-dle vai-rez.*

'Her hearing?'

'Yes. That is why I am calling you—because she isn't able to use the phone. She can't hear anything.' He says these last three words slowly and clearly, as if explaining to a child.

'So her ears are blocked? From the virus?'

'No. This is not the same as a bit of a cold and your ears go all stuffy, June. This is some kind of damage. It is not very common, but it does happen. And it is much more common for it to be only one ear.'

June blinks at the wall. 'But for her it's both?'

'Yes, both. She may regain the hearing, or some of it, anyway. But also she may not. We must wait and see.'

At dinner she says to the children, 'I'm going away tomorrow, for a few days.'

'Okay,' says Maggie, who is eight, through a mouthful of potato. 'Have you got an ex-tabition?'

'No. I'm going to visit my mother. Helen, remember her?'

'Of course,' says Esther, who is ten, with so much authority that it must not be true.

'I don't,' says Maggie.

'Well, you haven't met her, really. Only once, when you were just born, so you wouldn't remember.'

'Why can't we come?' says Cal, who is five. 'Are you going on a plane?'

'Just Mum, this time,' says Paul. 'Helen's a bit sick, so she can't have too many visitors.'

'Who is this person again?' says Cal.

'She's my mum. Your grandma.'

'But why don't I know her?'

His beautiful, solemn face. June feels the prick of tears. 'Well, she and I don't get along very well.'

The girls swivel, tuning in.

'Why not?' says Maggie.

June breathes deeply. *Get it right*, she thinks. 'Because she did something, a long time ago, and I'm still angry with her for it.'

'What did she do?'

'She . . . she just wasn't—I thought she wasn't a very good mother. And remember Anna, my sister? Well, I felt like it was because our mum wasn't doing a very good job that Anna went missing. I thought it was our mum's fault.'

Paul is watching her. She has never said this, she realises, to anyone. She's not sure she understood it herself.

'But *how*?' says Maggie. 'How was it her fault? What did she do?'

They don't speak about Anna much. She comes up in anecdotes, and when June parallels her own childhood with those of her children. *My little sister used to annoy me too.* And Anna is the other half of the 'we' when June says things like, *When we were really little the milk still got delivered to the house, in glass bottles with foil lids.* But they don't often talk about her disappearing, mostly because there is so much about it that June and Paul feel the children aren't ready for, and so when it does come up they—the children—become very reverent, and a bit self-important. June has overheard the girls telling friends, with pride, *My mum had a sister and she disappeared.*

'Mum?' says Maggie. 'How?'

'Well, it wasn't. It wasn't at all her fault. I just thought it was.'

'I thought it was Felix's fault our cubby fell down, that we built at kindergarten,' offers Cal. 'But it acsherly wasn't, the cubby acsherly got blowed down in the wind.'

'Shh, Cal!' Esther flaps a hand. 'Mum's trying to talk.'

'It's all right,' says June. 'I've finished.'

'Well,' says Maggie, 'now you know it wasn't her fault you can stop being angry and everything will be all right again.'

'Can I please leave the table?' says Esther. 'I want to practise my handstands.'

'Have you had some salad?' says June automatically.

Esther sighs and places one or two shreds of lettuce on her plate.

'Essie,' says Paul. 'Come on.'

Cal says, 'Felix said sorry to me anyway. Even though it wasn't his fault. I think he did it just to make me stop crying. I can be very annoying when I cry.'

She books a flight for the next morning. Packing seems a difficult task. She takes down a small case and opens it on the bedroom floor but does nothing further until late, almost midnight. Paul is already in bed. June dithers, makes a pile of clothes on a chair, adds things, takes them away, puts them back again.

She sinks to her knees. 'I don't think I want to go.'

'She's asked for you to come. She wants to see you.'

'Yes, she's *sent* for me.' June makes imperial, open-palmed gestures.

'She's gone *deaf*. She must be freaking out, the poor woman.'

'It's probably the least of what she deserves,' mutters June.

Paul puts his book down. 'This could be a good thing. A chance to sort some stuff out.'

She gives a surly laugh. 'I could cry annoyingly until she's forced to apologise for something she didn't do.'

'You could,' says Paul. 'Although that might not work, since she won't be able to hear the crying.'

June grinds her teeth and folds a t-shirt. 'I *am* angry,' she bursts out. 'I *do* blame her, for so much. I mean, does she really think that what she's offered, over the years, could possibly be enough? I don't think there's any way to stitch things up. I just don't know where to *put* all this anger.'

'You're never going to get what you want from her. But isn't some kind of relationship better than none at all?'

'So it has to be on her terms?'

'Well, wouldn't that be better than nothing?'

The injustice of it—that she, June, must be better, do a better job, be a better person than Helen. For herself. For the kids. For Paul. Bloody Paul, with his standards, his constancy, his rigour.

'Look. I'm going!' June puts her elbows on the bed and lays her hands flat, palms up. 'Okay? I'm going.'

Behind her the pile of clothes slides off the chair and onto the floor.

She dreams about the visit. Her mother has a guru, an enormously fat man, fair and pink like a baby, with a round, serious face. He is dressed in ballooning silken robes, soft green and crimson— he sinks onto a cushion, like a collapsing, loose-petalled rose.

'The treatment will begin,' says the guru, waving plump fingers, and in comes Helen wearing an old flowered dress that June had forgotten. Helen is young again, she is younger than June. It's the old Helen, from before.

'Anna,' says the old Helen, and holds out her arms.

June is Anna. She looks down at herself. She is Anna wearing her bathing suit, the one-piece with the blue-and-red pattern that did up with a clip at the back of the neck. Her legs are

Anna's—there's the scar on her shin. Also, somehow she can see her own face, which is Anna's face, Anna the girl, perhaps eight years old.

Helen's arms go around her, and she is shaken by Helen's crying. 'It's so sad,' says Helen. 'Isn't it sad?'

'What is?' says June, who is also Anna. But it doesn't matter what it is—she is crying too, she cries and cries, lavish, voluptuous crying, she never wants it to stop.

At the airport she looks up Helen's website. Helen gazes out from the screen, bright-faced and white-smiled. June doesn't know if this is the work of Photoshop or cosmetic surgery, but she imagines that she will find out soon enough. Against a leafy backdrop Helen's hair tumbles; one gently tanned shoulder shows. There are pale streaks at her temples that, highlights or grey, have an artful, intended look. *Classy* is the word that comes to mind.

June scans the departure lounge. The women awaiting the flight to Maroochydore are mostly young, and dressed as if for exercise—leggings, sneakers; *active wear*. They have skin browned by sun or chemicals and their hair is mostly long, straight and bleached. One passes in a whoosh of perfume, thongs snapping. Startling purple toenails; heels smooth and pink. June tucks her own dry, unadorned feet further under her chair. The effort these women go to! The waxing and plucking and treating and buffing. And not even for any special event—just for everyday life.

She returns to the screen, and feels a stirring of admiration for her mother's skill. Helen looks beautiful but real. She looks as if she's not trying. And she does not look like a woman in her sixties. What discipline, what work, must lie behind this casual-seeming facade. *Capture your everyday bliss*, it says under Helen's photo, and June can't help a snort. She pictures Helen and her clients—who are, presumably, wealthy, dissatisfied retirees—on a beach, wearing white, their tanned arms reaching for the bliss that they believe themselves entitled to, which they will hunt down and capture on a daily basis.

On the plane she is seated next to a man who introduces himself as Gerald. Gerald has a sun-ravaged bald head and a moustache. His eyes are watery blue. Gerald has been visiting his daughter and grandchildren in Melbourne. He shows June photos on a digital camera.

'I'm on me own now,' he says. 'Since Brenda passed—that's me wife.'

'Oh,' says June. 'I'm sorry.'

Gerald gives a nod. 'Yes, breast cancer, very sad. Nearly four years ago.' He settles in his seat. 'I do intend to move down. Be closer to Deb and the kids and that. But I just can't seem to get meself sorted out.'

'Well, it's a big thing, to move, especially interstate.'

'It is. And I can't think what to do with Brenda's orchids.'

'Orchids?'

Gerald presses buttons on his camera, then passes it to June. The screen shows the interior of some kind of shadehouse. Greenish light, benches crammed with pots, strappy curved leaves and spiny stems and fleshy-looking flowers, big, small, pink, red, purple, white, yellow.

'Wow,' says June. 'That's an impressive collection.'

Gerald smiles. 'She was proud of it.'

'And now you take care of them?'

'Oh, well—' he tilts his head '—I just follow the rules.'

He shuts the camera down, and there's something in his fumbling fingers, a bravado and a vulnerability, that sends a stab of sadness through June. Her eyes fill. She has a strong and inappropriate urge to touch him, to take one of his hands, to put her head on his shoulder. 'You must miss her,' she says, very quietly.

Gerald either doesn't hear or pretends not to. He bends to the small backpack lying by his feet, zipping the camera into one of its pockets. When he straightens, he folds his arms and says brightly, 'And are you heading home today?'

June swallows. He is right to change the tone, to turn the page, to keep them both within appropriate territory. Still— even though it is possible he hadn't heard what she said—she feels left behind, exposed. 'No,' she says. 'I live in Melbourne. I'm visiting my mother.'

'That's nice.' Gerald takes the in-flight magazine from its pocket and opens it, sinking further into his seat.

June turns to the window, looks down at clouds. The sense of having been dismissed is ridiculously severe. Gone is the feeling of pity, and the wish to comfort. What she would like to do now—the compulsion has come upon her with adolescent intensity, and no warning—is to say something shocking, something petulant.

Actually, she imagines saying, *it's not nice at all. What makes you think it would be nice? Brenda might have been nice, and missing Brenda might be nice in its own pathetic way, but my mother's not nice, visiting her won't be nice, and I'm actually not very nice either, so you're probably right to have stopped talking to me.*

After a while she gets up, squeezing clumsily past Gerald's legs without giving him a chance to stand and let her out. She goes into the toilet and sits down, and under the fluorescent light, in the roar of the air-conditioning, forces out a couple of dry, wrenching sobs.

*

There is no further communication with Gerald. When she returns to her seat he rises and gives her a smile, and after the plane has landed he does the same again before entering the shuffling line of disembarking passengers. She doesn't see him at the baggage carousel, or anywhere else. Her imaginary speech, however, continues.

You see—as she collects the keys for her hire car—*my mother has summoned me, Gerald, because it suits her right now. She is afraid, and she's decided it's me who should comfort her. But what about the times I've been afraid? When I've needed her? Well, then she's been too busy. She's always been too busy. Lately she's been busy doing yoga with bored rich people. Meditating. Drinking chia juice.*

And as she drives up the highway: *I haven't seen my mother for eight years, Gerald. My mother hasn't met my youngest child. She's only met my partner twice. She calls me sometimes on the phone, but you know what? I almost never answer.*

In Noosa she doesn't drive to Helen's house. She finds a backstreet parking space, near a supermarket. There's a cafe, in which she orders coffee and a sandwich.

Why am I here, Gerald? Good question.

December last year had been the twentieth anniversary of Anna's disappearance. Helen had asked June then if she would visit. This, after numerous attempts at phone calls, was done via email.

I thought we could have a little ceremony, of sorts, wrote Helen. *Look through photos. Talk.*

I can't, wrote June. *Sorry, too busy.*

She wasn't too busy, even with Christmas coming. She could have managed it.

The day—December the ninth, the last day Anna was seen, sleeping in her bed—passed, marked only by two ignored calls from Helen. It was a Thursday, but at dinner June drank three glasses of wine to Paul's one. This was only a few weeks before Shelly Beach, before Paul's declaration of uncertainty. Once the kids were in bed she had a bath, alone, and later wandered the house, alone—everyone else asleep—in her pyjamas, drinking gin and orange juice from a mug.

She took out a notebook that she'd pinched at some stage, early on, from the boxes labelled ANNA, which Helen kept in the spare room of the townhouse she moved into after Avoca Street. She read, in Anna's fanciful cursive, *Tonight I got up on the roof and watched the sun going down and it's like the most massive high you could possibly get, and I was straight sober. It comes from sadness, isn't that funny.*

She should have done something. She would have—would she have?—if bloody Helen hadn't barged in, tainting the occasion, putting her paw prints all over it, wanting to *look at photos*, to *talk*. Wanting to *share*.

She would have liked to have gone to Red Rocks, to the beach, alone, to sit in the shelter of one of the low dunes and half-close her eyes so all she saw was a blurred glitter of blue and red and gold. Dig her toes down to where the sand turns cool. Breathe in the ti-tree, the salt, the silty earth of the scrub behind her. Maybe swim, launching flat into the shallows, floating on her back, water in her eyelashes making tiny sunlit explosions. She would have liked to have been dazzled into thoughtlessness.

If she could be empty enough in her mind then something might happen, some trick of memory: the sense of a body alongside hers, the lightest underwater graze of a fingertip, a bony knee. Images flaring in the fizzing light—blue bathers straps, the wing of a shoulderblade, a bird-like dive. Perhaps even a voice, burring faint through the water: *Junie! Junie, come on!*

Outside the window of the cafe cars turn in and out of the super-market. Touristy-looking people move along the footpaths—hats, sunglasses, toddlers in pushers. Glossy-leaved branches dip in the breeze. Then she sees Dev. Unmistakable—tall, bald, tanned, dressed in immaculate linen and Birkenstocks, carrying a shopping bag made of something woven; hemp, perhaps. Before she can do anything—like hide under the table—he passes, not glancing in.

Relieved, guilty, she bolts the rest of the sandwich. She really must go to Helen's, where she is supposed to be. She can't skulk around the town like a fugitive.

Some time ago she'd had coffee with an acquaintance, another painter. Lisa, the woman is called. For some reason—they were on the topic of mothers, perhaps—June showed Lisa Helen's website.

Wow, Lisa said, *she looks about forty.*

Then June showed Lisa Dev's website, the home page of which has a photo of Dev, shaven-headed, shirtless and slick-skinned against darkness, grinning in the glow of an outdoor fire.

Spiritual manhood, Lisa read aloud. *Claim your natural mas-culinity.* She glanced up at June. *No way. What do they do?*

They go into the 'bush', said June, *which I think is a semi-cleared block of land not very far from Noosa, and they build a sweat lodge and get naked and sit in it and sweat and tell stories, and cry. And then, when they've finished, Dev has to go back and dismantle the sweat lodge and scatter the materials around so the next group can 'discover' them and use them to build their own sweat lodge.*

Lisa's laugh was so loud that the people at the next table turned to look.

June actually doesn't know if it's true about Dev dismantling the sweat lodge each time, but she assumes it must be—how else would it work? She felt guilty, though, after the conversation with Lisa, for making fun of him. She's only met Dev a couple of times. She knows nothing about him, really. He seems like a nice enough guy—and sincere, despite the ridiculousness of his occupation. There is a shadow behind this guilt, another layer. Might Helen, with her suggestion of *a little ceremony*, not also be entitled to earnestness, to genuine motives? June ignores this.

The last time she saw Helen and Dev was after the birth of Maggie. They appeared at the hospital, a surprise visit, but only stayed for an hour or so before they had to go somewhere else—the surprise visit, it seemed, happened to coincide with a life-coaching conference. June, exhausted and hormonal, burst into happy tears at the sight of her mother—something that had never happened before—but then when the conference was mentioned became sullen. Paul and Esther were due to arrive later in the day but Helen was apparently not able to wait long enough to see them.

What a shame, said Helen. *You'll all have to come up and see us some time instead.*

At this June's sullenness hardened into anger. *Yeah*, she thought, *I'll drag myself out of my hospital bed, shall I, and Paul has to get back to work soon but how about I just tuck my newborn and my toddler one under each arm and jog up the coast to see you, Mum, easy as that.*

June's stitches had been hurting, but not too badly; she could have waited until Helen and Dev had gone. Instead she made a point of ringing for the nurse and asking for painkillers, sitting up with a wince to swallow them and ignoring Maggie, who had begun to cry in her plastic crib. She pretended to be busy refilling her water glass as the crying intensified, and then was ravaged by crisscrossing blasts of righteousness, guilt, satisfaction and self-loathing as Helen picked up the baby and tried to soothe her.

Shh now, shh now, said Helen, holding the bawling Maggie as if she was a tray of drinks. June was about to intervene with a long-suffering sigh when Dev stepped forward, taking the baby into his large hands, where she immediately fell silent.

Hello, said Dev to Maggie, in a hushed voice. A smile softened his big, sharp-boned face. *Look at you*, he whispered. *Look how* new *you are.*

The room stayed very quiet. June experienced a joint-loosening surge of love for her tiny daughter, who was gazing silently up at Dev. Then—shame, thick and unbearable. How could she contaminate this newborn with her resentment, allow such ill-feeling into the same air that was entering her child's pure and eager lungs?

She had tried, with Helen, in those early years, when the children were very young. She'd called and later Skyped regularly, encouraged the children, once they were old enough, to speak with their grandmother on the phone or computer. She had contemplated a visit, the winter Maggie was one, and again the next year, but by then June was pregnant with Cal, and it all seemed too hard. And she did hold on to the resentment. She made efforts to hide it from the children, but it was there.

She can manage a trip to Indonesia, she said to Paul, after witnessing Facebook photos of Helen and Dev on beaches, under palm trees, *but she can't find time to come to Melbourne and see her grandchildren.*

Eventually it came to seem a blessing, in a way. *It's just easier not having contact with her*, she told Paul, and her friends. *I don't like who I am when I'm around her. I don't want to expose my kids to that.*

Dev has reappeared. He stands on the footpath outside the window, only two feet away, shading his eyes with his hand. His brows slide up; his muffled voice says, 'June?'

Shit. June jumps to her feet. A teaspoon goes flying, skitters under the counter.

She meets him in the doorway. 'Hi, Dev,' she stammers. 'I was just—I just had to . . .'

Dev's teeth are brilliant, his skin burnished. When he kisses her cheek there's a waft of something herbal. 'Hello,' he says. 'You are here. Lovely to see you. Do you know, it has been such a long time, I wasn't sure . . .'

'It's me.' June wrestles with her bag; the straps are twisted. 'Only, what, eight years older and more exhausted!' She is speaking too loudly; her smile feels like a grimace.

'Do you have a car?' says Dev.

'Yes! Yes,' she gabbles. 'Hire car, I picked it up. At the airport.'

The stiller he is, the more frantic she seems to become, as if some mysterious transference is taking place. *How will I keep this up?* she thinks. *I'll die in a minute, explode with tension, and I haven't even seen you-know-who yet.*

'Where is your car?' says Dev.

'Just, um . . . Oh, there it is, right there.' She stabs a triumphant finger at the far side of the road.

'Well, mine is just up there.' His pointing is elegant, clear, assured. It's like semaphore. 'So you can follow me, and you don't need to worry about the maps or anything. Okay?'

*

The house is modern, an assemblage of blindingly white box shapes, hemmed with cringing shrubbery. June glances in the front windows as she wheels her case up the path. One shows a wall of built-in wardrobes and a huge bed with expensive-looking linen; the other bookshelves, a fit ball, a desk.

Inside the door Dev indicates a shoe rack. 'Please,' he says.

June kneels and undoes her sandals. She is aware of how rumpled she is, the stickiness of her skin. As she rises, she rakes her fingers through her hair.

Dev takes her case and deposits it in a doorway. 'This is your room,' he says, then goes on, down the hall.

June follows him into a hangar-like kitchen-living area. More white—walls, rug, couches. A huge, wall-mounted television. Large, framed, black-and-white photographs of beaches. An immense dining table, completely bare. At the far end of the room, folding glass doors look out onto a courtyard: bamboo, wind chimes, a stone Buddha, another oversized table.

On one of the couches, with her back to them, sits Helen. She does not turn around.

'Ah,' says Dev, 'you see? This is weird, isn't it? She doesn't even know we are here.' He moves around the room in a curve, taking slow, sideways steps, bringing himself with almost comical caution into Helen's line of sight. 'Hello,' he murmurs, mouthing exaggeratedly and circling one large palm like a mime cleaning an imaginary window.

Helen's head turns, sharply, and then she speaks. In a strange, stilted, very loud voice, she says, 'Oh, you're here.'

Dev continues his mime. 'June,' he murmurs, sweeping both hands in a gesture of presentation.

Helen shifts around on the couch. She sees June, and a smile comes over her face.

'Hi,' says June.

'Junie,' honks Helen in that odd voice. 'Junie, you came.'

'Hi,' says June again, helplessly. She takes a step towards the couch, over the back of which Helen has extended her arms.

This is not the Helen from the website, polished and casually glam. Nor is it the busy, well-groomed Helen who breezed into the hospital room and held the crying Maggie with stiff arms, as if about to put her away in a drawer. It is not the smiling Helen from the Facebook photos, a flower in her hair, skin aglow with light from a postcard sunset. This is an old woman, crumpled, sag-faced, hair in a snarl at the back of her neck, her bare eyes small and underscored with wrinkles.

June takes all this in very quickly, with shock, as she approaches the couch. She briefly touches one of Helen's hands, leans to peck the soft cheek. Helen smells like the old Helen—her moisturiser, an apple smell—but also musty, slightly sour, the smell of a sick person, of someone who has dispensed with regular washing, who spends her time under blankets, who has removed herself, or been removed, from life.

'Hi, Mum,' says June, moving around the end of the couch to sit.

Dev has gone away, into another room. June wishes he hadn't. She doesn't want to be alone with this person, who is Helen. Because now this person is doing something unexpected. This person is crying, but it's not in the way June remembers Helen crying—which was weeping, really, loud and wet. Nor is this an instance of the Happy Tears, which coursed freely from shining, joyful eyes and down over trembling, softly smiling lips, and which were usually accompanied by insistently reaching arms. This is shameful crying, tight with fear. This crying is not a performance, or a release, or a comfort. Nobody would feel better after crying like this.

'Sorry,' says Helen in her megaphone voice, taking a tissue from her sleeve. 'I just—I feel terrible. I can't hear anything except for this God-awful buzzing, it's so loud, and it *never stops*. I can't sleep. I can hardly walk; I feel like my balance has gone. I can't even speak properly—my voice inside my head gets lost under the buzz, but then Dev tells me I'm shouting all the time.' Her lips pull back; she shreds at the tissue. 'It's all so awful. What am I going to *do*?'

This is it. The moment, or at least *a* moment—the kind of thing Paul was alluding to. An opening, an opportunity. For what? Forgiveness? Compassion? June delves inside herself, but nothing is there. Not the right things, anyway. What she feels is excruciated, horrified, awkward. With a mixture of repulsion and fascination she takes quick glances at the stretched-thin lips, the whitened teeth with their unfortunate dark fillings, the exposed, greyish gums, at the naked-seeming, reddened eyes, at the moles and freckles that have over eight years asserted them- selves in various ways—darkened, risen, spread—at the crepe-y skin between the chin and the throat, at the wrinkles, wrinkles, wrinkles. In between these glances she stares down at her own hands, which are clamped between her thighs. She can't stand to behold this suffering, but also she can't bring herself to touch this creature, to give comfort.

Side by side they sit, one snivelling and dabbing with the tissue, the other rigidly, almost broodingly, enduring.

Dev returns. 'I think it is time for some tea,' he says, from between the spotlessly white kitchen benches.

Helen's tears have stopped. She takes a deep breath and squares her shoulders, tucks her tissue away. She turns to June. 'Now,' she blares, 'how are *you*?'

'Fine,' says June, not thinking to move her lips clearly.

Helen picks up a small notepad and a pencil from the table, puts them in June's hands.

Fine, writes June, and shows Helen.

As if mute as well as deaf, Helen gives a thumbs-up, grinning, eyes still red, sniffing a bit through pink-rimmed nostrils. Here is the old Helen—the bravado, the jauntiness, the rallying smile.

And here is June's anger, a vast, hot flood of it. She springs to her feet as if electrocuted. 'Toi-let,' she barks, pointing, and walks quickly from the room.

'First door on your left,' says Dev as she passes.

She sits on the edge of the bath with her face in her hands. 'What is this about?' she says aloud. 'What is *wrong* with me?'

When she returns, Dev is still making the tea. The kettle and toaster have their own cupboard, with its own little bench inside; the other benches gleam emptily, as if for display purposes only.

She stops at the entrance to the room. 'Um,' she says, 'Dev, I'm not feeling very well. I've got a bit of a headache. I think if I lie down for a while I'll probably feel better. Is that—okay?'

Dev turns to her. 'Yes, of course,' he says in his formal manner. She almost expects him to click his heels. 'Are you sure you wouldn't like some tea first?'

'Oh, no thanks, I think I'll just . . .' She begins to retreat, glancing at the couches, at the oblivious back of Helen's head. 'Could you please tell Mum?' Then she goes, before he can answer.

The spare bedroom is small—a double bed, a straight-backed chair, a tall chest of drawers made of dark wood, something

Asian in its design. She lies down. The bedding isn't as luxurious as what was glimpsed through the window of the master bedroom, but it's good quality, and smells fresh. It hadn't been true about the headache, but she doesn't feel good. She feels pretty bad, in fact.

She wakes up, remembers where she is, stays lying there for a long time, then at last rises and troops wearily back out.

The enormous room is empty. The bamboo in the courtyard has darkened, merged with the fence; the sky above is a very deep blue, paling at its lower reaches. A light has come on at the base of the stone Buddha, illuminating the undersides of his belly and chin. The table between the couches has been cleared. The couch cushions have been plumped.

'Hello?' ventures June.

'Hello,' comes Dev's voice, and in a few moments he emerges from the hallway. 'Ah,' he says, stretching his arms over his head as if he is the one who has been sleeping. 'Feeling better?'

'Yes, thanks.'

'Helen has also been resting. Here she comes.'

They settle again on the couches. *Take two*, thinks June. This time Dev brings wine, which she is profoundly grateful for, and a small bowl containing some kind of dip, a plate of crispbread studded with seeds.

'Feeling better?' says Helen.

June nods. The wine is certainly helping. It soothes, it ameliorates. She sips, and sips some more.

'You look tired,' Helen's voice lurches. 'Doesn't she look tired, Dev?'

Dev seems unbalanced by this. He blinks for a few moments, then says to June, 'I think perhaps this is your mother worrying about you. I think you look very well. A little tired, but very well.' Then, to Helen, he raises his eyebrows and shakes his head, then shrugs, lifts a hand, palm down, and rocks it to make a *so-so* gesture.

June almost laughs. It's like a game, in which answers must be reduced to blunt objects: *yes, no, maybe.*

They all lapse for a while into sipping and crunching.

Then Dev says, 'So, June. We don't see much of you.'

A pinprick of discomfort penetrates the wine haze. 'Um,' says June. 'Well, no.'

'I find this quite strange,' says Dev. 'Helen, she doesn't have any other family. You are the only one. And yet . . .'

With her brave and uncomprehending smile, Helen looks back and forth between the two of them.

'I think,' says Dev, 'that she is very sad about this. That she doesn't have a relationship with you.'

A fragment of crispbread has caught at the back of June's throat. She coughs, and drinks more wine. Helen goes on watching, smile in place.

'What,' says June eventually, 'makes you think that?'

'What makes me think she's sad?'

'Yes.'

'She tells me.'

This is not pleasant, this conversation with Dev, but with its subject right there, grinning jovially and understanding nothing, and with the help of the wine, it has rapidly come to seem bizarre, unreal.

There is a sense of something coalescing. Because of Helen's handicapped presence, because of these statements being made by Dev, because of Paul, back at home, things have aligned, and June doesn't know if they will again. It's another opening, and it's one she can enter—she thinks so, anyway—and, inexpertly and without caution, she goes in.

'Well,' she says, brushing crumbs from her shirt, 'she certainly hasn't told me that.'

'Perhaps,' says Dev, 'she is afraid to.'

'Afraid? Of what?'

'I think, of rejection.'

'Rejection!' June finds she has finished her glass of wine. She seizes the bottle and pours herself more, her mind a furious Rolodex of grievances. What to say? Where to begin? What the hell—anywhere.

'Listen, Dev.' She takes a swig, sets the glass down, jabs a finger. '*She* rejected *me*. She—she smashed up a whole family, because she got bored, because she couldn't be bothered with it, because she just couldn't help putting herself first.'

It's coming easily. She can feel her lips flying, the eruptions of words. 'And then—you've seen what she's like, with this braveface stuff. Nothing can be bad, everything must be wonderful all the time. So then we get, *Everything's fine, it's for the best. You kids are fine—you're fine, you're fine, you'd better be fine. Be fine, and if you're not fine then I don't want to know about it.*'

Helen's face at the edge of her vision is puzzled. June leans forward. She feels inflated, huge with rage. She keeps going: 'And then—once things were over with the first boyfriend, when she must've got a glimpse of what she'd thrown away—then we'd have to watch *her* blubbering, crying about how sad everything was. Then *we* were supposed to comfort *her*.'

Helen is no longer smiling. Her expression is one of alarm. 'What are you talking about?' she says in her blundering voice.

'June,' says Dev. He is sitting very still, hands on knees. 'All I was—'

'Hold on.' June gestures with her glass, spilling a bit. 'There's a lot you probably don't know, Dev. There's all the stuff about Anna. Anna was cutting herself. Anna was fucked up. Anna had serious problems, and *she* just let it go on—and I bet she'd tell you it was because she thought Anna just needed love, and freedom, and that really Anna was going to be fine—fine, fine, fine, because we were all going to be fine, in fact we would be better than fine, we would all be *happy*, deliriously happy, we would all dance around with her while she took all her clothes off and had sex with whatever disgusting man—' She swallows. Her mouth is full of saliva. She feels like a boxer, as if she should be popping out her mouthguard for a swill of water. She almost spits, right there on the floor.

'Are you talking,' honks Helen fearfully, 'about Anna?'

'Yes!' June nods extravagantly. 'Well done, Mum.'

'June,' says Dev.

June raises a palm to him. 'I was talking about Anna,' she says. 'What was I saying again? Oh yeah—and she'd say Anna just needed to be allowed to be herself or whatever, to find herself, but really it was because *she* was too busy with her own conquests to pay attention.'

She pauses again, for breath. Dev appears to have given up trying to get a word in, and Helen to comprehend; they both sit, watching, waiting. This changes things—June rapidly begins to lose her bluster. She battles on, but the boxer's sweat is evaporating, and she begins to notice a horrible, childish tone in her own voice, a plaintiveness. She is slipping, and she's not sure into what.

'And I was worried it would happen to me, too. Anna's stuff, the cutting. The drugs—the need to, I don't know, scrub yourself out. I just had to hold myself together, just hold on, and she never once asked me if I was all right. If I missed Anna. She'd just crap on about her work—and there'd always be some man, you know, who she'd talk about with this *look* on her face. She was just this, this, sexual *monster*—in, well, in my mind, anyway.' She is faltering. 'I know this isn't the actual truth,' she says in a flat tone, eyeing Dev. 'This is just how it was for me.'

Dev nods slightly, but doesn't say anything.

'And then . . .' June sighs. She feels, very suddenly, wrung out. She is face down on the floor of the boxing ring, wishing for someone to undo her gloves. 'Then there was Dad going off the rails. He went crazy, and I had to deal with that. Completely by myself. I was eighteen, and there I was trying to drag him off the streets and make him, you know, eat and sleep—and I didn't know if he would get better, or worse.'

The room is very quiet.

'I think I'm finished,' she says.

'What on earth,' booms Helen, 'was all that about?'

Dev ignores her. He addresses June. 'All I am saying, all I am telling you, is what I know, now. Which is that Helen is sad that she does not have a relationship with you.'

'I can't stand it!' cries Helen. 'I have *no idea* what anyone is talking about!'

'Well,' says June to Dev, 'I'm sad about that too.' There is a wobble in her voice that she hadn't seen coming. She heaves a trembling sigh. It's not the longed-for crying from her dream, the deep and glorious relief, but her eyes have gone blurry, and there is a fizzing feeling in her nose.

'June. Junie.' Her mother has the pad and the pencil, and is thrusting them at her. 'Please. I need to know what you're so upset about.'

The pad is small and her writing comes out big and shaky, so she can only manage a few words to each line.

Anna was
lost and
I blamed
you
and
all I know is
how to be angry
I'm sorry
I love you
and I'm
sad we
don't

She doesn't know how to finish. She gives up and hands it over before she loses her nerve.

Helen reads, then sits, head lowered. Her breathing is audible. She fiddles her veiny hands together. When she looks up at June, her eyes are swimming.

Here we go, thinks June. *Here comes The Weeping.*

Helen opens her mouth.

'Mum. No.'

Helen's mouth closes. She tilts her head like a begging dog.

'No,' says June again, the word falling in a clod. '*I* am sad.' She taps herself on the chest. 'Me.'

She stays a week. She sticks it out. Atmospheres slide over them and settle, for moments, minutes, hours—breezy and humorous; oppressive, pressurised; gently sad—and are enjoyed, or undertaken, or ridden out.

They sit at the inside table; they sit on the couches. They sit in the courtyard, by the stone Buddha, beneath the chinking of birds. They go for short walks to the end of the street and back, to where the bushland starts, Helen taking dubious steps, sometimes slanting off sideways, horror-show smile always in place.

They drink tea. They drink wine. They eat tidy meals, mostly prepared by Dev.

'I'm still a terrible cook,' says Helen.

Helen talks, in her new, runaway voice, and June writes things on the notepad. Sometime June talks, out of forgetfulness, desperation, vindictiveness.

'I can't believe this,' she mutters. Or, 'You would think that.'

Once she stands behind Helen's chair and whispers, 'You don't know how much love small children have. How much of mine was wasted on you.'

Things, writes June to Paul in a text message, *are being said.*

'I miss the birds,' says Helen in the courtyard. 'Are they singing, Junie? Can you hear them?'

Did you know about the cutting? June writes. *Anna? Self-harming.*

'No,' says Helen, the word dolorous, heavy. 'Oh God,' she says, and puts her fingers, with their thickened knuckles, to her eyes.

Did you ever even worry? writes June. *About me? Once Anna was gone.*

'Yes!' cries Helen. 'Of course I worried about you. I was *consumed* with worry—about you, and about John. But, oh God, Junie, you were hard to love. Don't you remember? I'd ring you up and you'd give me the brush-off, and I'd try to take you out, for lunch, or dinner, or to a movie, and half the time you wouldn't even show up, and then when you did you'd treat me like, well, like I was your *enemy*.'

Hard to love?! scribbles June, and then, *I don't remember any of this.*

'Well, to show love to. I came along to all your art openings and you barely spoke to me. I always felt like you and your friends were sniggering behind my back. I'd have to work myself up to seeing you, I'd have to *steel myself*.'

That's not how I remember it. I thought you'd just moved on, from everything. Anna. Dad. Me.

Helen stares at her with an expression of exaggerated disbelief. 'Anyone would think,' she blares, 'that these are not the same events we are both talking about.'

'Everyone's fighting here,' reports Maggie over the phone. 'Essie's being mean, and Cal is just a total *poo*.'

'That sounds—hard.'

'I hate them both.'

'I can still remember,' says June, 'how good it felt to bite my sister, when we were fighting. When things had really reached a crescendo. I knew I was going too far, I knew I'd get into trouble, but it just felt so good to sink my teeth into her.'

'Mum!'

'Well, you just said you hated both of your siblings, and called Cal a poo.'

'Yes, but that's not nearly as bad as biting your sister who disappeared,' says Maggie. Then adds, with inspiration: 'And then *showing off* about it.'

'Well, I didn't know when I bit her that she was going to disappear.'

June thinks of nineties Helen, her harshly cropped hair, her work suits, mid-length skirts and big-shouldered jackets, the red nail polish. Her skin had been paler then, her make-up bolder—stark eyeliner, ovals of blush, lips to match the nails. All the effort showing in the hard edges, the drawn-on lines. Helen's high heels on the kitchen floor in the mornings, her diet breakfasts, black coffee, half a grapefruit.

'At boarding school,' says Helen, 'there was a girl with orange hair. Bright orange. Like, well, like an orange. And she peroxided it and it went green.'

Fresh fish. Fresh ginger. Coriander. Lime. A sunset behind the bamboo. The Buddha leering over his up-light.

That Bhudda, writes June. *Spelling? Buddha? Looks like he's ready to tell a ghost story.*

'It came free with the outside table,' honks Helen.

Helen says, 'When you said moved on, did you mean given up? Because of course I had to move on. We all did. Even John, in the end. But giving up, that's something different. Giving up *hope*, I mean. You can't, even if you want to. I've wanted to! It causes so much pain. It's not a rational thing.'

They watch television—cooking shows.

'What's she saying? Quick!' Helen elbows June. 'Where's the notepad?'

Texture excellent, June writes. *Too sweet tho.*

'Oh, but he's my favourite!' cries Helen. 'He's the one I want to win!'

'I had no idea she was into this stuff,' says June to Dev, but he doesn't answer—he is also enthralled, hands on knees, face thrust slightly forward, eyes on the screen.

'Hey, Dev, you know the sweat lodge,' says June to Dev, and giggles. 'Do you have to take it apart again? Each time?'

The handle falls off the inside of the bathroom door while June is in there. She can't fix it, and she can't get the door to open. Dev is out. June hammers with her fist for a while and calls, uselessly, like a child, 'Mu-um! Mu-um!' Then she sits on the edge of the bath and waits.

After a long time she gets up again and looks through the cupboards and drawers for something to write with but finds nothing. She begins to tear toilet paper into the shapes of letters. H. E. L. She is just starting the P when a shadow appears under the door and there is a dampened knocking, as if made with the heel of a hand.

'June,' comes the clumsy voice. 'June? You in there?'

June leaps up and hammers again, squats to stuff the toilet-paper letters under the door, rises to resume hammering.

The door swings open. Helen's face is lit up. 'Junie!' she says. 'I felt you banging, with my hands! Through the door!'

Out in the courtyard Helen examines the toilet-paper letters, laying them on the table. 'Helen,' she says proudly.

June collapses with laughter, snatches up the pad.

Not Helen! HELP!

A mild breeze dances the letters.

*

Helen connects a laptop to the enormous television and dims the lights. She and June sit side by side on the couch.

'John did this,' says Helen. 'Got all the old photos scanned and sent them to me. Once he'd met Kathy and stopped being angry.'

She says it almost with humour, as if John's anger had been a whim, arbitrary and undeserved, and June has to contain a gush of irritation.

But then the photos. Suspended within the TV's wide black mouth, their colours rich and filmic, even the ones that are over- or underexposed, flash-blasted, unflattering. Baby Anna on her back on a rug, sun-dapples on her face, thumb plugging her mouth. A slender John with June and Anna on the beach at Red Rocks, June aged perhaps four, in underpants, face blurred as she bends to a plastic bucket; Anna nude, her toddler body caught between John's knees, stubby fingers, fat grin under a hat. All of Anna's primary school photos, tracking her increasing frogginess, her hair in various shades of ginger and sometimes chlorinated green, her mouthfuls of evolving teeth.

The smiles, the eagerness—June is sure she can't bear it, but Helen goes on wielding the mouse, unfurling Anna after Anna against the black. She speaks, also, a one-sided commentary, answering her own questions.

'Grade two? Three. Those teeth! Mrs Murchison, God she was drip . . . Now where was that? It was somebody's party, wasn't it, a picnic at the Botanic Gardens . . . You girls got those roller skates for Christmas, remember? And Anna's were too big, we had to stuff the toes . . .'

She halts, finally, at one of Anna and June sitting at Nan's kitchen bench. It must be around the time of the break-up— Anna frowns into a *Choose Your Own Adventure* book; June's book lies flat, hiding the cover; her pubescent nipples disrupt the front of her t-shirt. Faux-timber laminate. Glasses of milk. Slices of fruitcake.

'Shall we stop here?' says Helen.

June draws in breath. She is one giant, live, nerve ending. She nods.

'Or do you want to keep going?'

Not, writes June, *if we want to stick to happy memories.*

Helen laughs like something deflating. She closes the laptop and switches off the TV. Then she puts her hand over June's on the couch between them.

June's lips are numb. She bends forward, dropping tears into her lap.

On June's last morning they go, early, to a beach. June drives, obeying Helen's stentorious directions. She parks and they walk. They pass houses like Helen's, white and modern, black SUVs in their driveways, plush lawns. They pass rickety fibro shacks that make June think of the island—houses with cobwebs and perished canvas window awnings. They descend a hill covered in tall trees, and turn onto a narrow path—no more buildings now, only trees—and wind up and around and along until they come to stairs down to the water.

The beach is a small, clean semicircle between cliffs, its narrow sweep of pale sand bookended with dark rocks. Tranquil, luminous, blue-green waves. It's like an ad for a beach. At the far end a grey-bearded man is exiting the water, naked. Helen nudges June. The man claps one hand to his mouth and the other to his groin and does a comical little jiggle to his towel and clothes. Helen waves; June hisses at her to stop.

The sea is hardly colder than the air. June dives under. She swims out, away, but when she pauses she finds she can still stand, the water just up to her chin. She turns around. The bearded man is a miniature figure, dressed now, ascending the steps. Helen, about halfway between June and the shore, breast-strokes, blank face, closed eyes.

June feels the wave behind her, and has barely time to snatch a look at it before she launches herself, head down, right arm windmilling. She feels the lift, the slip of the water being sucked back below her. She joins her hands over her head, and kicks, and kicks.

PART FIVE

BELGRAVE

Not far from the train station there is a path. You don't have to walk up it for very long before you feel alone in the bush. Completely. Everything else very far away.

Ferns have curling shoots with insides no person has ever seen. The ground is damp in a permanent way. Dark brown marks on the tree trunks, from rain dripping, running down.

The sun shines. The ferns make lace. The tree-trunk marks have their own brown gloss. The ground steams.

Not far from the train station there is a path. It can take a while to feel alone. In the bush. Completely. Everything else left behind.

Ferns have curling shoots, tender, private. The ground is damp, the tree trunks marked from drips, deep brown.

The sun begins to shine. Everything goes lacy, glossy, and steam comes from the earth.

Keep walking.

Not far from the train station there is a path. Leave everything else behind and walk until you are completely alone. Completely.

Tiny green hairs inside the curls of fern fronds. Damp ground. Tree trunks streaked dark.

Shining sun, steaming earth, lacy ferns, bark brown and glossy.

Look up. There are places for climbing.

Not far from the station there is a path. It doesn't take long to feel completely alone. Just you. Completely. Everything else gone.

The insides of fern fronds curled and new. Lush damp ground. Dark wet bark.

Sun in everything, lace, gloss, steam.

Run. Laugh, your hair pink and gold.

Not far from the station there is a path. You trail behind the others so you can feel what it would be like to walk completely alone, to not have to jostle and shove, to not have to tear everything up with your noise.

You blunder your finger at the curl of a frond. You want to lie right down in the rich leaf pulp, which is steaming, and just watch. Grimmo comes back to check on you. Oh yeah, he says, it's kicked in. You can't speak, you close your eyes and there is a net of fleshy purple flowers, squelching open and shut.

Ahead, higher, the voices of the others rip the soft air.

Not far from the train station a path swarms. Get in it. Be conveyed. A tunnel, a passage, glittering white. Papery wavings.

Put your finger in a just-born green curl. This air, tissue layers, dancing spangles, should be dense, should mean wading, slowness, but it has no weight—it allows, lovingly it swirls and resettles. Nothing is still. Nothing is just one colour. Black, white, yellow, crimson, blue, silver. In the air, the trees, the ground, on the underside of every leaf. Colours, and millions of tiny suns. Quivering orbits, somersaults, vibrations. You could watch them forever, but now look up at this lace, green, woody, wet-gold, quivering. And the hearts of the trees, brown and deep.

How far up have you gone? Your feet don't even touch the ground.

Not far from the station there is a path. You have been here before but that was with Grimmo and the others. Now you are alone, in the bush, completely. Everything else left far behind.

Oh God, it's all still here. It's even closer. Those fronds curling whether anyone sees or not. The damp ground, the saturated bark.

The sun again, steam and gold and dapples, who needs acid, your heart is a puppy, you have to skip to keep pace.

This time you will climb higher—far, far up.

Not far from the station is a path. You know this path, but still it's a surprise how quickly you feel alone in the bush. Completely. Away from everything.

The tiny fronds curled new and uncaring. The ground damp and rich and uncaring. The trees with their drip marks not caring who walks between them.

Where is the sun? You need its dapples, its gloss, its heat on the ground.

Far, far up, what if it's not the same as before?

Not far from the station there's a path and walking up it is different each time.

You are alone in the bush, completely, everything else very far away.

You are alone but the rest of the world feels close.

You are with Grimmo and the others, big and loud, every step blaring.

You are tripping, time slowed to syrup, one leaf a universe.

You are drunk, listing to the edge of the path.

You are stoned, dry-mouthed, laughing into your sleeve, the trees smeary, the ground jittering.

You are sober, silent, small on the hillside, nothing but legs, lungs, heartbeat.

Each time there are fern fronds curled tight and new. Each time the damp ground, the marked trees.

Each time you are climbing far, far up, to something.

Not far from the station there is a path. You barely take two steps on it and the rest of the world is wicked away. You are alone in the bush. Completely.

Hello, ferns. Hello, tender curling shoots. Hello, ground, always damp. Hello, tree trunks with long brown stripes.

Sun this time, that's nice; hello, sun. Switch on the dapples, the gold spray, the warm and dewy loveliness.

Up you go, far, far up, to something beautiful, or bad, or to nothing.

Not far from the station there's a path. And here you are, on it again. You should feel alone. Completely alone, in the bush. But of course you're not. Can you feel us, watching?

Ferns, ferns, ferns. Ground, ground, ground. Trees, trees, trees.

Sun. Or no sun. Beautiful or ugly, nice or not nice.

Far, far up, an ending. Or not.

Not far from the station there's a path and God you are sick of walking up it.

Even baby fern shoots can be ordinary. The brown drips on tree trunks, boring, boring, boring.

The light is grey and flat, the ground slippery with decomposed leaves. Something is wanted of you—we want something of you—but you just keep walking, as boringly as you can.

You yawn.

Far, far up will be the same flat light, the same wet ordinariness. Good.

Not far from the station there's a path and you thought you knew what to expect but it doesn't like a smart-arse. You are alone in the bush, completely, the rest of the world left behind. You will need to take this seriously.

You thought you were finished with those ferns, but they catch at you all over again, their newness, their aloofness, their frailty. And this ancient hill clangs cold emptiness through you, forgettable speck. The trees nurse their dark lines.

The sun comes out and everything is so beautiful you can hardly breathe.

Get up there, far, far up, to where you're supposed to be.

Not far from the train station there is a path. You have to walk a long way up it before you feel completely in the bush. And then not quite completely—the rest of the world is not all that far away.

Fern shoots curl. The ground is soaked, as if it could never be dry. Dirty brown stains on the tree trunks.

There is no sun. The ferns drip. The trees are ugly.

Far, far up, there is a place, very steep, for running, blindly.

Not far from the train station there is a path. You could never be alone on it because terrible things wait behind the trees. You want to go back to the rest of the world but you can't.

The vile curls of ferns, the wet marks on the tree trunks, poison.

Fragments of light vanish. The ferns offer their awful secrets. The trees come closer.

Far, far up is a place for slipping and falling.

Not far from the train station there is a path. A person would have to walk some distance up it to feel completely in the bush. Completely. The rest of the world very far away, left behind.

Ferns curl. The wet ground is not as cold as might be expected. The tree trunks bear dark lines, descending.

When the sun goes down the ferns still curl, the trunks still stand. The ground stays strangely warm.

Far up, there is a place, between rocks, that no searcher, none of us, would ever find.

Not far from the train station there is a path. Which leads around and around and up a steep hillside, a path soundless with leaf mould, cut between ferns and tall, patiently dripping trees. Further along, higher up, there are vertical slabs of rock, slick and wet, and huge boulders sunk in greenery, and from time to time the feeling of space off to one side.

Higher, higher. The path becomes less certain. The air sharpens. There are places for looking out, and down. There are places for being careful. There are places where the ground is very suddenly just not there.

Far, far up, you stand on the edge of a place for slipping and falling.

Far, far up, you sit on the branch of a tree. How you could get there, so high, we have no idea.

Far, far up, but not as far as the places for slipping and falling, you are in between two rock faces, at the bottom of a long and secret drop, in a private hollow, very tight. You are upside down. We can't see you but we know you are there.

You are a girl, pink-blonde, gappy grin, long limbs and flat chest.
     You are a baby, soft and curled.
     You are fifteen, slight, with small curves like add-ons, gnawed fingers, obstreperous hair.
     You are whole. You glow and are well.
     You are thin and broken. One of your legs is bent the wrong way. One of your arm bones sticks out. One of your eyes has been swallowed by the pale slug of its swollen lid. One side of your head is pushed in.
     You needed help but you didn't want it.
     You wanted help but you didn't know how to ask for it.
     You didn't need help; you would have been okay.

You look at us. You smile. You are sweet, you are lost, you didn't mean anything, there was an accident.
     You won't look at us. There was no accident, nothing accidental happened.
     You look directly at us and you are so angry we can't look back at you.
     You will never forgive us.

None of these things is the truth.
     There is a truth but we can't get to it.
     And this isn't Belgrave. This isn't anywhere.

But this is all we have: the train station, the path, the ferns, the ground, the trees, the places for falling or resting or hiding or flying away from.

(Or choose a different starting point: the city street, the car of the drug dealer, the park at night, the bus terminal, the bridge over the river.)

This is all we have, these infinite strands of possibility—to fabricate, to arrange and rearrange, to worry at, to tend.

Which is tedious, painful and exhausting, and which makes us feel sick.

Which is necessary.

Which has no ending.

What else, then? Anything else?

Yes. We still have:

—You in my arms at three months, gummy blind smile into sunlight, the milk in my body pulsing, ready, thick with love.

—You at Nan's on the couch with your cut leg, after the stitches— after the blood, the screaming, Dad bundling you into the car, beach towel soaking red. All of that over, everything hushed and gentle, but the fright still there, the seriousness. The blue bedspread brought out to tuck around you, the hospital bracelet proud on your wrist. For once not shy of tenderness, I give you an apple, and gravely you accept it. *Thank you, Junie.*

—Your skinny fingers, your elbows, you angling yourself around the bannister in your pyjamas, morning hair, toast crumbs. Taking my big hands with your very small and sticky ones: *Dad, look, my tooth is almost falling out.*

—Pot smoke. School uniforms. You on the roof beside me, your arm against mine for a moment, warm.

—The kitchen at Avoca Street on a Sunday morning, late. You coming in, smelling of cigarettes, shadows under your eyes, your clouded gaze, *Hi, Mum.* You leaning into me, your arm around my neck, your teenager's fingers—bitten nails, half-moons of chipped polish, cheap ring from St Kilda markets—in my hair.

And even now, without you, we still have:

—A golden evening, three parrots skimming dauntless under the backyard grapevine, their calls brazen, explosive, the ruffled air cool on my cheek. 'Mum!' calls Cal, amazement in his round eyes, his splayed, fat fingers. 'Did you see that? Those bright birds?'

—Breaking down in the hills near Dev's bush block and standing alone by the side of the road in the humming slowness of a summer afternoon. Purple clouds, green light, the smell of rain, the tick of the car's engine. Camphor laurels garlanding the fence line. Two horses jumping a narrow creek bed—red mud, dry stones—and cantering, with playful head-shakes and flags of tails, diagonally up the slope.

—Buskers in Toronto's Union Station, a string quartet playing *The Lark Ascending* by Vaughan Williams. The smell of hot chocolate, the timeless, expectant busyness of train stations. The violin reaching, trembling, higher, higher, over the weaving crowds.

Damp earth. Sun, leaves, sky.

ACKNOWLEDGMENTS

This book was written with the generous support of the following organisations: The Australia Council for the Arts; Varuna, the National Writers' House; The Henry Handel Richardson Society of Australia; The Trawalla Foundation and the Stella Grass Trees Writing Retreat; Bundanon Trust's Artists-in-Residence program.

Thank you:
Jane Novak, Jane Palfreyman, Ali Lavau, Christa Munns, Sandy Cull, Tegan Bennett Daylight, Louisa Syme, Kate Ryan, Claudia Murray-White, Rowan Frew, Mick Turner.